D1236149

GUN
BOSS

Also by Jack Ballas
in Large Print:

Angel Fire
Powder River
Montana Breed
Hanging Valley
Iron Horse Warrior

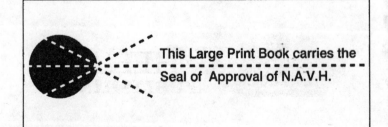

This Large Print Book carries the
Seal of Approval of N.A.V.H.

GUN BOSS

JACK BALLAS

WHEELER
PUBLISHING

Published in 2005 by arrangement with
Cherry Weiner Literary Agency.

Wheeler Large Print Western.

The text of this Large Print edition is unabridged.
Other aspects of the book may vary from the original edition.

Set in 16 pt. Plantin.

Printed in the United States on permanent paper.

Library of Congress Cataloging-in-Publication Data

Ballas, Jack.
    Gun boss / by Jack Ballas.
        p. cm. — (Wheeler Publishing large print westerns)
    ISBN 1-59722-124-4 (lg. print : sc : alk. paper)
    1. Large type books.   I. Title.   II. Wheeler large print
western series.
PS3552.A4673G86 2005
    813'.54—dc22   2005021683

To Cherry Weiner, my agent, who through her tireless efforts ensures I don't get lazy and take time from my computer. Keep pushing me, Cherry. You're a jewel.

As the Founder/CEO of NAVH, the only national health agency solely devoted to those who, although not totally blind, have an eye disease which could lead to serious visual impairment, I am pleased to recognize Thorndike Press* as one of the leading publishers in the large print field.

Founded in 1954 in San Francisco to prepare large print textbooks for partially seeing children, NAVH became the pioneer and standard setting agency in the preparation of large type.

Today, those publishers who meet our standards carry the prestigious "Seal of Approval" indicating high quality large print. We are delighted that Thorndike Press is one of the publishers whose titles meet these standards. We are also pleased to recognize the significant contribution Thorndike Press is making in this important and growing field.

Lorraine H. Marchi, L.H.D.
Founder/CEO
NAVH

* Thorndike Press encompasses the following imprints: Thorndike, Wheeler, Walker and Large Print Press.

chapter one

Trace Gundy took another swipe with the rasp, closely eyeing the hoof he dressed to fit the shoe. His horse swung his head as if to ask how much longer he had to stand three legged while getting new footwear. Gundy cocked his head to listen. Horses, many of them, were approaching.

He dropped the buckskin's leg and ran. His riders wouldn't return to the house this time of day. The sun stood at only ten o'clock. Dee was in the house alone. His gut tightened. He grabbed his gunbelt from a wall peg on the way. On reaching the barn door, gunfire sounded. He stopped, peered out.

Three men lay dead on the ground; at least eight, still in the saddle, fired at the house. Gundy thumbed off a shot. One of the eight, knocked backward, dropped to the ground.

He fired again, his bullet slammed another from his saddle. One rider, already off his horse, ran for the ranch house door. Gundy fired at him but missed. The man went through the doorway on the run, firing, a six-shooter in each hand.

Rifle fire from the bunkhouse dropped three of the riders. In only a moment the rider who'd entered the house came out running, looked about wildly, and headed for his horse.

Gundy thumbed off another shot. The raider staggered — but made it to his horse, and mounted. The four stared at Gundy, jerked reins, and raced from the compound. The whole thing lasted only a few minutes.

Dee — where was she? He sprinted for the house.

Two of his men lay just inside the door. Gundy ran to the kitchen. Dee, his wife, lay slumped by the stove, a large wooden spoon still in her hand. The acrid stench of gunpowder hung over the room.

Gundy turned her onto her back. Her dress, soaked with blood, showed four holes, one over her breast, another in her side, and two in her stomach. Their baby had been growing there.

Her eyes, wide and pain-filled, stared at Gundy. "Trace, the *gringo* did it. But, Trace, don't waste your life to get even. I love you too much for that. You and Paul build the ranch you always wanted." Her voice came out thin and reedy. "I — I love you so much, *mi amor*." She took a shallow, tremulous breath, bloody froth bubbled on her lips. She gripped his hand, hard, tried to say something, shuddered, and closed her eyes.

Tears, foreign to Gundy's face, streamed down his cheeks, his lungs convulsed, and he sobbed great wracking sobs. He had never cried until now, for the Mescalero Apache who raised him didn't allow it. He pulled her body to his chest, held her there, and rocked back and forth, keening to her through his agony.

Four days later, Gundy, tall, slim, stood by his horse talking to Paul Kelly, Dee's brother. "Gonna ask three things of you, Pablo: take care of Dee's grave, keep it weeded, an' put flowers on it when you can get them. Do the same for our men who died, kill every Comanchero you see, wherever they are, an' last, if I ain't back in a year the ranch is yours. The paperwork makin' it legal's in my desk."

Kelly stood there a moment, stared at the ground, then locked eyes with Gundy. "Amigo, get the ones who did this. If it takes the rest of our lives, the ranch will still be yours when you return — just get them."

"They ain't gonna get away, Kelly. I studied their horse tracks, an' I ain't gonna *ever* forget their faces. Every one o' them looked at me when they rode out. I'll remember them."

Gundy shook Kelly's hand, nodded to his crew, and took a last look around the compound that made up the ranch yard.

He had taken so much pride in his ranch, the huge adobe house, walls three feet thick for cooling in the summer and warmth in the winter, both needed for this high desert country. The bunkhouse, no less grand, stood about fifty yards from the house, and the stables and the cook shack were all surrounded by an eight foot adobe wall with glass imbedded in the top to protect against intruders. This time the wall had failed to do its job; the raiders came through the gate.

Again, his look swept the yard and its buildings, then he kneed his horse out the gate, headed north.

By his reckoning, the three breeds and one gringo would put nothing but distance between the Big Bend and themselves. They would not go to the New Mexico Territory; Comancheros were hated there as much as in Texas. The raiders were all of that outlaw breed. He thought they would head for Colorado where there was a large Mexican population. They could lose themselves in the settlements.

Well away from the ranch buildings, Gundy picked up their trail, heading northwest. He didn't try to follow their tracks. To verify they hadn't changed course, he cast back and forth at the end of each day until he spotted their horses' tracks. On the fourth day it rained — but he didn't need tracks now to know he'd been right. They headed for Colorado.

Across the Comanche lands, Gundy rode with care, staying to low ground, never skylining himself, never building a fire.

Days passed, and Gundy became aware he had changed. Even as an Apache he had known emotion, although there were many who thought him more savage than the warriors he rode with. Now he felt nothing. His heart was a cold, throbbing muscle in his chest. His thoughts, like ice, were frozen and calculating. His world centered on revenge. But at night he took Dee from the recesses of his mind and loved her all over again, feeling his heart swell, his throat muscles tighten, and his chest heave, trying to push tears from his eyes.

He would not simply kill the men he chased. They would die a slow, terrible death. The Apache had taught him the ways to kill slowly and horribly. He had not forgotten.

In Raton, the settlement at the foot of the mountains, Gundy asked questions about the men he chased. They had been in the town only five days before, all four of them.

At the foot of Raton Pass, Gundy shivered and shrugged into his sheepskin. Early summer had not warmed the late afternoon air. Where he sat his horse, the trail was over six thousand feet high. He thought to cross the mountain and stay a few days in Trinidad.

That night, high on the mountain, Gundy sat huddled close to his fire, one of the few he had known in past days. Pulling one of his two Hudson's Bay blankets tighter to his shoulders, he breathed the scent of the coffee he drank, a scent mixed with that of the mountain cedar surrounding him and the pungent smell of wood smoke. The smells and flicker of firelight were those he'd grown up with farther south in the Capitan Mountains. *And* he was on the hunt. He felt at home.

The same stars had shone on him when

he took the blankets from a Comanchero freight wagon. The bandits had stolen the blankets, great bales of them, and he returned the favor, but stealing only two. Trailing them to their leader and killing him had broken up the tight-knit organization of bandits — and in doing that he made an enemy of every Comanchero. The ranch he now owned had belonged to the bandit leader.

He should never have married Dee. Even before they married, the Comancheros hated him. He had killed too many of their kind.

Thoughts of Dee were always with him, and with the thoughts came the icy fire in his brain and his gut. By the next night, if her killers stopped in Trinidad, he would meet them.

Before his anger and hate could take control and stop any chance of sleep, he slumped down to rest his head on his saddle and watched the stars go away.

The sun already lighted the sky when Gundy saddled and left camp. He had waited for full daylight. To ride around mountain country in the dark could cause his horse to break a leg or pitch him over a cliff.

The climb to the summit pushed him to

the back of his saddle, against the cantle. But after another thousand feet, the ground tilted downward and he felt his weight shift. In the last town he'd heard it was only ten or eleven miles from the top to Trinidad. His pulse quickened and his neck muscles tightened. The thought of meeting even one of the Comancheros sharpened his Apache upbringing.

Another two hours he crossed the Purgatoire River and entered Trinidad. A flicking glance showed him a typical western town that meant to stay put. Brick and stone buildings intermingled with wooden structures stared at each other across a dusty street. A tin-panny piano sounded from one of the saloons. Gundy rode past the noise and continued to the end of the main street, studying each building and the horses tied to every hitch rack.

He stopped at a horse trough and let the buckskin drink, then rode around a dog sleeping in the dusty street and headed back the way he'd come.

Sunlight pushed against his eyeballs and he pulled his old black, flat-brimmed hat down to shade them. Almost back to the spot where he entered the street, the smell of coffee and frying bacon faintly tickled his nostrils. It had been a long time since breakfast.

He reined his horse to the front of where he guessed the tantalizing smells came from. The building was a neat, whitewashed, clapboard structure. Gundy climbed stiffly from the saddle and went in. He wasn't surprised to see only a couple of patrons. It was late for breakfast, and a little early for dinner.

A corner table, one with red-checkered oilcloth at the front of the room, was to his liking. A pretty black-haired girl, carrying a coffeepot in one hand and a cup in the other, came to wait on him. She reminded him of Dee in the carefree way she held her head and the smile that lit her face when she greeted him.

"Coffee?"

The words to ask what the hell she thought he came in for were on the tip of his tongue. He bit them off short. She wasn't to blame for Dee's death. He'd try to be civil.

He returned her smile and said, "Don't believe they's anything prettier than a girl carryin' a coffeepot."

She chuckled deep in her throat and poured him a cup of the steaming liquid. "What'll you have, cowboy? Never mind

15

the blarney, it won't get you one bite more than if you just sit quietly."

"Aw, heck. An' I figured it might get me the other half o' that steer I'm gonna eat."

She laughed again. "What you want *with* that half of cow?"

"Half dozen eggs, if you got any. An' fried spuds, biscuits, an' keep the coffee comin'."

She walked with the free stride of a girl raised in the mountains. And, Gundy thought, she knows she's pretty — but she wasn't Dee.

By the time she brought his order the place had emptied. "Sit an' talk if you ain't got nothin' else needs doin' right now."

"I just stirred the stew." She looked at the chair across from him, and he stood and held it for her. "I'll sit a few minutes."

Gundy studied her a moment. "Ma'am, want to ask you somethin'. In the last couple o' days, you seen four strangers ride in, tough-lookin' customers, one gringo, an' three breeds?"

She looked him in the eyes. "Why? You don't look like the kind who'd ride with *them.*"

"You seen 'em then?"

She nodded. "They were here. Dirty, rude, and insulting, they were. I told them

16

to leave or I'd get the marshal."

Gundy cut a bite of steak, swished it around in the egg yolk, and put it in his mouth. After chewing and swallowing, he said, "No, ma'am, I ain't the kind to travel with them. Them an' me got somethin' to settle." He wanted to tell her of their part of Dee's death — wanted to talk about it with someone. But it was too soon.

"Mister, three of them left yesterday. One of them, a breed, is still here. But please be careful. They all looked like bad men."

She didn't even know him but, Gundy thought, her concern was genuine. "Lady, it's them what wants to be careful, an', yes'm, *I* always am."

He finished his meal, paid the girl, thanked her for the information, and left.

Saloons bordered the street on both sides. Gundy stood by the door of the cafe and studied each person. Buckboards and big freight wagons, along with riders, trying to keep from getting run over, wended their way through the dust. As best he could, Gundy gave each person a careful look. His man wasn't among them.

He'd check the saloons on this side of the street first; saloons were where he was most likely to find the breed. He'd worry about the other three after taking care of this one.

He pushed through the bat-wing doors of the first watering hole he came to, slid to the side, and checked the men at the tables and the bar. Cigarette, cigar, and pipe smoke hung over the room in a layer, and the place smelled of stale beer, but he made sure the man he hunted wasn't there. In the second saloon, he followed the same routine, except he thumbed the thong off the hammer of his Colt. He didn't want to shoot his quarry — but he might have to.

Gundy went into two more saloons with no better luck. In the fifth, the Golden Nugget, he saw who he thought was one of the four, but dim light and smoke clouded his vision. He wanted to make sure. The man was talking with a girl, so not fearing being seen, Gundy slipped around the wall to within about ten feet of the man. He didn't stare at him, for a man can feel it when eyes are upon him. A whiplash-like glance told Gundy what he wanted to know. The breed sat there, laughing, drinking, like any other man in here. Angry bile rose in Gundy's throat. He swallowed and sucked in a deep breath.

He wanted this scum alive. He picked a table to the man's back, ordered a beer, and waited, but pulled his hat down over his eyes to partially hide his face.

Gundy watched the girls to see if they only danced, or also went upstairs with their customers. In that event he'd have a long wait unless he went up and dragged the man out of bed, which he was ready to do.

In the hour that followed no one went upstairs. He ordered another beer, sat there, and squirmed, wishing the damned breed would get tired of this place and leave.

From where he sat he could see the front door. The light above and below the bat wings dimmed, and after a while only a splotch of dark showed. It had been about noon when he came in here, now night had set in. He'd wait if it took a month.

The Comanchero had been drinking steadily. Gundy had two beers in all that time. His gold pocket watch, a wedding gift from Dee's father, told him it was ten o'clock. When he looked up from reading the time, the breed pushed himself to his feet, and a mite unsteadily headed for the door. Gundy followed.

Outside on the boardwalk, he waited for the man to either get his horse or head for the hotel. The breed went to his horse.

Gundy relaxed a little. His buckskin was also at the hitch rail.

The Comanchero reached for the reins looped around the rail and Gundy stuck his .44 in his ribs. "Don't reach for your gun an' you'll live a little longer."

Instead, the breed reached to the back of his neck for a knife. Gundy, in a chopping motion, brought his pistol down on the greasy head.

Not waiting for the man to fall, Gundy caught him by the collar and held him upright until he could get in front of him and hoist him like a bag of oats across his saddle.

"Hey! What're you doing with that man?" The voice came from behind Gundy. Damned if he would see this chance foiled. He looked over his shoulder. "Jest tryin' to get my drunk partner out of the saloons an' back to camp." The man he talked to had a star on his vest.

"We got a herd out o' town a ways. He was s'posed to be back by nightfall — last night, didn't make it, so I come for 'im."

The marshal leaned closer to peer at Gundy, grunted, and said, "If that rotgut he's been drinkin' don't kill 'im, the tender care you're giving him will. Go then, get out of my town."

"Didn't figure to be tender with 'im, Marshal. I had to stand the bastard's watch last night."

Gundy pulled a pigging string from his saddle and tied the breed's hands and feet to the cinch rings, mounted his horse, swung his hand up in a casual farewell, and rode toward the edge of town. The last thing he saw before clearing the town was the pretty waitress standing beside the road. She lifted her hand in a tentative good-bye.

chapter two

Gundy took the north trail out of town, headed toward Pueblo. After about a mile the breed started mumbling. Gundy wanted him wide awake — wanted him to know all that happened to him.

After another half hour the Comanchero grunted, "Hey, amigo, why you do this to me? Untie me. Let me go. I do nothing to you." Gundy only looked at his filthy head hanging at the side of the horse.

He rode another three hours, and figured he'd come about twenty miles from Trinidad, another ten miles or so and he'd be in Walsenburg. He didn't want that.

This trail, although well traveled in daytime, was deserted at night. Gundy figured anybody in their right mind would've made camp hours ago. Only the muffled clop of their horses' hooves broke the silent darkness. The air had a fresh, clean smell.

What he had in mind for the breed wouldn't stand for interference. Gundy thought to get into the mountains before he went to work on him. Then he could take his time.

He kneed the buckskin, left the trail, and headed west. After about five miles Gundy drew rein, dismounted, and went about making camp.

He went to the breed, cut the lashings holding his feet to the saddle, and again tied them. He did the same for the man's hands — then upended him from the saddle. Gundy had tied his hands and feet so tight he thought it would cut circulation. He didn't care if gangrene set in; the filthy bastard wouldn't have use for either extremity when he got through with him.

He opened a tin of beans, fried some bacon, and ate a cold biscuit sopped in bacon grease. Drinking coffee, he looked over the rim of his cup into the breed's eyes. Fear literally dripped from them. "Huh, you finally recognize me, eh, droppings from a dog?"

"*Si,* senor, I know you, but I 'ave nothing to do with killing your wife. Ranse Barton did that evil theeng."

"All o' you raided my ranch — you all die."

"No, senor, I beg of you, don't do theez theeng to me. I 'ave hear of you many years now, and 'ave always feared the Apache Blanco."

"The Apache Blanco was dead until you an' that filth you ride with brought him back to life. Where'd the others go?"

"I do not know, senor."

"Well, think on it overnight. You tell me an' I might kill you easier — right now I ain't figurin' on it."

"You gonna feed me, senor?"

"Don't push your luck." Gundy slid down against his saddle and went to sleep.

The next morning stars still sparkled in the black skies when Gundy kindled his breakfast fire.

He took a swallow of his second cup of coffee and turned his head slightly to hear better. The soft thud of a horse's hooves reached his ears. He faded into the darkness, away from the sound. Another few moments and a voice hailed, "Hello the camp."

"Ride in, climb down, keep your hands in sight — an' empty."

The rider materialized out of the dark. He kneed his horse so his left side was visible to the fire and stepped from his horse, holding his hands wide of his guns. He was a tall, spare man, and in the flicker of the fire Gundy saw he was tanned to a dark mahogany. He'd spent a lifetime outdoors, probably in the saddle.

"Set, an' pour yourself some coffee."

"Thanks, stranger. Jest finished a cup at my own fire an hour or so ago. But figure a man can always use another." He glanced at the breed and turned his eyes back to Gundy. "Trouble?"

"No. No trouble. Just got a little problem. Ain't figured how to kill 'im yet. Thing is, it's gonna be slow."

The rider stared at the Comanchero a moment. "He must've done you a great hurt, friend. Most men deserve a chance."

"You want to help 'im — try your luck, stranger."

A slight smile crinkled the corners of the rider's eyes. "No, I don't think I want trouble with you. You want to talk 'bout what he done to you?"

"Only to say, he killed my wife, him an' three others."

"Don' believe heem, senor. He eez the Apache Blanco. He always catch people like me weeth meexed blood an' keel us. He hate us." The Comanchero's eyes filled with hope; this rider was the only chance he had.

Gundy, using his left hand, poured himself and the rider another cup of coffee. He nodded. "I'm the Apache Blanco, all right, if you've ever heard of him. But three years ago, Lew Wallace, territorial governor of New Mexico, gave me a full pardon. I ain't done nothin' bad for seventeen years. Before that I was a kid raised by the Mescalero, rode with them on raids — raised hell in general. Done nothin' bad since."

The stranger stared at Gundy a moment, took a swallow of his coffee, and said, "Always wondered what you were like. Been hearing about you for years. I heard what that bunch did to you down Texas way a few weeks ago. Woulda bet my saddle you'd be after them but never figured to run into you."

A thin smile creased the corners of his mouth. "Somehow, I thought you'd be wider, taller, and one hell of a lot meaner-looking." His eyes swept Gundy from head to toe. "You're plenty tall, but built more like a fine sword." He nodded. "Figure you'd be a ring-tailed coyote if crossed. I ain't gonna cross you, Blanco." He finished his coffee and stood.

"Reckon I'll be getting along now."

While he was climbing on his horse, the breed, his voice thin and reedy, whined, "Senor, you cain't leave me like this. Help me."

The stranger's eyes flicked from the breed to Gundy. "Something you need to know. I got a pickup message on the four you told me about from Marshal Ben Darcy down in Marfa, Texas, two, three days ago. Since meeting you I figure to let you handle it your way." He reached in his shirt pocket and flipped out a badge. "I'm Deputy United States Marshal Lawrence Bean — and anyone asks me — I've never seen you in my life." Again that thin smile creased his lips. He kneed his horse into the wan light of the coming day.

Gundy broke camp, again slung the breed across his saddle, tied him securely, and rode westward.

By nightfall, deep into the mountains, tall ponderosa pines surrounded him. All day, and much of the night before, he had thought on what to do with this man he took into the wilderness. The gringo was the one he reserved special Apache treatment for. He was the one who killed Dee. This one, he decided, would get an even break, even though he didn't deserve it.

He shivered. The animal trail they followed was over seven thousand feet high. Gundy shrugged into his sheepskin, glanced at the breed, raised his eyebrows, and rode on.

Rain squalls or even snow showers were not uncommon at this altitude, regardless of the season. Finally he saw what he looked for. A deadfall had torn itself from the base of a cliff, leaving a cavelike hole in the side of the hill. The hole would make a good campsite.

Gundy set up camp first. It might take him a while to get what he needed from the breed. After starting supper, spreading his blankets, and cleaning and oiling his guns, he cut his Comanchero loose and re-tied him, although not as tight as the night before.

Gundy ate, deliberately left a few bites of beans and bacon, passed them before the breed's nose, held his plate so the Comanchero could see what was on it — then tossed the contents into the brush. This was the second day of no food and no water for the breed, but hunger would not bother him much longer.

Gundy cleaned his plate in a narrow stream at the bottom of the hill and re-turned to camp. "Where'd them other three go when they left you?"

"Gringo, I don' tell you nothin'. I'm hungry an' thirsty. You gonna feed me?"

Gundy smiled. "Ah, *si,* you will tell me. It might take a while but I guaran-dam-tee you'll tell me. An' I ain't never gonna feed you."

He threw more wood on the fire, then walked into the brush until he found a sapling about two inches in diameter. Using his Bowie knife, he cut it down and made two stakes, each about two feet long.

Back in camp he untied the breed's feet. He tried to kick Gundy, but missed. Gundy hit him across his shins with a stake, pulled his boots off, and retied his feet. Gundy held his head to the side, trying not to breathe. "You put on clean socks when the last pair rotted off?"

He drove one of the stakes in the ground, jerked the Comanchero's arms out straight, and put his knees on each elbow while tying his hands to it, then wrapped his fingers in the stringy, black hair and pulled him straight. The breed tried to curl up. Gundy backhanded him across his face, drove the other stake in the ground, and stretched the breed so his feet barely reached it. Gundy tied his feet to that stake.

The Comanchero's gaze followed him about the camp, his eyes wide, his lips quivering. "What you do weeth me, senor?"

"Gonna see if you really meant you wasn't gonna tell me nothin'."

Gundy delved in his possibles bag and brought out a spare cinch ring. "You ever rustle cows — blot brands?" He nodded.

"Yeah, know you have, so you know how to use a cinch ring."

He put the steel into the coals, and while waiting for it to heat, rolled and smoked a cigarette. He would rather have had his pipe, but reserved that smoke for when relaxing.

The Comanchero twisted his head to the side, and cutting his eyes downward held them on the steel ring beginning to glow a cherry-red.

"You cannot do theez to me, Blanco. Eet ees not human."

"Nobody ever said I was human." He pulled the ring from the fire. "You gonna tell me names and places, so suck in your guts. Don't want you to tell me too quick. First, gonna have a little fun." Gundy felt like he'd never talked so much in his life, but talk might make the breed fear the happenings more.

Holding the ring between two sticks, he pressed it to the bottom of the breed's left foot. Smoke and steam mixed with a scream ripped from the bandit's throat.

Gundy pulled the ring away and put it back in the fire. The breed whimpered. "*Madre de Dios,* stop this. You're worse than anything I ever hear. *Por favor,* stop."

Gundy again removed the ring from the fire — and crammed it against the right foot. Again the inhuman scream rent the air. "Wish you'd of washed your feet 'fore I started — maybe the stink wouldn't be so bad." He pulled the steel, now cooled to a bright gray, away and carefully placed it back in the coals. Then he slit both trouser legs as far as the breed's knees.

"Oh, please, senor, I tell you wat you wan' to know. Now I tell you." His whole face quivered. Sweat poured from it. His eyes were squeezed tight with pain. "Now I tell you," he repeated. "They all go to Denver."

"They didn't go to Denver. Think I'll cook you a little more — loosen your brain so you think better." He pressed the ring to the calf of the Comanchero's leg, only to see what had been a man go limp; his face, a pasty white, framed closed eyes. Gundy placed the ring back in the fire.

Every time Gundy burned the bandit, he thought he'd get rid of his supper, but when he'd begin to weaken, begin to feel he couldn't continue, he'd bring up a picture of Dee as he'd last seen her in that kitchen.

The outlaw stirred, opened his eyes, and lay there a moment. His eyes told Gundy he searched his brain as to where he was — and what happened to him. He glanced at the fire and began to sweat again. "I tell you now. They go to Leadville. They weel not stay there an' I don' know where they go then. Please do not burn me again, senor."

Gundy believed him. He drew the ring from the fire and let it cool. He stared at the man for a moment. "Thought 'bout lettin' you go, but cain't do that. Couldn't sleep if I did. In the morning I'm gonna strap a six-gun on you an' see if you can beat me."

"Blanco, I cannot beat you. Maybe no man can. Geev me a chance, Blanco."

"That's all the chance you got. You don't draw on me, I'll kill you anyhow. None o' you gave my wife or my men a chance."

Gundy checked the lashings on the breed's hands and feet, stoked the fire, and crawled between his blankets. Long after he lay down, he thought of what he'd just done, and felt no remorse. He closed his eyes, and behind his eyelids he saw pictures of Dee as she had been on their wedding night, and when she told him they were to have a baby, and as she looked when riding her favorite horse, her long black hair streaming behind, her green eyes sparkling and full of life. He thought of her until sleep took him.

The next morning before daylight, he put more wood on the fire, knelt close to the ground, and blew on the coals until flame sprang up. Then he put coffee on.

Overnight, a light snow dusted the trees, making them look a lighter green against the dull gray sky. Stringers of clouds hung veillike in the gorges, and some, only head high, coated him with beads of moisture. He pulled tighter into his sheepskin.

He opened another tin of beans, fried bacon, and opened a tin of peaches for breakfast. Again he withheld food and water from the breed.

Gundy cleaned the campsite, poured water from a small snowmelt stream on the fire, saddled his horse, and turned to the Comanchero. "It's a good day to die, dog droppings. Only you an' them other breeds gonna get some sorta chance. The gringo gets nothin'."

"Blanco, I can't beat you. You might as well keel me now."

"Don't do things that way, always give a man a chance."

He strapped on his guns, took one from its holster, and stuck it down in the man's belt. "When I cut you loose, take time to get the blood back in your hands, then make your play."

He cut the thongs holding the breed to the stakes and stood across the campsite from him. The bandit massaged his wrists. With his feet burned raw, he couldn't stand. Gundy waited, knowing the breed would try a sneak play.

The Comanchero slowly rubbed his hands and wrists. Long after Gundy knew he had full use of them, he still rubbed them. A gleam came into the black eyes, and the bandit dropped his hands into his lap close to the gun, still rubbing his hands.

Gundy made as though to turn his back. The breed's hand flashed to the six-gun.

chapter three

Gundy waited until the muzzle cleared the breed's belt, then, seeming to him like slow motion, he palmed his pistol and fired into the chest facing him. A black hole opened in the man's left shirt pocket.

The Comanchero jerked off a shot, his .44 still pointed to the side. Gundy squeezed off another shot. A black ring showed above the breed's belt buckle. Its twin welled a steady red stream. The stumpy bandit again tried to bring his gun in line with Gundy, but it settled ever so slowly to rest on his thigh.

"You 'ave keeled me, Blanco." He tried again to raise the gun from his leg. Then his eyes widened, glazed, and he toppled to the side.

Gundy stared at him, punched the empties from his handgun, reloaded, walked to the mass that had been a man, and picked up his pistol. "Three to go." He said it softly. There was no one to hear, but it gave him satisfaction to know he had done part of the job. Again, he felt no remorse.

Before riding, he cleaned his weapons, again looked at the breed, and left him lying where he had fallen.

Three days later he rode down the main street of Leadville. He wondered that men would live in such a place, cold the year around. The sides of the hills showed great raw scars, where men scraped, dug, and dynamited to rip silver ore from the gaping wounds. Houses huddled close together as though to protect each from the cold and snow. Chestnut Street was a quagmire and the continuing rain promised it would stay that way.

Gundy tied his horse in front of the Grand Hotel; it had been the City Hotel the last time he saw it.

At the desk he asked for a room, and water taken to it for a bath. "Mister, I'll put you on the waiting list. We don't have an empty room, haven't had in seven years. You'll probably have to wait about three weeks to get in."

Gundy shook his head. "No, reckon I'll sleep in the livery."

"Yeah. If they got any space left, even then they'll charge you to stay there."

"You seen two breeds an' a white man ride through here in the last week or so?"

"Yeah, they wanted a room, and when they found none were available, and wouldn't be for a while, one said he was going to ride on, was going to Red River; the other two, the white man and one of the breeds, headed for Cheyenne."

Gundy left. He thought to stock up on supplies, but changed his mind when he checked the prices. The storekeepers were getting their share of the silver taken out of the ground without the backbreaking labor or risk.

Gundy stood by his horse in front of the general store. He knew the area where all three of the Comancheros had gone. Which way should he go, north or south? If he went north he might never find the third man. If he went south, he thought he could cut back to the Denver trail at Raton, and head for Cheyenne after taking care of the man in Red River. He smiled and hunkered farther into his sheepskin. On the east side of the mountains it would be warm. He could stand a little heat.

He checked his possibles bag and saddlebags. He had enough provisions to last about a week if he lived off the land. He headed south for Red River, long known as an outlaw hangout.

Gundy, despite the reputation of the

town, was glad to see its lights. Ten days of some of the hardest riding he'd known lay behind him. His buckskin's ribs looked like he could play a tune on them. *He* felt about as gaunt as his horse.

He kneed his horse ahead and reined in at the hotel, rented a room, took the buckskin to the livery, left instructions for him to be fed grain every day, and went back to his room for a much needed bath and shave.

Then, stretched out on the corn-shuck mattress, he intended to take stock of what he knew, and think about how to go about finding his quarry. Before he could get his thoughts in line, his eyelids, as though they had weights on them, insisted on closing. After forcing them open for the third time he gave up.

The next morning when he stepped from the hotel he studied the town. Gray, unpainted buildings bordered the one dusty street. Pines on the hillsides pushed down to the backs of the buildings trying to take back what man had taken from them. Saloons, signs hanging over the boardwalk depicting them as such, seemed to occupy most of the buildings. But now he wanted breakfast.

In the town's only cafe, a woman who

looked like she doubled as a saloon bouncer at night waited on him. After eating, he sat over his third cup of coffee and studied the waitress, wanting to ask her some questions but decided against it. His best chance at finding the breed would be to look for him — and the best place would be the saloons.

After eating, he walked along the main street. This time of day he expected to see shopkeepers opening for business and the street full of housewives, shopping. Instead, miners filled the streets, and men with low-hung guns strapped to their legs. And the women he saw were hollow-eyed, haggard-looking, and overpainted. They came from the saloons after their night's work. It wasn't a town he wanted to spend time in.

He looked at his watch, too early for a beer but he wanted to start his search. He shrugged. A beer could last a long time if he nursed it. A careful study of the street showed the Best Chance as the busiest-looking saloon, a good place to start.

Gundy went in and waited for his eyes to adjust to the dark; there might be someone in here who knew him. He had enough trouble already without more finding him.

Several tables stood empty against the

back wall; he chose the one in the corner. A skinny girl, looking to be about forty, but more than likely about twenty-two or -three years old, came to the table. "Whatcha want, mister?"

"Beer."

"Can I sit with you? Buy me a drink?"

"Don't want no company, just bring me a beer." Gundy didn't mean to be unfriendly, but he had felt no other way since leaving the Big Bend. The girl's shoulders drooped a little at his words.

She brought his beer, he paid her, and when she turned to walk away, he said, "Lady, I didn't mean to hurt your feelin's." He picked a quarter from the change on the table and handed it to her. "Buy yourself a beer, I just don't want no company." She smiled, and it brightened her face such that she almost looked her age.

Gundy pulled his pipe from his vest pocket, tamped and lighted it. Sitting alone, no conversation, his back to a wall, nobody to bother him, he relaxed.

He'd been there only a few minutes when a tall, bony man came to his table. "Ain't friendly to sit here alone like this, stranger." He squinted at Gundy, studying him. "You *are* a stranger — new to our town, ain't you?"

40

Gundy took his pipe from his mouth and carefully placed it on the table, looking at the man all the while. "Ain't lonely, an' now that you asked, you ever see me before? If you ain't, then I'm a stranger. I figure on stayin' one. Get lost."

"Wh-what'd you say? Why damn you, that's right unfriendly."

With his left hand, Gundy picked his pipe up and stuck it in his mouth, drew his handgun with his right, and rested it on his leg. The skinny, hatchet-faced man obviously hadn't seen Gundy pull his .44. He reached for the edge of the table and tossed it to the side, spilling Gundy's beer. He set his feet to get closer to Gundy and cocked his fist to swing. Gundy lifted his .44 and held it at arm's length pointed dead center between the man's eyes.

"Now it'd be right unfriendly o' you to swing that fist. If you do, I'm gonna spill more than a drink, gonna spill your brains over most o' this room. Sit down, an' when that little old girl comes back you're gonna buy me a beer."

"I'll be damned if I will."

Gundy smiled. "Naw, now you see, you're wrong again. You won't be damned if you do, you'll be dead if you don't. See how messed up your thinkin' is?" He still

41

held the pistol about two inches from the man's face.

The man's eyes crossed trying to focus on the bore of the Colt sticking in his face. The corners of his lips creased, his eyes crinkled at the corners — and he laughed.

He went to the table he'd just thrown to the side, set it upright, dragged it back in front of Gundy, pulled up a chair, and sat. Still smiling, he said, "Stranger, you got a mighty convincin' way about you." He held out his hand. "Name's Slade, folks call me Blacky."

Gundy frowned. He had heard of Blacky Slade, the leader of all outlaws in this part of the territory, and now, he decided, Slade must be crazy. Here he sat with a gun sticking in his face, and he grinned. Gundy, still frowning, shook his head, then holstered his pistol.

"Mister, you must be one o' the loneliest bastards I ever seen. You just went to some length to make my acquaintance." He shook Slade's hand — with his left. "Name's Trace Gundy. Now, you gonna buy me another beer?"

Slade looked over his shoulder. "Cindy, bring us a couple beers." To Gundy he said, "I really was only tryin' to make your acquaintance. I like to know who comes and goes in this town."

"Why?"

Slade squinted at Gundy. "You never heard of Blacky Slade?"

Gundy shook his head. "Not that I recollect," he lied. "You a known man?"

"Some say I am. A few marshals an' sheriffs lookin' for me. You don't need to tell me who you are. I've heard about Trace Gundy many years."

Gundy frowned. Would his reputation follow him the rest of his life? "Don't believe all you hear, Slade. 'Sides that, I been pardoned, free to go where I want, an' do most anything I want inside the law."

Slade stared at Gundy straight on. "You got any fight with me, Blanco?"

Gundy, trying to think how to answer, swept the room with a glance. As the leader of these outlaws, how loyal was Slade? Enough to protect them from a killing? He decided to answer with the truth. "That depends, Slade. I come here to kill a man. You stand in my way, you an' me got trouble."

Slade shrugged, raised his eyebrows, and said, "If I could stand in your way, must not be me you're lookin' for. So, that bein' the case, any trouble you got with somebody else ain't no business of mine."

Gundy gave him a thin smile. "It ain't you, Slade."

The skinny outlaw picked up his beer, held it out in a toast, and said, "Here's to no trouble 'tween us."

Again using his left hand, Gundy drank. His caution drew a smile from Slade. Gundy swept the room with a glance. The breed wasn't there. He finished his beer and stood. "Thanks for the beer. I'll buy you one next time."

Slade nodded.

Gundy walked from the stale air and darkness of the saloon into the crisp smell of the outside and bright sunlight. He filled his lungs and searched the street for the next place he'd look. He settled on the Pine Cone. It had nearly as many horses in front as had the Best Chance.

This saloon was not quite as large as the last so he shouldered up to the bar, quickly looked at each man there, and turned to leave.

"What's the matter, partner, not thirsty this time o' day?"

Gundy looked at the lanky cowboy and saw only friendly interest in his eyes. "Thought I was, then figured since I just ate breakfast, an' it's a long time 'til dark, I'd wait awhile."

44

The cowboy nodded. "Reckon you're right, but there's darned little to do in this town besides drink an' lie around with these women." He grinned. "You ever see such a bunch of pure-dee ugly women in your life?"

Gundy chuckled. "They might look better if a man had been punchin' cows about a month with no time in town. An' if them women had a bath anytime during that month." He held up his hand in a friendly wave. "See yuh."

The next saloon was no better — or worse, but the Comanchero wasn't there. Gundy checked three more with the same luck. All the while he pondered how to get the breed out of town and on the trail with him without having an all-out gunfight. He decided he'd play the cards the way they fell.

Gundy had been looking in places that had good business. Now he scraped the bottom of the barrel. The place he stood in front of had raw, unpainted shiplap for siding and a rusty tin roof. He elbowed his way past men who were obviously the town's riffraff. He tried not to breathe the stench of unwashed bodies, and the place had only two lanterns lighting it. His eyes took longer to adjust than he liked. Those who had been in there awhile would see him long before he had that advantage.

He pulled his hat down on his forehead, and keeping his head lowered, he stood against the wall. Finally satisfied he could see as well as he ever would, he looked up — right into the eyes of the man he was looking for.

A man stood between Gundy and the breed and before Gundy could clear a space between them, the Comanchero pushed and shoved his way to the door with Gundy only a few steps behind.

Gundy jammed his way to the street into the bright sunlight, only to catch a glimpse of the breed turning the corner between two buildings.

The streets were almost empty of people. It was time for the noon meal. Gundy ran to the corner of the building, stopped, and carefully peered around it. Empty. He ran toward the back and slowly poked his head out to see. A bullet knocked slivers into his chest. He drew back, poked his pistol out, triggered a shot, spun and ran to the front of the building, rounded it, ran to the other corner, and again headed toward the back.

Reaching the corner of the building, Gundy dropped to the ground and poked his head around far enough to see. The breed stood close to the stand of trees that pushed up to the back of the saloon, his side toward Gundy, his eyes locked on the space Gundy had just left.

Gundy stood, walked into the open, and, his voice soft, said, "You lookin' for me?"

chapter four

The breed spun, firing blindly — three times. A shot knocked a board from the corner of the shack they stood behind, another tugged at Gundy's vest, and another went into the dirt at his feet.

Gundy triggered off all six shots in one continuous roar. Despite how fast it happened, Gundy watched each bullet hit the breed, four in the middle of his chest. The last one knocked his nose back into his face, tearing off the back of his head. A crowd gathered. Gundy swallowed hard, the brassy taste in his throat choking him. That bullet tugging on his vest had been too close.

Gundy, his face feeling like leather and his eyes burning like white-hot steel, asked those around him, "He got friends here who want to take it up?" It came to him, the six-gun in his hand was empty. He made a border shift, holstered the empty gun, and stood with a full cylinder facing them.

Gundy's gaze centered on each in the

crowd, boring into them. One by one their eyes lowered. One of them said, "He wasn't known hereabouts. And even if he was, *I* ain't gonna be the one to face that draw o' yourn. The way you shifted and drawed without me bein' able to see you do it? Uh-uh, not me, stranger."

Gundy nodded and waved the barrel of his pistol for them to head back to the street. Most of them glanced at the man Gundy had killed, lying in the dust, and left.

When Gundy again stood alone, he walked to the body, looked down at it, and felt only a twinge of remorse at having taken another life. This man had been a party to killing his wife, and there were two more of them.

He holstered his gun and reloaded the empty one. Not until then did he go to the livery for his horse, ride to the hotel for his gear, and head out of town. Two left, and one of them was the gringo.

He stayed that night in Eagles Nest, and again grain-fed the buckskin.

Early the next morning he headed for Raton, but before he could reach there, he would travel through Cimarron Canyon, to his way of thinking one of the most beautiful places he'd been.

And for the first time since Dee's death,

he found himself looking forward to something other than vengeance. Some of the hardness went from him. His chest loosened, his heart seemed to pump warm blood instead of ice. But the gringo was still out there ahead of him. Gundy wouldn't allow himself to soften now.

He camped that night in a deep copse of trees alongside the Cimarron River at the bottom of the canyon. Water tumbled over rocks, soothing Gundy's raw emotions. He liked the music of it, but wondered whether the bubbling and gurgling would cover sounds of approaching men. It was worth the chance.

After eating, he lay against his saddle, listening to the water and smoking his pipe. What would Dee think of what he was doing? Despite what they had done to her she wouldn't want him wasting his life on a vengeance trail, she would want him to go on with life, build his ranch, maybe get married again after a suitable time. Yeah, she'd want all that for him. His face muscles tightened. She wasn't looking at it from his side of the coin. He'd never rest, or do any of those things, as long as her killer and the breed lived.

Weeks passed and the cold Gundy had

known in Leadville and the comfort of Cimarron Canyon thawed in the searing heat of the plains. Pueblo, Denver, and Fort Collins lay behind him.

During his ride, the distant blue mountains took on white crowns, and with passing days snow crept farther down their shoulders. Winter would soon be upon the land.

Cheyenne spread in front of him. Looking at it, Gundy didn't see the town, he saw only the end of the trail. With any luck the gringo and the breed would both be here and he could turn the buckskin's nose to the south again.

Despite his yearning for home, Cheyenne's opulence pushed itself into his mind. Stopping his horse at the end of the main street he counted no less than twelve variety halls that served most entertainment needs: theater, saloon, gambling, and women. Finding his prey here would not be easy.

He stopped at the cheapest-looking hotel. If he didn't find the men he looked for he would have to find a job and a place to winter. He wouldn't write Kelly for money.

After stashing his gear, he went to the lobby, picked up a newspaper at the desk, and sat to read. Even though not an old building, the room in which he sat smelled musty. Maybe he noticed it more because of the time he'd spent outdoors. He finally put the paper aside and leaned his head against the cushion.

Where could he go from here? The men he hunted could have caught the Union Pacific and headed east or west, or they could have ridden north.

He was tired, tired of riding, tired of killing, tired of not being home. But where was home? Dee no longer was there to hold tight to him in the night, no longer there to welcome him at the end of a day. And there, he was known as the Apache Blanco, a name it seemed he would never live down. Also, he had two more men to take care of before he shed the teachings of the Apache.

He stood. He'd not had coffee since breakfast.

Out on the street he looked both ways and sighted a small cafe about a half block away.

Sitting, with his coffee and a piece of apple pie in front of him, Gundy studied the people and wondered at how much each cowtown and its people were alike, yet these people were different in small ways. Some seemed to be more what he would call city folks. Their clothes were not quite as rough, some wore suits instead of Levi's.

Many wore string ties. Gundy couldn't see much use for a necktie; he couldn't wipe sweat with it, couldn't tie it across his face to ward off dust, couldn't . . . Well, hell, he couldn't use one for anything except to choke him.

He finished his pie and coffee and went out on the street. Cheyenne was too large a place to ask if anyone had seen two riders that fit the descriptions of those he wanted. While standing in front of the cafe, he counted at least fifteen men of the size and build of the ones he looked for, except they had the wrong face. The way he would describe a face wouldn't turn up any who'd seen them.

Gundy had heard somewhere it was best to stay still and let those you wanted come to you. He again looked down the street. Too many places to check out. A bench in front of a store, on the shady side of the street, came under his gaze, a vantage point about midway in the business district. Gundy crossed the street and sat on the smooth, worn board slab.

People moved up and down the street like a sluggish stream. Gundy sorted them out, studying each one. About midafternoon the throng thinned. The man Gundy took to be the proprietor of the store came out and stood by his side. "Reckon if I use your bench much longer, you gonna charge me rent on it."

The man chuckled. "Nope, set long's you want. Been watchin' you though. You lookin' for somebody?"

Gundy hesitated. "No. Been ridin' a long time, ain't seen nobody much and figured to set here an' look a spell. Cheyenne's gettin' to be a pretty good-sized city. Ain't seen one like it, 'cept maybe Denver."

The man nodded. "Railroad's brought in a lot of people, track workers, all sorts of them workin' for the U.P., and a lot of Texans are up looking for ranchland. Yeah, we got us a pretty good town growing here." A customer walked into his store, and the storekeeper turned to follow. "Set long's you want, young man." He chuckled again. "I promise, I'll not charge you rent on that bench."

Gundy sat there until after dark, went to his room, slept, and was back early the next morning. He followed the same routine for four days.

Opening for business on the fifth day, the store's owner looked at Gundy, a crease between his brows. "Young man, I don't know why you're here, you're welcome to stay long's you like, but you're not just lookin' *at* people. You're lookin' *for* someone."

Gundy stared at the dusty street a moment, then locked gazes with the man, he'd learned his name was Renton. "Yes, sir, reckon I done used your bench long enough I owe you an answer. I'm lookin' for a couple of men what did me a bad wrong."

Renton stared at him a moment. "Well, Mr. Gundy, I'll not ask the nature of the wrong; I'll just say, I hope you find them."

Gundy nodded. "Thank you, sir. I'll find 'em. Ain't gonna rest 'til I do."

Renton nodded and went in the store.

Gundy was allowing himself thirty-five cents a day to eat on. He'd have a morning cup of coffee, one at noon, and then a quarter for supper. He'd moved out of the hotel and was camped down along the Crow River, but was back at his bench early each morning.

The seventh morning, his vigil paid off. At first, he thought he was wrong, but then the young breed, who had almost walked by him, glanced, looked away, and again snapped his head in his direction. He ran.

Gundy launched himself from his seat, caught him in less than ten steps, grabbed his collar, and tossed him to the ground. The breed had no gun that Gundy could see.

"Comanchero, I'm gonna take you outta this here town. You gonna tell me what I want to know. Then I'm givin' you a gun. Gonna kill you."

The young man looked at Gundy, his black eyes wide, with a trace of fear lurking in their depths. "Senor, I know you have theeze theeng to do, but I must tell you, I 'ave never keeled anyone. I deed not even shoot. I 'ave never had a *pistola* in my life."

"What were you doin' with that bunch, then?"

"*Mi hermano,* me brother, as you would say, take me weeth heem. He promise *mi padre* he well take care of me, so he make me ride weeth heem, 'til you keel heem in your *yarda,* then the Senor Barton take me weeth heem. I 'ave no home, so I go weeth the senor."

Gundy stared at the young man for a long moment, stared into the almost fearless but honest eyes, and felt his heart pump warm blood again. He believed the youth's story.

"Where is the man you traveled with?

56

Think I done seen every puncher, railroader, an' city man in this town. Ain't seen either o' you 'til today. Where you been? Where's the gringo?"

"Senor, I 'ave a job weeth the railroad. They teach me — how do you say eet? *Sí,* they teach me to make the fire in the engine. I 'ave been on the trip." The young breed shrugged. "Senor Barton, he ees not here. He ees gone."

Gundy felt like he'd had a knife stuck in him. He went flat. "Get on your feet, boy." The breed stood, looking at Gundy's holstered gun all the while. His eyes shifted from the Colt to look into Gundy's eyes. "*Sí,* senor, the Senor Barton ees gone, many days ago."

"You know where he went?"

"*Sí.* He say he go to see his brother in a place called Milestown in the Montana country. He ees gonna be a partner with heez brother een a cantina."

Gundy studied the youth. He had no reason to kill him. The boy had not wronged him in any way. He'd simply been in the wrong place at the wrong time. For only the second time in as many months, his heart thawed. He felt like whistling.

"*Muchacho,* I will not harm you. You seem like a good boy. Barton's a different story. Go now, go about your business. You can work without fear."

The young man's eyes looked as though he'd seen death — and it had walked away from him. "*Gracias,* senor, I know you must avenge, ees that the word? *Sí,* that ees the word, you must avenge what he did to you. I 'ave heard him brag about it. Again, senor, thank you for my life. I go now?"

Gundy nodded. The young breed walked swiftly away, then broke into a sprint, looking over his shoulder every few yards.

Gundy walked to his campsite, packed his gear, counted his few dollars, saddled up, and rode out. Rance Barton's date with hell had to be postponed until Gundy could make sure he had the means to survive the winter that day by day pushed summer a little farther south.

He figured to get work on a ranch somewhere around Milestown, then in the spring he'd scout Milestown until he knew every store, saloon, creek, everything about it. He had a hard two hundred seventy-five or more miles ahead of him.

The first night out of Cheyenne, he made a dry camp. He'd crossed Lodgepole Creek and didn't want to push his gelding trying to make it to the Chugwater. He had been in short-grass country for quite a spell, and his horse had had no grain in some time.

He found out the next day he could have made it to Horse Creek and had a fire, along with water. Buffalo chips were getting scarce, and here on the plains he found no wood. He scouted the banks of the Horse and gathered enough limbs and twigs to be sure of fire enough to boil coffee that night, in case he couldn't make it to Chugwater Creek by nightfall.

Between Cheyenne and Douglas, Gundy made only the one dry camp, but from there to Gillette he was looking for sinkholes, ravines, anywhere there might have been water for the gelding — and him. It was not until he crossed the Belle Fouche that they again drank their fill.

He stopped overnight at the settlement of Gillette, bought coffee out of his few remaining dollars, and asked the storekeeper the best way to get to Milestown.

"Pardner, don't know how long it'll take you to get there, but outta here, bear a little east and you'll come across the Little Powder, ride along it 'til it forks into the Powder, then cut straight west 'til you come to 'nother stream — that's the Pumpkin. Ride along it 'til you come to the

Tongue — *it* runs right down the side o' Milestown. Cain't miss it. Course, I'd say you got 'bout week an' a half, maybe two weeks ride ahead o' you."

"Pard', I done come a lot farther'n that. I'll find it, and much obliged."

Eight days later the weather turned raw. Cold rain set in, and Gundy figured he'd better find a place to hole up for the winter. He looked at his money again. Three dollars wouldn't take him far, and Rance Barton could wait; besides, Barton would stay in Milestown and leech off his brother. Dee would want him to take care of himself first. Gundy found it a little harder with the passing of the days and weeks to keep the cold hatred he'd carried so long. He'd get to Barton in his own good time, but first he had to make sure he had a place to winter, or he wouldn't get there at all.

He topped a hill, and spread out before him was the sweetest-looking ranch he'd seen in months. It looked like a good place to find a job.

Riding toward the ranch house, he noticed a sad lack of young beef, course they might have sold the young stuff off before winter set in. He nodded. That was what he would have done, save feeding through the cold months.

The gelding plodded down the side of what Gundy took to be the bunkhouse. No fire showed through the window, and no lamplight. What with the time and the dark dreariness of the day, Gundy wondered at the desolate look and rode to the veranda of the main house.

In answer to his knock, footsteps sounded inside, then a woman's voice. "Yes? Who is it?"

"Ma'am, ain't nobody you know. Just wondered if I could use your barn or bunkhouse to get in out of the weather. Also, ma'am, if you're hirin', I could sure use a job."

A bar rubbed against the rough wood inside and the door opened a crack.

Gundy knew she stood there studying him. "Ma'am, I ain't much to look at, bein' drenched like a drowned pup; fact is I probably ain't much to look at any time, but I'm a worker."

A chuckle from inside and the door swung wide. "C'mon in, cowboy. I was about ready to set for supper. You're welcome to share what I fixed." Gundy made a quick swipe to remove his hat, wishing his hair wasn't plastered soggily to his head.

He stared — couldn't help it. The soft

woman's voice, with the lilt to it he'd heard through the door, came from the most handsome woman he'd seen since Dee. Her face was strong, maybe too strong to be called beautiful, but the beauty was there, and Gundy drank it in. Brown hair, blue eyes, and a figure with everything — enough of everything — in the right places.

"You gotta pardon me for starin', ma'am. Didn't expect to see a woman so all-fired pretty." His face turned warm. "Aw now, I shouldn't of said that. Make you think wrong of me."

Again, she chuckled. "No, cowboy. I won't think wrong of you. Fact is, it sounded good. I've not had a compliment in ages."

Gundy glanced about the room. It was nicely furnished with sturdy, comfortable pieces. "If, after seein' me, ma'am, you'll still let me eat supper with you, I'll go out to the bunkhouse an' shave an' clean up a mite."

She nodded. "Go do that then, while I fix the biscuits."

Gundy put on his only pair of Levi's that weren't faded and worn so thin you could read a newspaper through them. He'd washed a shirt only the day before. Finished dressing, he glanced at his gun, stepped toward the door, turned back, and swung the worn gunbelt around his waist. When he felt presentable he walked through a thin mist to the house.

"Well, you did come back. The biscuits and coffee are ready, so set up to the table." Standing at the stove, she looked over her shoulder at him. "What name you using up here, cowboy?"

"My own, ma'am. Trace Gundy."

"Trace Gundy, nice name. I'm Joyce Waldrop. Folks call me Joy."

"Nice to meet you, Mrs. Waldrop."

"Joy's the name, and let's talk about that job you're looking for while we eat."

chapter five

They sat in silence until almost halfway through their meal, when Joy went to the oven for more biscuits. She brought a jar of honey, placed it in front of Gundy, and studied him a moment. "Mr. Gundy, I'll be as honest as I know how. I need help. I have two old, stove-up punchers. They do all they're able to, but there are many things they can't handle, and I can't afford to hire anyone. My calf crop disappears almost as fast as they are weaned, and I don't know how to catch the rustlers." She looked at her plate a moment, looked up, and locked gazes with him. "Mr. Gundy, I noticed you wear your gun like you know how to use it, but I can't ask your help for what I could pay."

"Who does the cookin' for your crew?"

"I do. Why?"

"Well, ma'am, I was just thinkin'. I need a place to hole up for the winter. I *could* make that into late spring, see if I might ferret out them rustlers for you." He allowed his eyes to crinkle at the corners, about as much as he'd smiled lately. "The only catch is, you'd have to feed me, an' if you have a stray cartwheel or two along the way, I need some new Levi's."

"Mr. Gundy, I can't let you do that."

"Call me Trace, ma'am."

"Deal — if you'll call me Joy."

They shook hands.

He stood and went to the door. "Reckon after I help with these here dishes, I can take my gear to the bunkhouse?"

"In my house, Mr., uh, Trace, I do the dishes."

"Yes'm, but just wonderin', ma'am, where's the menfolks? Bunkhouse was dark with I rode in."

Her smile lighted her face like one of those gas lights Gundy had seen. "Today's Saturday. Where you come from, don't people go to town then, Trace?"

Gundy returned her smile, thinking her a pretty nice lady. "Yes'm, they surely do. An' where I come from is down Texas way, Big Bend country."

"I thought as much when I saw your Texas rig. Put your horse in the stable, stash your gear, and if you would, come back. We'll have coffee and I'll sketch a rough map of my ranch. Seems like you're working for me."

Gundy nodded, went to his horse, and led him to the stable. She'd said *her* ranch. He wondered if there was a *Mister* Waldrop. Yeah, had to be. She was too pretty to be long unmarried in a country hurting for women.

He stashed his gear, cleaned and oiled his weapons, made up one of the empty bunks, and lit a fire in the potbellied stove in the middle of the floor. A glance showed fourteen bunks with no bedding or gear on them. In better times quite a few men had worked here. He headed back to the main house.

After coffee and getting the ranch boundaries committed to memory, Gundy said he'd turn in. He figured to cover as much of the ranch as daylight would allow the next day.

"Trace, the weather's rotten. Wait 'til it clears a bit."

"Ma'am, my experience with cow critters an' a ranch don't allow for many off days. I'll start in the mornin'."

On the way to the bunkhouse, he thought about the look on her face when he said he'd get started the next day. Almost like she shifted part of her load to him. It had been a relieved look. Money or not, he was glad he'd stopped here. But come spring, he'd find the gringo. He was tempted now to go on into Milestown, find the gringo, and get the whole thing over with. He shook his head. The way to find Barton and take care of him was not to stick his head in a hornets' nest without knowing what he was getting into.

Then he thought of Joy. She was in trouble — bad trouble. She could lose her ranch. What would Dee want him to do? He knew the answer to that question before he asked it of himself. He could almost hear her say, "Trace, don't you dare leave that poor woman needing help. You do what you can for her, then, if you must, find the gringo and rid the world of him."

The morning again dawned drizzly and cold. Gundy stirred the fire and went to the pump for coffee water. He didn't figure to disturb Mrs. Waldrop this time of day. Calling her by her first name was going to take some getting used to. He was on his way back to the bunkhouse with the water when she called from the front door.

"Trace Gundy, don't you dare ride out of here on an empty stomach. Breakfast's on the table. Come in and set."

"Aw, ma'am, didn't figure to bother you this time of day."

"Get in here. When you asked who did

67

the cooking around here, I took that as meaning you meant to be fed if you worked for me. Well, cowboy, you work for me so come on in."

A half hour later Gundy rode out feeling a lot better.

Joy's brand was the Flying JW, and her ranch spiked into the vee where the Pumpkin flowed into the Tongue.

While riding, Gundy kept a mental tally of the young cattle he came across. He rode down the Pumpkin to the Tongue and headed up it. The rain had been light enough to not affect the water level, and the dry summer kept the river low. By mid-afternoon he had seen only a half-dozen yearlings, all heifers.

He read every track he came across. He saw the same two sets of tracks several times and took them to belong to horses ridden by the two ranch hands. He'd check their ponies to make sure.

The fence needed mending in several places. Some of the breaks he took care of. Others, he made a note to come back to with a spool of wire and fence posts.

He got back to ranch headquarters about eight o'clock that night. The bunkhouse was dark, but showed a flicker of firelight from the stove. The men must be back.

Joy had a lamp in the window. While putting his horse away, he looked at the other ponies in the stable, checked their hooves, and verified the prints he'd seen belonged to them. He washed his face and hands, combed his hair, and knocked on the door.

"Come in, Trace. I saw you put your horse away. You work late hours, don't you? Dinner's warm, so set and eat."

At the table Joy put a heaping plate of venison, potatoes, greens, and biscuits before him, then she brought them each a cup of coffee. She gave him a direct look, like men look at each other. "Tired, Trace?"

He shook his head. "Just hungry. I'm used to long days." He cut a slice of meat and studied her a few moments, wondering if he should tell her how bad things looked.

After a minute he decided she could take any kind of news head-on. "Ma'am, you probably know it a'ready, but 'bout all you got left is old stuff. All day, I figure I ain't seen over ten, maybe fifteen yearlings."

She gazed into her cup a few moments, then again hit him with that straight-on look. She nodded. "I know. I've tried tracking little bunches away from my land, but I'm not any good at it. They'd have to leave a trail a blind man could follow for me to stay on it."

Gundy swallowed the rest of his coffee and stood to pour another cupful when she took it from his hand. "I'll get it, just sit still. You've had a hard day."

"Joy, you're gonna spoil me. I ain't used to that sort o' thing." He again sat and slanted a look over his shoulder. "Ma'am, I ain't bragging', just tellin' you like it is. I been known to track smoke across granite rock. The Apache raised me from a spindly legged colt to full grown. If them rustlers leave any sort o' trail I'll find 'em, an' when I do I'll see if I cain't read to them from the book — make them leave your stuff alone."

He stood to leave. "If the weather's tol'able tomorrow, I'd sort o' like for you to show me where you tracked 'em to. Maybe that'll give me a little start."

Joy studied him a moment. She liked the way he took hold of a problem. He was a clean-cut man, looked her in the eye when talking to her, seemed open and honest — and she needed help. There were so many things she couldn't do. Trace seemed so capable, a far cry from the two old punchers she had. Oh, they did what they were told, but the fact remained, they had to be told. Trace went out and looked at things, found what had to be done and did it. She'd known him less than a day, but she trusted him. She was used to making snap judgments about people and had seldom been wrong. Putting her trust in him couldn't cause her to lose much more. She faced up to it, if she didn't get help soon she was going to lose the ranch. It was all she had.

"We'll leave after breakfast. The boys'll be here then. And, uh, Trace, would you sort of take over and lay out their day's work?"

Gundy tipped his hat, nodded, and left.

Snores greeted him when he entered the bunkhouse. He always moved quietly, *that* lesson he learned from the Apache. He crawled into his bunk without waking them, then he lay there and stared at the firelight flickering off the ceiling beams.

He thought of Dee, and found he could think of her without bitter hatred welling into his throat. He still had every intention of killing the gringo, killing him brutally, but he now knew he could do it without anger spoiling his thinking.

From Dee, his thoughts turned to Joy. She was a lot of woman, but seemed willing, more than willing for a man to take over and run things. She readily agreed to showing him what she knew of the rustlers, and she'd shed telling the men their daily chores right slick. She shifted that job to him without batting an eye.

The next morning at breakfast Joy introduced Gundy to the men; Slim Baden, a fat man — Gundy figured to ride some of the fat off him — and Bob Lawton, a puncher he thought he'd get some good work out of with a little push. They acknowledged meeting each other in the bunkhouse.

"Men, Mr. Gundy will be laying out the work from now on. If he says do it, take it as though I said it."

Gundy locked gazes with each of them and saw no reluctance to take things like she said.

Joy brought the coffeepot to the table and served each a full cup.

Gundy pushed back from the table a bit in order to look at them. "Men, know you done seen where fence posts're broke, and wire needs to be restrung. Get the wagon, load posts an' a spool o' wire. Next time I ride fence I don't want to see a break anywhere."

He looked at Joy. "The weather's too nasty for you to get out in. Don't want a sick boss."

"If you men ride, I can, too. I'll clean the kitchen first."

Gundy told the men to head out, he'd saddle Miss Joy's horse. When they left the house, Joy led him on a straight line toward where she'd lost track of the rustlers. They rode in silence until Gundy pointed to a bull showing more than a little longhorn blood, but mixed with Hereford. "Notice your brand's a Flying JW. This been your ranch from git-go?"

"No, Trace. My husband started it soon after Fort Keogh was built. JW was his initials, too. James was his first name."

Gundy pondered this awhile. She didn't say more, and he didn't push it. If she wanted to tell him what happened, she'd tell him.

They rode northeast, crossed the Pumpkin, and rode another half hour until they came to a cedar break growing out of a limestone outcropping. She pointed to the ground, devoid of growth. "This is where I lost their trail the last time. They've taken anywhere from five to fifteen head at a time, some branded, some not, but most unbranded. I know, because I've ridden this range almost every day. You get to know your cows pretty well seeing them that often." She pinned him with that penetrating look she had. "Trace, I just plain don't know what to do."

He squinted at the ground, not expecting to see a track in this weather. "Joy, were you able to tell if they kept the cows sort of on a straight line from where you picked up the tracks?"

"Yes. They did."

"At different times when you tracked them, did they all head in this direction?"

"Yes."

Gundy reined the buckskin back toward the ranch house. "Come, I'll ride home with you. Need some supplies. Coffee, flour, bacon, a couple tins o' beans. Gonna be gone a few days, want to see what ranches are in the direction you pointed me. Want to take a look at the brands. An' if they's any unbranded stock on your place, tell Baden an' Lawton to round 'em up and start brandin'."

Joy cast a puzzled look at him. "Trace, you're taking a great deal of interest in getting this place back on a paying basis. Why?"

He pushed his hat to the back of his head. "Well, ma'am, we got a sayin' down where I come from, it's 'I ride for the brand.' Maybe you folks up here say the same thing. It means they ain't a damn, uh, 'scuse me, ma'am. It means they ain't nothin' you won't do to make things right for it, fight, work, even die for it. That's the way I work for my brand."

She sidled her horse close to his, and placed her hand over his on the pommel. "Bless you, Trace. I don't want you to die for my brand or be hurt in any way. You take care of yourself."

A tingle Gundy hadn't felt in a long time went from his hand straight to his heart. He had never expected to feel such again. He gripped the saddle horn hard. Joy removed her hand, and a pretty blush swept up her face, but she didn't remove the straight-on stare.

"Ma'am, reckon I always take care, but I'll get the job done. You can bet your last dollar on that."

"Trace, I *am* betting my last dollar. I shouldn't saddle you with my problems, but like I said, I have nowhere else to turn."

"Think maybe you turned to the right place. I'll get it done." He looked ahead of them. The ranch house was only over the next hill.

Four hours later Gundy reined in at the spot Joy lost the trail of the stolen cattle. Riding slowly he cast back and forth, looking for broken cedar twigs, rocks that appeared to have been overturned in recent weeks, or maybe a deep gouge in the limestone. Joy had told him it had been only three weeks since the last cattle disappeared.

He found no sign that day, or the next, but he held his northeasterly course. On the third day he saw broken twigs twice, and then saw a gouge where a shod horse had slipped on a side slope. Blood pumped into his chest; his hair tingled at its roots.

By his reckoning he was now east of Milestown. When he reached the Powder, hooves had cut a good trail where they entered the water to ford the river — and again where they came out on the other side. He had seen no cattle anywhere, and these cows were tight-bunched, driven cows. He was on the right trail.

Following their trail now was easy. The rain hadn't gotten this far so horse tracks showed plainly. Gundy climbed from the gelding and studied each set. He would remember them.

Caution rode with him, not wanting to happen upon riders. He couldn't pull his gun and start shooting, couldn't accuse anyone of rustling. He wanted to make sure of what action to take — wanted to make sure the cattle were Joy's.

There was a new settlement, Ismay, about fifty miles east of Miles. He didn't want to ride into it. Anyone seeing him might remember, and he wanted to remain a stranger to all in this area where he thought the rustlers might be headquartered.

Before reaching Ismay, he rounded a hill and saw a ranch of sorts spread before him, at least there were cattle, but no ranch house or outbuildings. He ducked behind a boulder, rode his horse into a ravine and ground-reined him, then went back to the boulder to study the setup, to make sure there were no riders in sight. Then he wanted to see what the brands looked like on those cattle. He studied the terrain about fifteen minutes and saw no riders.

Satisfied he was alone, he rode into the pasture, sort of a bowl surrounded by cedar and a few stunted cottonwoods, but the grass was good, almost fetlock deep.

There were, by his best reckoning, about a hundred fifty head in this one holding area. Most of the brands he looked at looked legal enough, but he spotted several he'd bet his hat and horse had been blotted. The only way to tell for sure would be to peel the hide back and look at the underside. Gundy shook his head. Far from home range, if he got caught they'd hang him from the nearest tree. And then he found what he'd been looking for all along; two big steers with a Flying JW on their hips. They'd probably been in the brush when the others had their brands blotted. His gut tightened. Someone was sure to be watching these cows. A slight pull on his Winchester eased it in the scabbard.

He kneed his gelding close to a white-faced yearling steer, one with a pretty good set of horns. Longhorn and Hereford, he thought. The brand had not yet healed over.

The steer drifted away from him. Gundy kneed his horse to stay with it, leaned from his saddle to take a closer look, and heard an angry whine close to his ear, followed closely by the sharp report of a rifle shot. A raw coppery taste flowed from under his tongue, his gut muscles knotted.

Gundy slapped his heels into the buckskin and headed away from where the shot sounded. His horse dug in and went belly to the ground, running all out. Two more shots followed, close together. The trees came at him like they, too, were running, trying to help.

Firing at a man who didn't have a rope

on a cow not his or a fire built with a running iron laying in it was unheard of. Whoever fired at him was not an honest rancher.

Once into the scrubby cedar, Gundy pulled his rifle and left his horse. Two more shots followed, clipping twigs from the scrubby tree he rolled behind. He jacked a shell into his Winchester and waited, hoping they'd think one of their shots found him. He pondered riding away, then a cold seething anger took hold. He'd found proof they'd rustled Joy's cows, they wouldn't have strayed this far from home range, and somehow when people shot at him, he had a tendency to shoot back.

Minutes passed, finally after what seemed hours a rider showed at the far edge of the pasture still holding his rifle in his hands. He sat his horse and Gundy could see his head move from side to side as though studying the surrounding area, looking for sight of the man at which he'd fired. Gundy smiled. *That* one had not been raised by the Apache, he hadn't the patience.

He centered his sights on the rider's chest and raised the barrel slightly to allow for distance, then hesitated. He thought to give the man some warning. He shrugged. The rider hadn't warned *him*. He squeezed the trigger.

chapter six

From where he lay, it looked like the rider went limp, threw his rifle from arms that could no longer hold it, and slipped off the side of his horse. Some of the knot left his gut. He waited.

His Apache training said be patient, but the practical side said, "Someone might have heard the shots and will high tail it to see what they are about." Too, there might be more than one rider across the pasture. Patience won.

He searched each side of where the rider left the safety of the trees, looking for motion, tops of trees moving, a glimpse of a horse stepping from cover to cover, anything. Then he saw what he looked for. A rider bent low over his horse's neck scooted from behind one bush, hurrying to the next.

Gundy drew his sights on the side the rider would probably come from, sucked in a deep breath, held it, and tightened his grip on the trigger.

Only a moment passed, and in what

seemed slow motion, the horse's head appeared, his neck, and then the rider. Gundy squeezed the trigger.

The rider jerked and fell from his horse. Not until then did Gundy run for the buckskin waiting patiently about fifty feet away. He hit the saddle in a running leap. He'd found what he came for, but knew when he came back the cattle would have been moved.

Milestown lay due west, a trip through it to the ranch would give him a chance to look the town over and see where the Tongue flowed into the Yellowstone, how the town sat in relation to the two rivers, and he wanted to take a long-distance look at the saloon Rance Barton's brother had going. Gundy didn't tie the rustlers to anyone in Miles so he didn't fear being seen there. If their headquarters ranch was close to Ismay, that was probably where they'd hang out.

Several times during the next couple of hours, Gundy pulled in behind boulders or scrub brush and searched his back trail. Finally satisfied no one followed, he relaxed — a little.

After crossing the Powder, he angled a bit south, wanting to circle Milestown and come in to the west of Fort Keogh, wanting the fort between him and Milestown.

All afternoon a black bank of clouds hovered to the west, hiding the sun. Soon, Gundy again rode in a slow drizzle. Dark began to slip in under the trees, pushing dreary daylight to the tops of hills. He looked for a place to camp, one where he could have a fire and hot coffee. He'd scout Keogh and Milestown in daylight, when he could see what surrounded him.

A deep ravine cut to his left. He kneed the gelding down it. About a quarter of a mile into the earth's gash he found a shoulder ten or fifteen feet up its side, rode to it, searched the rim on both sides, and the direction from which he'd come. Satisfied his firelight would not be seen, he made camp.

Leaning against his saddle, he wondered why he had taken on a chore that might get him killed before he could find the gringo. Joy was a mighty pretty lady, but he wasn't interested in her as a woman, or any other woman for that matter. Dee's memory was still on him. So why was he doing it? He shrugged. Hell, he had to earn his keep somehow, and he wouldn't see her lose all she and her husband had worked and fought for. With that thought, he pulled his blankets and slicker over him and went to sleep.

During the night, the clouds moved to span the sky from east to west, and the drizzle of yesterday had turned to a steady cold rain. Gundy broke camp on an empty stomach, shivered, and looked sourly at the plentiful supply of soggy wood. A lot of good it did him. He wished he'd covered some of it with his ground sheet. Too late now.

About midmorning he forded the Tongue and came onto Fort Keogh. He pulled off the trail and waited for a cavalry patrol to pass, thinking they were going out to harass some poor band of Sioux trying to find food for their families.

Gundy stayed on the trail to Miles, but studied every foot of it. Not far from the banks of the Tongue he came on a lone but large unpainted building, bleached gray by the weather. The gringo's brother must have been in business quite a while, or his saloon had been something else before becoming a saloon. He rode past the front and reined his horse off the trail. Pulling his slicker under his seat, he squatted at the base of a large cottonwood.

His eyes locked in on the doors of Barton's place. After a while the doors opened and two young soldiers, propelled by a boot to their rear ends, stumbled out the door and fell in the mud by the hitching rack. They stood, looked at each other, brushed hands down their mud-soaked trousers, trying to clean them as much as possible, and staggered toward the fort. Drunk and broke, Gundy thought.

Barton got them drunk, took their pay, and threw them out. Wonder how many dollars from the fort end up paying for watered-down whiskey, diseased women, and crooked card games in that cesspool yonder? He sat there another hour and watched the dregs of creation, real hard cases, along with many young soldiers go in and out of the tavern.

Gundy stood. He'd seen enough. He would have liked to go inside and truly verify his suspicions, but was fearful of running head on into the gringo and having to use his gun. He didn't want that. His plans for the gringo were not for nearly so quick and merciful a death.

Only a couple of miles and he crossed the Tongue to sit at the end of Milestown's main street. It was a sea of mud sandwiched between two rows of sun- and rain-bleached buildings.

He kneed the buckskin down its length, passing the livery, feed store, and was abreast of a store depicted by a sign swinging in the wind that said it was Leighton's General Mercantile Store. Gundy glanced to the other side of the street and saw the jail. On a whim, he reined over and dismounted.

Inside, Gundy watched a grizzled, old lawman swing his feet off the desk and look sourly at him. "Hope you got no trouble that'll cause me to get out in this weather."

Gundy shook his head. "No, sir, just wanted to make your acquaintance. I'm new to these parts." He stuck out his hand. "Trace Gundy's the name, my real name."

The marshal's eyes crinkled at the corners, and he took his pipe from between his teeth. "Good to meet a man who gives me his *real* name. Marshal Bruns here. What can I do for you?"

"Not a thing, Marshal. I really did come in here just to get acquainted." He pulled his own pipe from his sheepskin. "Mind if I smoke?"

"Help yourself."

Gundy took his time in packing and putting fire to his pipe. "Come by the fort a while ago. Then, just the other side o' the river yonder, two or three times I seen young soldiers get thrown outta that saloon. What's the Army say about that?"

The marshal leaned back in his chair and stared at Gundy a moment. "Why, Mr. Gundy? Is that some concern of yours?"

Gundy felt the blood rush to his face, and his eyes tighten. "Marshal, anytime I see people, whatever amount o' money they got, or whatever color they are, gettin' kicked around, I figure it's some of my concern."

The marshal stared at him a moment, gave a jerky sort of nod, and said, "Yes, Mr. Gundy, I believe you're really troubled by what you saw, so I'll tell you straight. The Army would like to shut that place down. *I* would like to burn it to the ground, but I got no legal right to do it."

Gundy liked what he heard, and he liked the man at whom he looked. He decided to tell it like it was, but not all of it. "Marshal, if you look through your posters you'll prob'ly find one on me. I'll tell you here an' now, contact the governor's office in the Territory of New Mexico an' they'll say I been pardoned of all charges down yonder. I ain't been in no trouble since I was nineteen years old. Them posters call me the Apache Blanco."

86

The old marshal smiled, or at least the wrinkles on his face crinkled all over and Gundy took it for a smile. "Son, I didn't know nothing about Trace Gundy, but I damned sure know about the Apache Blanco. I wouldn't of known you. I figured you'd be a cross between a grizzly and a mountain cat. Hell, you look 'bout like any other clean-cut young man. And I got nothing on you. I know about your pardon. But thanks for coming by to let me know you're in these parts."

Gundy nodded. "Thanks, Marshal. I got a favor to ask o' you. One o' them brothers what owns that there saloon across the Tongue might be askin' 'bout me. 'Preciate it if you say you ain't never heard o' me. One o' these days I got a score to settle with him, but I ain't gonna do it in your town. Gonna do it in my own time, an' my own way."

Bruns pierced him with the iciest blue eyes Gundy had seen since leaving Texas. "Son, ain't gonna ask what you got in store for him. Don't want to know, but good luck."

They talked while Gundy finished his pipe, and Bruns suggested he make the man's acquaintance across the street, Leighton was his name, owned the general store. "Good man to know, Gundy, and he's as fair and straight as any man you'll find."

Gundy nodded, looked at his pipe, and figured to knock the dottle from it when he got outside. He stood. "Reckon I'll go see 'im then, 'fore I go back to the ranch. Workin' for Miz Waldrop out yonder on the Flyin' JW."

Bruns nodded. "Good woman, Gundy. She needs a good hand."

Gundy angled across the street in mud halfway to the tops of his boots and went in the store. Leighton walked over, introduced himself, and asked if he could show Gundy anything.

Gundy grinned. "Not 'less you're givin' it away, Mr. Leighton. Just stopped to say howdy. Marshal said you was a right nice man to know."

They were the only ones in the store, so they talked. Leighton found that Gundy worked for Joy Waldrop and told him if he was broke to go ahead and get what he needed, he'd carry him for it. Gundy shook his head. "No, sir. Reckon I like to stay clear o' owin' folks, but thanks anyway." After a while Gundy left, climbed on his horse, and headed for the ranch.

It was after dark when he rode into the

ranch yard. Baden and Lawton were playing checkers by the light of the stove. Lawton glanced up when Gundy came in, his slicker dripping a puddle onto the floor. "You et yet?"

"No, but ain't gonna bother Miz Joy this time o' night."

"Better do it. She'll be mad if you don't. Says least she can do is to be sure we eat good."

Gundy put his hat back on and headed for the house. The door swung open as soon as he stepped to the porch. Joy stood there in her slicker. "Just coming out there to get you. Don't you dare *ever* go to bed hungry. I don't care what time it is, I'll fix supper for you."

He put wood in the stove and sat. After bringing him coffee, she busied herself putting his supper on to heat. Not until he had food in front of him did she pour herself coffee and sit across the table from him. "The boys have been grumbling about working so hard, but somehow I get the feeling they like it."

Gundy chewed, swallowed, and nodded. "Ma'am, a cowboy ain't happy 'less he's growlin'." He studied her a moment. "You run this place all by yourself?"

"Yes. A horse fell with Mr. Waldrop a

year ago." A flicker of pain crossed her face. "Saddle horn caught him in the stomach, tore him up pretty much inside. He lived only two days."

"Aw now, Miz Joy, I shouldn't of asked. Didn't mean to stick my nose in your business."

She smiled. "No, it's all right. I'd rather have told you myself. Losing him still hurts, but our time together left many good memories. I put them back where I can remember when I'm alone. It's time to get on with life." She stood, poured more coffee, and looked across her shoulder at him. "Find out anything while you were gone?"

"Ain't sure. Know I found a couple o' your cows, but they was a couple men with rifles makin' like they didn't want me lookin' too close."

"Did they shoot?"

Gundy nodded. "Yes'm. Clipped a few branches off a tree I hid behind, but they stopped that after a while."

"Oh, thank goodness you weren't hurt. Did you shoot at *them?*"

He cast her a frown. "Miz Joy, when folks fire at me I always shoot back, just sort o' rubs me wrong not to." He took a swallow of coffee and locked gazes with her. "Ma'am, know I killed one an' hit the other. Don't know how bad."

Joy, peering deep into his eyes, said, "I knew it would come to this. I'm sorry I got you involved, Trace." She placed her hand over his. "I don't want you hurt, so please, this ranch isn't worth getting you men shot. Just stop now and we'll weather it somehow."

Her small, work-hardened hand resting on his stirred memories, feelings he wasn't ready to deal with yet, but he didn't know how to get his hand from under hers without being too obvious. "Joy," he reckoned he might as well call her by what she'd asked him to. "Joy, we ain't gonna stop now. I'm in this up to my ears. That rustlin' ain't gonna go away 'less we do somethin' 'bout it." He pulled his hand from under hers and stood. He took a couple of paces across the room and returned to stare down at her.

"Gonna tell you somethin', ma'am. When you hired me, you took on all o' me. They might be some better able to help you, but I ain't made their acquaintance yet. Tell you somethin' else. I ain't no outlaw. Ain't wanted in no state, nowhere, so you can rest easy 'bout that." He picked up his cup. " 'Nother thing, ma'am, I'm in this to the end. If you fire me, I'm still gonna go after 'em. When they shot at me, I bought into the game to the end."

"Why, Trace, why are you doing this for me?"

"Don't know, Joy. Ain't doin' it just for you. Rustlers, whether here, Texas, wherever, need to be wiped out. An' the reason I'm doin' it? Well, seems like I'm the one, so no more about us quittin'."

He walked around the table and again sat. "I'm takin' a couple o' days to ride around the ranch and see what jobs I can turn the boys loose on, then I'm goin' back to where I found your cows. Don't figure 'em to still be there, but I'll find 'em. Then I'm gonna take a look-see on the back side o' one o' them hides." He slanted her a questioning look. "How many head you figure's been took from you?"

She frowned, staring into her empty cup, then looked into his eyes. "Somewhere around eight hundred fifty head, maybe a few less, but not many."

Gundy pursed his lips and whistled silently. "Them's a lot o' cows, ma'am. Hope I can find most o' them."

Three days later the weather cleared, the men were busy putting new railings on the

92

corral, and Joy stood in the ranch-house doorway watching Gundy ride from the yard.

Why did she put so much trust in this man she'd known only a little over a week? She had practically turned over running the ranch to him. She admitted he stirred feelings in her she thought were dead, feelings she had sworn to herself she would not let happen again. The pain was too great to chance experiencing another time.

His slim strength seemed to say, "Let me handle it, I'm used to this sort of thing." She was tired of taking losses she had no knowledge as to how to take care of. And the two old men working for her were good ranch hands, nothing more. She couldn't picture them bracing a bunch of cattle thieves. Trace went about getting things done like he'd had a ranch of his own at some past time. He had that quiet confidence about him that engendered trust.

She watched Trace top a hill and disappear from view. She filled her lungs with a breath of cold air, still looking at the spot where she lost sight of him. She went slowly back into the house, reluctant to give up the picture of him riding away on her business. To keep her mind busy, she cleaned the kitchen, then the house, but still couldn't shake Trace from her thoughts.

He had told her after riding her range that he couldn't find a single cow that hadn't been branded, and the fence had been mended. The boys had done a good job.

For the first time she didn't worry about the ranch and jobs she knew had been neglected in recent months. She hummed while she worked. She would not worry about Trace. He would take care of himself. But all that day and into the night she did worry about him.

chapter seven

Gundy rode to the pasture where he'd seen the cattle. Knowing where he was going, it took only two days. He stopped behind the same boulder he first stood behind the day he had the shootout. For over an hour he studied every tree and clump of brush, watching for sign he was not alone. The branches of a cedar moved, trembled, bent. Gundy drew a bead about head high and waited. A spot of red and brown showed through the branches. His finger tightened on the trigger — and a huge longhorn steer pushed into the clearing. His breath escaped in a silent whistle. He eased pressure on the trigger.

Gundy had been right about them moving the cattle. The big steer was the only animal in the bowl. He climbed back on the gelding and rode to the edge of the clearing. As many head as had been here would not be hard to trail.

About halfway around the perimeter, he picked up sign a large number of cattle had been bunched and pushed into the brush.

Earth pounded to fine dust, broken branches, and cow pies left sign even Joy could have followed. His gut muscles tightened.

If he thought to come back and trail the stolen cattle, it was a safe bet those who had taken them would figure on his doing that. Abruptly he kneed the buckskin at right angles to the direction of the tracks, and stayed on that course for about a mile, then started a slow circle figuring he'd again cut their sign. A couple of hours later he came on their trail again. He still didn't follow them. Instead, he crossed the tracks and started another circle. He glanced at the sky, it was getting late and colder. He shrugged into his sheepskin.

In the next two days he crossed the trail eight times. From the pasture they headed in an east by northeast direction and never varied. Gundy figured they would pass to the north of the new settlement of Ismay. He hooked his leg around the saddle horn, pulled his remaining money from his pocket, and counted it. Two dollars and sixty-five cents. He'd spent thirty-five cents in Milestown for breakfast and a pair of socks. He headed for Ismay.

Looking down at the town from the top of a hill showed it as about the size of Milestown. He rode down the hill, crossed

Fallon Creek, and sat at the end of a street bordered on each side with structures of raw, unpainted lumber. The largest building looked to be a saloon. A beer would taste good.

Small chance of anyone knowing him, but he used caution.

The room was empty except for four riders standing at the bar, a long, highly polished piece of furniture. Gundy was surprised to see such in this country, then thought it must have been brought in on the Northern Pacific that ran down the southern edge of town.

He pulled his hat low over his forehead and went to the end of the bar.

"Beer," he said when the redheaded bartender looked at him.

After getting his beer, he drank slowly, knowing he'd best not have another. His remaining money would have to last the rest of the winter.

He wasn't eavesdropping until he heard one of those at the other end of the bar say, "Barton and that brother o' his been spendin' all their time back there in Milestown . . ." then he lost what followed.

He studied the four a few minutes, decided he'd never seen them before, and walked to stand next to them. "Howdy, you men look like cow nurses. Know of an outfit what's hirin'?"

They swung their heads to look at him. The closest one, a squat, bowlegged puncher, raked him from head to toe in a look that hesitated when it got to his tied-down holster. "Naw, the boss ain't takin' on no range bums to feed all winter."

"Mister, I'm not gonna take offense at your words, but if you don't pull in your horns I'm gonna read to you from the book. Now, I'm askin' again, your boss hirin'?"

A large man, small head, huge shoulders, standing on the other side of Bowlegs, pushed his friend aside. "Cowboy, offense or not, he ain't takin' on no bums."

Gundy went cold inside. He wanted to avoid trouble with this ruffian, but knew it wouldn't happen. If it came to a fight, he had no doubt but what he'd have to take them all on. He grinned at the big one, and at the same time brought his fist up from around his knees. It connected with the man's chin. Biggun backed a step, tripped, and fell flat on his back. The other three surged toward Gundy. He palmed his .44 without thinking and thrust it in front of him.

"Y'all wantta meet whoever brung you

98

into this world, take a swing at me or draw them guns. Either way, you gonna die."

They stopped as though they'd walked into a wall. "Back up, now, right now."

They backed to the end of the bar. Biggun rolled to his knees and launched himself at Gundy's legs. A jerky, chopping motion, and Gundy brought his handgun down behind his ear. He sprawled flat on his face at Gundy's feet.

"Your mamas should of taught you to treat strangers more kindly." Gundy took his beer from the bar with his left hand, and backed away a few steps so he could see all four of them. "Now shuck your hardware and leave it on the floor." He motioned to a tall, thin puncher standing slightly forward of Bowlegs and the other cowboy. "Real carefullike, bend over an' undo Biggun's belt." The man did as told.

"Now, drag your big-mouthed partner outta here. Come back for your guns next time you're in town. I'm stayin' long enough to finish my beer. Git!"

"Mister, if I ever cross your trail agin I'm gonna blow your damned head off," the thin puncher said.

Gundy let a cold smile show, then stared into the puncher's eyes. "Sure is surprisin' how much respect you done learned to show. Callin' me 'mister,' now that's right nice." His face again froze. "Get outta here, now, before I change my mind an' give y'all back your guns, one at a time. Then you got real trouble."

Bowlegs and Slim, dragging Biggun between them, motioned the last man to come on and left.

"Son, don't know who you are. You handle yourself mighty well, but you just bit off a real hunk o' trouble, probably more'n any one man can handle. Those punchers ride for Lem Barton's Box LB, the saltiest outfit in these parts." Gundy turned from watching the surly bunch out the door. The bartender shook his head and continued. "I never seen a man get a handgun out any faster'n you did, but that's a mean bunch, an' there's a whole lot of them."

Gundy tossed down the rest of his beer. "Partner, sometimes a man's tired an' he ain't of a mind to take nothin' off'n nobody." He put his glass back on the bar, and aware he still held his pistol in his right hand, holstered it.

The redheaded bartender reached to refill Gundy's glass.

"Reckon one's enough, gotta watch my money."

The redhead grinned. "Have another, on

the house." He stuck out his hand. "Name's Dawson, call me Red."

"Since you put it that way, don't reckon I can refuse." Gundy shook Dawson's hand. "Trace Gundy here."

While Dawson drew another beer, Gundy gathered the guns and belts from the floor and handed them across the counter. "I'd take it kindly if you'd give me time to get outta town 'fore you give these back . . ." He shook his head. "Naw, that wouldn't be right, it'd put you in a bind. I'll take 'em with me. Tell that bunch I'm leavin' their guns across the creek yonder at the end of the street."

"Much obliged, Gundy. I try to stay outta these things." He pulled a sawed-off Greener from under the bar. "When I find I can't, I just sortta choose what side I want to win and dive into it headfirst. This little helpmate's made the difference."

Gundy smiled, drank the rest of his beer, held up his hand in farewell, and said, "Hope I'm on the side *you* choose."

He'd rebuckled the four gunbelts and carried them looped over his left forearm. On leaving the saloon, he looked up and down the street before stepping off the boardwalk to his horse. None of his adversaries were in sight, but the cold knot between his shoulders told him they watched.

He crossed Fallon Creek. Out about a hundred yards the trail bent to the right, and in the bend a thicket of small trees shielded the rutted roadway from view. He pulled in behind the clump of saplings. He had no doubt the four had saddle guns. He opened the loading gate on his Colt and shoved a sixth shell into the cylinder.

In only a few seconds the drum of horses' hooves sounded on the hard-packed road. They were close-bunched, and almost rode him down before they could stop their horses.

"Hold it there. I can empty every saddle before one o' you gets a rifle smokin'."

They stared at him. Gundy studied their eyes. None of them showed fear. If they were wearing handguns, every man jack of them would try his luck. He grinned at them. "Ain't it hell, boys? Two losers in one day." Slim fondled the stock of his rifle. "Uh-uh, don't try it. Your mama didn't raise a damned fool." Slim drew his hand back, his look dripping pure hatred.

"Tell you what I'm gonna do. I'm askin' you to get off your horses, one at a time, and stand off to the side. Turn your horses so you can climb down on the side I'm on. You first, Biggun."

They did as he told them, and stood shoulder to shoulder holding their horses' reins.

"Now, ground-hitch them horses an' start walkin' back to town. I'll turn your horses loose about a mile out. Figure they'll head for the barn though, so you men got a pretty good walk ahead o' you, 'less you rent a horse from the livery. I'll hang your guns over the horn."

Bowlegs said, "Cowboy, we ever meet agin, fill your hand. Ain't no talking gonna take place. Start shootin'."

"That goes for all of us," Biggun said.

The devil crawled back on Gundy's shoulder. "We can take care o' that little problem right here, one at a time."

Their eyes showed hesitation, but still no fear. They seemed to think if he was that eager, he must be *very* good with his handgun. "We'll wait for the right time, cowboy, this ain't it," Biggun growled, having elected himself as their spokesman.

"All right, start walkin'." Gundy waved his pistol barrel toward town.

They trudged off, occasionally kicking at trail dust and glancing over their shoulders at him. When they waded the creek and were safely on the other side, Gundy gathered the reins of their horses and headed in the opposite direction. He watched their backs. They were as salty a group of hard cases he'd ever seen.

Still shielded from their eyes, he left the trail and headed cross-country. About two miles farther, he tied the ends of each horse's reins to the one on the other side of his neck, looped them over the saddle horn, turned them loose, slapped them on the rump, and said, "Go on now, get to the barn."

They trotted off a few feet, turned their heads to see if he followed, then tried cropping the sparse grass growing from the limestone formation and couldn't. The reins wouldn't allow them to get their heads down. Now, if they headed home they'd save him a lot of time trying to find the Box LB. He could follow them.

Gundy waited a moment. A big bay gelding finally decided the barn was the best place in Montana and headed out. The other three followed.

The Box LB horses set a pace that allowed Gundy to check the ravines and long swells of land that lay around him. He seemed to have the world to himself. The sun sank toward the horizon, and the horses picked up their gait.

Dark settled in, and Gundy trailed the

horses by sound alone. An hour into the night, Gundy topped a rise and looked down on a good-sized spread, judging by the lamplit windows.

He sat his horse about a quarter of a mile from the buildings and wondered if he dared try to get closer. Did they have sentries spotted around the area? Were the hands all in the bunkhouse from the day's work? Would any be leaving? He could ride in like a wandering puncher and ask if they had any grub left from supper, but he wanted to do this without being seen.

He decided to chance getting closer.

Moccasins would allow him to get to a window and have a look inside, but his were back at the ranch.

He ground-hitched his horse and worked his way toward the lights, not looking at them as they would dim his night vision, not much but maybe enough to get him killed.

Move a few feet, stop, search about him, listen, and move again. Gundy was at home now, he'd done this since a small boy.

The ranch yard opened before him, about fifty yards from the closest building. He sweated despite the cold. He squatted with a cedar at his back, allowing him to blend with the darkness. Ranch hands, in ones and twos, came from a square building nearest to him. Cook shack, he figured, because they went from it to a long, low log structure a little farther out. Gundy thought it might be the bunkhouse.

Another hour he sat there pulled deep into his sheepskin. Finally, the lights went out in the cook shack. No one stirred about the yard. Lamplight still showed from the main house. Gundy dropped to his stomach and worked his way, a few feet at a time, toward the light.

He picked up a hand to move forward another few inches. He froze. Something stirred only a few feet in front of him. Gundy tested the air and smelled dog. The wind was in his favor, the Great Spirit stood with him tonight, unless the mutt came his way. Gundy didn't move, hardly breathed. The pup sniffed the ground, then wandered back toward the bunkhouse.

Gundy relaxed, aware that every muscle in his body was tight as a rope on a lassoed steer. This was a helluva time to think of it, but crawling to that ranch house wasn't the smartest thing he'd ever done. Ain't gonna take no prizes in a brain contest no way, he thought, and inched forward again.

A half hour that seemed a week passed,

and he rose enough to see into the lighted room. A man stood with his back to the window. From the back, he looked like the gringo, but he and his brother might look much like one another.

Gundy's gut crawled, his chest tightened. Standing here with his head poked above the sill of a lighted window was begging to get shot. He lowered his head and again searched the yard around him. Still nothing. He hoped the pooch had curled up somewhere and gone to sleep. He pushed his head above the sill again.

The man inside walked to a cabinet, poured himself a drink, and turned toward Gundy. Every line of his face had been etched in Gundy's memory that day a few months ago. Gundy's hand went to his gun, stopped, and he forced himself to relax. Can't kill 'im here. Gonna wait an' do it my way — the Apache way. This is the end of the trail though, I know where he is, an' I'll do it in my own time and place, he thought, and lowered himself from the window. Now he knew where the gringo was, and more importantly, when he solved Joy's rustling problem, he would solve his own. Things worked out in strange ways, and, he'd always thought, everything happened for the best. Maybe at the moment they didn't seem so, but all a person had to do was wait awhile and the good overshadowed the bad. He grinned into the night. Worked again, he thought.

He took as much care in leaving as in getting to the house. But getting Joy's cattle back had become a far greater problem.

chapter eight

Gundy found his gelding and rode west from Barton's ranch. He didn't want more distance between himself and Joy's Flying JW than need be, but he wanted a close look at Barton's cattle the next morning.

His horse crossed a small stream after a couple of miles, and Gundy made camp on its bank. Knowing, unless it was roundup, there wouldn't be night herds posted, he made a fire and cooked supper. After eating, he slouched against his saddle, drank coffee, and thought about the day's happenings.

Not one of his problems had gotten easier. He could wait to take care of the gringo until things were right; fact is he didn't want to tie killing the gringo to getting Joy's cows back. With Joy, her lack of operating money and men, he could see no way of solving her problem.

One man fighting the Barton crew would fail from the start. It had to be done in one big push, and that would take men, a lot of them. He went to sleep trying to think of a solution.

The next morning when the sun edged red above the distant plains, Gundy sat his horse on a knoll, giving him a view of a great part of what he supposed was Barton land, much of it dotted with cattle.

His gaze swept every inch of the land closest to him looking for riders. If he got caught doing what he was about to do, he could be hung for rustling or shot. Neither option appealed to him.

Convinced he could do it and get away, he rode toward the bunch of cows nearest him. He checked every cow there, looking for what he hoped would prove to be a blotted or altered brand. He cut out a big brindle steer and hazed him to the west, moving faster than any cowboy would normally drive beef. But Gundy wasn't worried about this critter losing weight, he wanted to get somewhere fast, where he could butcher the steer and peel its hide.

This time he stayed below the crests of hills, not wanting to skyline himself. When about ten miles from the Powder, he made camp, hobbled his horse and the big brindle animal, ate supper, and went to sleep.

The next day, about noon, he crossed the Powder and breathed easier. Wasting the whole carcass of a beef didn't set well, but he could figure no other way of doing it.

About sundown, he sighted a couple of tipis and headed their way. Close enough, he recognized two families of Sioux. They were supposed to be on the Pine Ridge Reservation, but it wasn't uncommon for them to leave and hunt for meat. Their families were starving. The government and crooked Indian agents stole rations supposed to go to the Indians and lined their pockets with the profit.

Gundy drove the steer close to their camp. A squat, powerfully muscled warrior stood warily by the flap of his tipi.

"You come take us to reservation?"

Gundy shook his head. "No. I am the Apache Blanco of the Mescalero. I am your friend. I bring meat."

The Sioux warrior looked dubious. "Why you do this?"

"I need only a part of the hide. I don't want to throw away the meat, so I give it to you." Gundy smiled. "I want to slice a small hunk of it for myself."

The Indian eyed the steer, hunger in his eyes. "We help kill." Together, they slaughtered the steer, bled it, and Gundy took the hide and a thick steak. "I'll take this hide away from here and bury it so no one can accuse you of stealing."

The wife of the Sioux and a woman from the other lodge were busy butchering the beef when Gundy rode from their camp. When alone he spread the hide and looked at the underside of the brand. It had been altered from an I Bar T. He had all the proof he needed, but the law might want more. Right now *he* wanted to know he was on the right trail. He cut the brand out, buried the rest of the hide, and made camp.

The next morning about ten o'clock Gundy rode into Milestown. He didn't have enough money to tarry long, so he headed straight for Marshal Bruns's office.

"What you doing back in town so soon, Gundy? Thought it might be a couple of months 'fore I seen you again."

"Got somethin' to show you, Marshal." Gundy unrolled the strip of hide and laid it out on Bruns's desk, face up. Then he flipped it over. "They didn't even take the trouble to do a good job of blottin' this one, an' they's a lot more like it out yonder."

Bruns pinned Gundy with his gaze. "Why you tellin' me? I got no authority outside o' town."

Gundy nodded. "Yeah, I know, but I

want to tell you who's doin' it. Comes time for a showdown, don't want you stoppin' me from doin' what I got to do. Showdown'll pro'bly happen right here in your town."

"Damn! Was afraid you were gonna say that. Okay, tell me what you know."

Gundy laid it out for him, what he knew to be fact and what he suspected. When finished, he eyed the marshal. "Bruns, Miz Waldrop can't afford to lose even part of her calf crop next spring. I figure to see it don't happen."

"You got an interest in that ranch, Gundy, or the lady herself?"

Blood surged to Gundy's throat. "Gonna let that pass, Bruns, but I'll tell you this right now. I got a ranch o' my own down in the Big Bend of Texas, one hundred seventy thousand acres. I got no money 'cause I won't send home for any. I'm gonna kill the bastard that killed my wife, then I'm goin' back to Texas. No, I ain't got any interest in Miz Waldrop's ranch, 'cept I figure to see her get back on her feet an' be able to run it 'thout nobody stoppin' her. As for the lady herself? That ain't none o' your damned business." He pulled his hat down hard on his head and turned to leave.

"Wait a minute, Gundy. I owe you an apology. Sorry I asked what I did, but *I* don't want anyone taking advantage of her situation either. I'm a happily married man. Her husband was my friend. You could say we're on the same side."

The heat drained from Gundy's head. Embarrassed at having blown up, he pushed his hat back, wiped his brow, and grinned. "Sorry, Marshal. But I meant what I said. If I can stop whoever's stealin' her cows, I'm gonna do it, whatever it takes."

"And if it's outside of town, I'll take my badge off and help you. Call on me if you need me."

Gundy stared hard into Bruns's eyes a moment. "Marshal, I might just do that."

Gundy left and went across the street to say howdy to Leighton, then he circled the town, studying the back of each building. After that, he crossed the Tongue and circled Barton's saloon. There he had only to take a hard look at the front and left side of the building, as well as the escape route on two sides. The Yellowstone and Tongue rivers protected the other two sides. A plan began to form in his mind how to get the gringo away from town and where to take him. He was no closer to figuring what to do about Joy's stolen cattle.

Having seen what he wanted, he headed for the Flying JW.

On the way home he rode fence awhile, then cut through several bunches of cattle. Everything looked well taken care of, except the lack of young beef. Finally, he turned toward the ranch buildings.

He hardly recognized the place when he rode up. The rails around the corral were freshly whitewashed. Not a post was broken. At the stable, boards that had been sagging for lack of proper nailing were snugged to the framework. He smiled to himself. All those old reprobates needed was a good solid shove in the right direction. Too, he knew it wasn't all his doing. Joy had taken hold and was acting like the owner again. He liked to think he had given her the heart to keep trying.

His horse picked up his gait and stepped fancily toward the stable. Gundy took care of him before going to the house to give Joy a report.

She greeted him at the door. "Trace Gundy, I'm so glad to see you." She stood back and looked at him from head to toe. "You're all in one piece, I see. Thank heaven for that. I just knew when you left here you'd get into trouble."

115

Gundy stood there and looked at her. She had a sparkle in her eyes that hadn't been there before. Her hair was neatly combed and put up in a bun at the back. Why, she was one of the prettiest women he'd ever seen. But then, he'd thought that the first time he looked at her.

He smiled. "Ma'am, if I'd known how pretty you were gonna be, an' what a good welcome you'd have for me, I'd a come home sooner." He sobered. "Soon's dinner's over, an' the boys go to the bunkhouse, you an' me, we gotta talk. I done found out more'n I figured."

Her eyes locked on his. "Why sure, Trace. We can talk now if you want. Supper's ready, and it's still an hour until the boys get in."

He smiled again. "Reckon I just wanted an excuse to sit an' drink coffee with you. We can talk now if you want."

She colored prettily. "Trace, you don't need an excuse to have coffee with me. We'll wait until after supper. I'd like that, too."

He tipped his hat, nodded, and said, "Reckon I better go clean up a mite." He rubbed the stubble on his chin. "Reckon I better shave, too, if I'm gonna have coffee with the boss."

Back in the bunkhouse, he bathed, shaved, and dug out his best Levi's. They were faded and had a couple of patches on the knees — but they were clean. He'd had a bath in the Powder, if he dared call it such. The water had been so cold he'd gotten in and out almost before he could get wet.

He'd finished buttoning his shirt when Baden and Lawton came growling into the bunkhouse. "Workin' us to death. Ain't never worked so hard," Baden said.

"Yeah, I'm a mind to quit. Ever since that Gundy come here, Miz Joy seems changed. She done took hold of this here ranch. You notice she's tellin' us what to do every day."

Gundy knew they hadn't seen him yet, but he couldn't hold back the laugh. "You two spavined, broke-down old goats ain't about to quit. You never been so happy as you been the last couple o' weeks. An' you're both glad Miz Joy done took charge. This place is beginnin' to look like a workin' ranch again."

They looked at him, looked at the floor, then gave him a sheepish grin. "Gundy, you're right, Miz Joy seems like she's gitten' over Mr. Jim gitten' killed like he did. You done made her want to git on

117

with livin'," Lawton said, and looked toward the door. "C'mon, let's go eat."

"Whoa up there. You two gonna get used to another thing. You ain't gonna put your feet under that table yonder in the big house less'n you wash up first, every day. Now get after it. When you get there, I want to be able to see the skin underneath all that dirt."

They looked at each other, looked at Gundy, and really did some first-class grumbling. He laughed, and when he put the small shard of mirror on the post to shave, Baden said, "Now gosh ding it, that there is a shore 'nuff reason to quit."

While they cleaned up, Gundy cleaned and oiled his guns, thinking he kept them cleaner than Baden and Lawton kept themselves, but then his life had often depended on his weapons.

The three of them ready, they trooped to the house. Gundy noticed Joy didn't miss their appearance. It was only a glance at all three, but that glance swept each from head to toe. A slight smile creased the corners of her mouth.

During supper, Gundy joshed the boys a bit, and got growls from both, which caused Joy to laugh. A look passed between them that said how pleased they were she could again laugh at small things.

For dessert, she served them hot apple pie with thick cream poured over the top. Lawton rubbed his stomach, looked at Gundy, and said, "Reckon you told Miz Joy we wuz about to quit. She ain't fixed us no pie like this for some time. Done it so's we wouldn't pay no mind to you workin' us so hard."

Straight-faced, Gundy replied, "Nope. She knows sweets'll give you more git up an' go. Figures she'll get more work outta you that way."

"Well gosh ding it, if I'd a knowed that, I wouldn't of eat so much," Baden said, and loosened his belt over his ample stomach another notch. Again, Joy laughed.

Gundy and the boys stood to leave. "Trace, why don't you stay and give me that report on what you found?"

He nodded, filled his coffee cup, and again sat. He pulled his pipe from his pocket and quickly shoved it back.

"Oh, smoke your pipe while we talk, Trace. I like the smell, makes me know there's a man in the house."

They sat through a comfortable silence, drinking their coffee, Gundy smoking. He felt her gaze and looked up into her eyes.

"Why are you doing all this, Trace?

You're no run-of-the-mill cowhand. You've either had your own spread or ramrodded one."

"Yes'm, a little of both I reckon. For right now, think I better tell you what I know 'bout your cows, an' the part of it I'm guessin'." He'd tell her about himself when the time came, but there were other things she needed to know now, things that affected her.

"Miz Joy . . ."

"Oh, Trace, please stop the miz and ma'am. Surely we're better friends than that."

He flushed. "Yes'm, reckon we're getting that way. Anyhow, what I want to tell you is, I know where your cows are. At least I think I do, yours an' maybe a whole bunch o' other folks'."

"Well, why don't we get together and go take them back?"

"Ain't that simple. Don't know who them other folks are what owns them other cows, an' it's gonna take a whole bunch o' fightin' men to do the job. Them cow thieves got a big ranch with a salty crew, a *big* salty crew surroundin' 'em."

Joy pierced him with that gaze he'd learned meant she was way ahead of what he'd told her. "We can't do it without getting a bunch of men hurt. I don't want that to happen. I don't want *you* hurt doing a job I should do myself."

Gundy stiffened. "I ride for the brand, ma'am. Where I come from, that means I do whatever I have to in order to make the brand pay. Gonna think on this awhile. Come up with an idea that'll work, then we're goin' after your cows."

Not breaking her gaze, she said, "You're quite a man, Trace Gundy. I'm thinking any woman you befriend can count herself a *very* lucky person."

His face turned hot again. "Thank you, ma'am. Them's mighty kind words, but we better wait an' see if I can stand in boots big enough to deserve them." He stood. "Reckon I better get to bed. Tomorrow, wantta get a pretty good count of how many head you got left."

She nodded, an amused look in her eyes. "All right, Trace. And I'll get out the tally book then, and we'll see how bad I've been hurt."

On the way to the bunkhouse, he wondered if he was being unfaithful to Dee. Joy stirred him as no woman had since the raid on his ranch. He fought the idea. She was a beautiful woman, a nice woman, a strong woman, but he wasn't interested in her like a man is to a woman — or was he?

121

chapter nine

The next morning Gundy awoke to frost and a cold wind blowing out of the north. Joy said, over breakfast, snow would soon fall. Well, he'd at least have a warm place to eat and sleep through the deep-freeze months.

When he topped the buckskin, he had to ride the kinks out. Danged horse hadn't been this frisky since he left Red River.

He rode straight south, looking for a bald hill Joy said marked the south boundary of the ranch. About seven miles out he sighted it, an outcropping of limestone, and turned back north, working back and forth from east to west.

The cattle he saw were in good shape for the onset of winter. Every hundred head he counted, he made a mark on a slip of paper he'd brought for the purpose. The middle of the afternoon, he tied his bandanna from the top of his head to under his chin and pulled his hat down over it, tight. His ears felt like they'd break off if he touched them. The temperature plummeted.

By the time he reached the ranch soon after sundown, he counted thirty-three marks on his paper. If left alone, there would be a good calf crop. He intended to see them left alone.

For the next two weeks Gundy worked with the two punchers getting everything ready for winter. A powdering of snow dusted the land in the middle of the third week. Joy thought it too early for such.

That night at supper he asked how many ranches there were in the area. She counted on her fingers, mumbling the brands to herself. She looked up. "Five, six counting this one. Two between here and the Rosebud, one west of here, and two more to the south. Why?"

He frowned. "Just thinkin'. Stands to reason if you're losin' cows, others must be, too. Think I'll visit 'em an' see. Gonna leave in the mornin', be back in 'bout a week."

The first ranch he visited, an easterner, by the sound of his words, greeted him with suspicion. "What business is it of yours if we're losing cattle?"

"I'm reppin' for Miz Waldrop. She's losin' cows. We wondered if she was the only one."

He'd said his name was Ted Bilkins. His

eyes shifted to the side, then to the ground. "We might have lost a few, but not enough to worry us. We're not hunting for a shootout over them."

Gundy stared at him a moment. Feeling sorry for him. He wouldn't last. Out here a man fought for what was his. He tipped his hat and rode off.

Crossing Bilkins's range, Gundy saw only a few yearlings, the same indication of wholesale rustling he'd seen on the Flying JW.

The next ranch, the Circle BR, was a different story. When he hitched his horse to the tie rail by the front door, a frosty-haired man Gundy judged to be in his mid-fifties came out. "Howdy, stranger. Name's Runnels. Step down an' rest your saddle."

Gundy liked the man right off. "Name's Gundy." They exchanged handshakes. "Need to talk awhile, Runnels. I'm reppin' for Miz Joy over east o' here."

"Hear tell she's a fine woman. Knowed 'er husband 'fore he got killed. Good man, good cowman. Never met *her*. Come on in. Coffee's on the stove."

Sitting at the kitchen table, Mrs. Runnels brought them each a cup of coffee. "You men can take care of yourselves from here on. I have things to do."

"Yes'm. That's the way it ought to be," Gundy said.

"Notice you smoke a pipe. Pack up an' light up. I'll git the coffee after we drink this. Danged woman's gettin' so she bosses me around all the time."

Gundy chuckled. From the little he'd seen of the two, he figured they carried on like this all the time, had spent most of their adult lives hassling each other, and loved every minute of it.

"Now, young man, what you ride all the way over here for?"

Gundy stared into the sharp blue eyes and thought to come right to the point. "Runnels, you losin' most o' your young stuff, mostly yearlin's?"

Runnels looked into his empty cup. He seemed to have aged ten years at the question. After a moment he looked into Gundy's eyes. "Son, you crossed my range. You see many calves?"

"No, sir, but thought I'd ask. Your neighbor, Bilkins, told me it wasn't none o' my business. He didn't seem interested in doin' nothin' 'bout it no way."

"City man," Runnels grumped. "He won't last out here much longer."

"You ever try trailin' them cows you lost?"

125

"Tried it, but lost the trail every time on hard ground. Figure I've lost maybe four hundred head."

"Miz Joy's been hurt worse'n that, 'bout eight hundred."

Runnels whistled. "Whew! She gonna make it?"

Gundy shook his head. "Not 'less I do somethin' 'bout it, and right now I don't know what to do. I trailed 'em. Know where they are, an' even with bein' able to prove they're stolen the bunch that took 'em are hard cases down to the last man. Got nobody to help me."

Runnels frowned, put fire to his pipe, looked in the bowl, then shook his head. "Soon's I got the place in shape for winter, I let all but four of my hands go. The ones I kept ain't fightin' men. Probably handle a rifle right nice, but ain't fightin' men. Know what I mean?"

Gundy nodded. " 'Fraid I do. We got a couple like that on the Flyin' JW."

Runnels leaned forward. "What you got in mind, Gundy? What we gonna do?"

A thrill went up Gundy's spine. Runnels had said "we." He took it to mean Runnels would join the fight when the time came. "Don't know. Right now I want to see how many ranchers in the area are losin' cows,

126

an' how many men we can count on from them. Looks like you an' me are the only ones so far, but I gotta see three more ranchers. Bilkins is out. Far as I'm concerned, he'll be out when we divvy up the herd when we get it back." He stood. "Runnels, soon's I come up with a plan, I'll let you know, an', er, why don't you an' the missus come over to see Miz Joy. Think she'd like to see another lady."

Runnels grinned. "Son, tell you now. We'll do that. I b'lieve it might get my missus off my backside for a while." He put his hand on Gundy's shoulder. "Good luck with your plan. We need it. Say, it's gettin' late. Stay the night with us and get an early start in the mornin'. Looks like snow an' deep cold 'fore mornin'.'"

Gundy had been hoping for the invitation. "Man, I was hopin' you'd ask. Didn't relish sleepin' out yonder in some ravine tonight."

"Ma, make the bed in the spare room, Gundy's gonna stay the night." Gundy figured Runnels's yell could be heard down at the stable.

Miz Runnels made the bed, then got busy on supper. She never missed a chance to sling a barb at Runnels who winked at Gundy each time. Speaking so she'd be sure to hear, he said, "See what I was tellin' you, Gundy? It's a true wonder I ain't beat down to a nubbin the way that woman mistreats me."

Gundy, feeling his grin stretch to his ears, shook his head. "Yeah, Runnels, I sure feel sorry for you. Most men would give their best saddle horse just to have a few days of the life you've got. Poor mistreated old man."

Miz Runnels looked at her husband. "See there, Pa, what I been tellin' you all these years? You're the luckiest man alive to have me." She sobered and looked Gundy straight on. "And, Mr. Gundy, I'm gonna tell you this, knowing he's gonna throw it back at me every day from here on, I'm the luckiest woman alive to have that there man of mine."

Somehow Gundy knew they had told each other those very words many times. It made him feel warm inside, and for some reason he felt closer to them for sharing their feelings with him.

The rest of the evening they searched for a way to get the cattle back without men getting hurt. But for all their talk they knew the only way to get them back was to go in with guns.

The next morning Gundy was ten miles away when the sky lightened. A light snow fell and seemed to get heavier.

By noon, the wind blew the pellets horizontally. Early, too early for this, Gundy thought. The cows would suffer, many of them would die. If they drifted to barbed wire, that's where they'd stop and suffocate from rime ice in their nostrils or freeze to death. He'd heard of thousands of head lost during the great die-ups in Texas.

He'd noticed no unbranded cattle on Runnels's range, and knew Joy's cows were branded. He nodded into his sheepskin. He'd cut the wire, let them drift. It would make the gather harder come spring, but that was better than skinning carcasses.

By nightfall, although he had to guess when that was, the leaden sky seemed to sit right on top of his shoulders, Gundy had cut Runnels's fence, and Bilkins's and Joy's fence also. He looked for a place to camp.

He stayed close to Pumpkin Creek, looking for a cut-bank he could crawl under and build his fire so as to reflect back on him. It had to be large enough for his horse. If the gelding died, Gundy knew he would be next.

He found what he wanted and spent an hour in the semidark gathering wood enough to last the night, then built a fire ringing his hole under the bank. He cut branches from brush along the water's edge and weaved a front to his shelter, keeping the fire inside it.

Thick ice covered the creek. Gundy used his Bowie knife to chip chunks of it for coffee, thinking the temperature must be close to zero.

After a while, satisfied he'd done the best he could, he cooked supper, the best part being the thick black coffee. As soon as he drank the coffee, he melted more ice so his buckskin could drink.

Through the night he replenished wood on his fire. He'd never heard of a man dying from lack of sleep. What he reckoned was about two in the morning, he stumbled along the bank searching for more wood. Gauging what he gathered by what he'd burned, he collected enough to last into midmorning.

A sickly, gray dawn seeped into his shelter. Gundy stood and climbed to the top of the bank. The snow showed no letup. He crawled back into his hole thinking he'd best wait it out.

Several times that day he checked the weather and gathered more wood. An early storm like this couldn't last much more than a day or two. Each time he came back he patted the gelding's neck and ran his hands down the strong flanks. He'd never seen a horse grow such a heavy winter coat, and at the same time marveled once again how well nature protected its animals.

When living with the Apache they judged the severity of the coming winters by the thickness of animals' coats, the amount of food stored by them, and many other natural signs. The white man could learn a lot from those who lived *with* nature. White men tried to conquer and destroy it. The Indian adjusted to it.

The second morning the wind had slackened, and snow fell in short flurries. Gundy put his fire out and saddled up. That afternoon he reached the Denton Ranch, told him essentially what he'd told Runnels, and found that he, too, had let most of his riders go, but he thought a couple of those left might handle guns right well. Gundy left Denton with his promise to support the plan, when he had one.

Ben Purdy, it turned out, had lost only a few cattle, his ranch was farther from the area, but he promised to support the rest of the ranchers.

Purdy was a grizzled old man, with a mane of white hair that stood out in all directions. Even when he laughed, Gundy thought he looked fierce as an old grizzly bear with a sore paw. "Son," he said, "tell you like it is. We gotta git rid of all the scavengers in this here neck of the woods. I done had to fight the Sioux, but I understood them and why they fought. I was trying to take their way of life away, but these here lowlifes what're stealing cows ain't fit to live. They're an abomination against mankind. Yes, sir, I'll help with men, guns, supplies, whatever it takes. Let me know when."

"How many men can you spare for this, Mr. Purdy?"

"I got fifteen" — he rubbed his jaw — "reckon keep five here on the ranch." He nodded. "Yep, figure ten men'll do it."

"Soon's I figure where to get another ten or fifteen men, I'll tell you 'bout it an' we'll go get 'em."

Purdy walked to his horse with him. "Why don't you stay the night, son? Eat supper, get a night's sleep, and an early start in the morning."

It was in Gundy's mind to decline, but looking at the old man, he had the feeling Purdy liked him and wanted to get better acquainted. Gundy liked Purdy too. "Sounds like a right good idea. All right, I'll head home in the morning."

That night, sitting over a healthy glass of whiskey, Gundy told Purdy he'd probably begin seeing several other brands on his place because he'd cut the fence during the storm.

"Hell, son, before we had all this here barbed wire out here, we always had brands from other ranches. We'll just cut 'em out and head 'em home, or wait 'til roundup and your rep can cut 'em out."

Gundy nodded. "Way we used to do it, sir. Thank you."

Gundy rode toward the Flying JW the next morning feeling much better. His biggest problem had been cut in half. It would be a lot easier to find ten or fifteen fighting men than twenty-five, and Joy could count herself lucky. Out of the four ranchers Gundy met, there was only one weakling.

During his two-day ride home, the beginning of an idea muddled around his head, both where he could get the men and where he could get money to pay them. He'd think on it a little.

chapter ten

He rode into the ranch about noon of the second day. Joy stood on the porch and watched him put his horse away. Gundy felt a warm glow, thinking it was nice to be waited for, maybe even worried about.

His horse cared for, he headed for the bunkhouse.

"Trace Gundy, you come right on up here and eat your dinner. I've looked for you for three days now."

"Aw, ma'am, I cain't come in your house dirty as I am. I'll clean up and be there in a minute."

"Stop only to wash your hands and face. Your stomach doesn't know you're dirty. Come on up."

On the way to the house, Gundy hoped the boys wouldn't see him going in to eat dirty as he was. They'd have a conniption fit after the dressing down he'd given them about being clean.

"Now, sit down while I dish up. I'll make fresh coffee. You could float a horseshoe in that on the stove."

"Ma'am, I like it like that. Let me have a cup of it, don't bother with makin' more."

"Now you hush, it's no bother."

While eating Gundy told her about the fine neighbors she had, that he'd invited the Runnelses over to visit, and about the storm, and cutting fence to prevent a die-out.

"Sorta took a lot on myself, inviting folks to come see you, but seemed as how you could do with seein' another woman. An' cuttin' the fence, well, ma'am, I seen cows die by the thousands durin' blizzards when they couldn't drift with the wind. Couldn't stand to see the same thing again."

Joy stared at him a moment. "Trace, you invited the Runnelses because you care. You cut fences for the same reason. You're a very thoughtful man." She continued looking at him. "And I thought I told you to call me Joy."

"You did, ma'am, but, well, it seems sorta like I'm takin' liberties with you." As soon as he said it he felt his face turn red. "Aw, what I meant was . . ."

Joy choked on laughter, then, straight-faced, said, "You can take any kind of liberties with me you want, as long as I tell you it's all right."

Gundy didn't dare look her in the eye.

135

He stared at his plate. "Yes'm, didn't think of it that way."

When he told her about Bilkins his face hardened. "Ma'a— uh, Joy, when we get the cows back to those what owns 'em, we ain't givin' none to Bilkins."

"Oh, Trace, that's not fair. They're his cattle."

Gundy shook his head. "No, ma'am. Out here a man works and fights for what's his. He ain't got the gumption to help us fight, they ain't his cattle no more."

He felt her studying him. "Trace, I said a little while ago you were a thoughtful man, a kind man, and you are. But it seems you can be very hard at times."

"Yes'm. Reckon I can be. When you feel up to it, I'll tell you some of why I'm like I am."

"Tell me now, Trace. I want to know. Somehow, I feel it's important that I know you."

"No, Joy, but I'll tell you soon. Want to get your cows back, want to do right by you first."

"Why is it important you do right by me?"

"Don't know. Just know I gotta do it. Reckon some of it's 'cause you took me in, gave me a job."

She smiled. "Trace, a man as good as you are around a ranch wouldn't have had to look for a job. I'm certain you had a good one where you came from, could still have it if you wished, but something's driving you. Want to tell me about it?"

He shook his head. "Not yet, Joy. I gotta get some things straight in my head first, then I'll talk to you 'bout me."

That night Gundy lay in his bunk, and in the flickering light from the stove stared at the ceiling. Guilt gnawed his guts. Dee hadn't been dead but a little over six months, and he had all but stopped shadowing her killer. Yeah, he still intended to kill the gringo, but it had ceased to be the only reason he lived.

He shouldn't be thinking of anything but the gringo. He should have killed him and headed for Texas. He could have lived off the land on the way home. He could have wired for money if that was his reason for delaying. Hell, he could have done a lot of things, but here he was working for a woman, thinking about her in ways he shouldn't be. *Was* he thinking about her like a man thought of a special woman?

He admitted she wasn't just any woman. He knew she hadn't taken Dee's place — would never do so. But was he making a

137

place for her, her own special place? That he wanted to help her didn't mean anything. He would do the same for anyone in trouble, wouldn't he?

Gundy didn't get much sleep that night. He had allowed himself to think further than the next meal, and didn't like it.

The next morning he rousted the boys out and told them they were going to try to find the drifted cattle. And they would drive any of Runnels's cows back to his range. The two grumbled and growled through breakfast. It was cold enough to freeze the horn off an anvil, but they saddled and went with him on the thankless task. And they spent the next two weeks at the same job.

They frequently stayed away at night, wanting to be close to the job the next morning. During the last night before Gundy thought to return to headquarters, they camped close to the Tongue.

Drinking coffee before turning in, Slim Baden took a healthy swallow and eyed Gundy. "Boss, you figure to ever let us go in town again? Hell, I ain't had a drink in a month or more. I'm gitten drier'n a Texas water hole in August. Think maybe a drink would fix me so's I could work harder."

Surprised, Gundy snapped a glance at

him. Neither of the two had called him "boss" before. "Baden, Lawton, want you to get somethin' straight. Miz Joy's the boss. I'm just sort of an unofficial ramrod 'til we get this ranch runnin' smooth again. To answer your question, reckon I ain't been thinkin' much about what you boys might want. Wanted to get things goin' good. Yeah, when we get home go on in town. Tie one on if you got enough money. If I had any, I might join you."

Ignoring what Gundy said about who was boss, Lawton said, "Boss, we got a few bucks, c'mon, go with us. We'll buy the drinks."

Gundy shook his head. "Don't reckon so, boys. I'd like to but from here on I want someone to stay close to the ranch. Don't like the idea of a woman bein' alone out here. I'll stay home this time. When you get back, I might go in. But from here on in, I want at least one o' you here all the time, an' don't get far from your guns."

"You 'spectin' trouble, boss?" Lawton asked.

Gundy laughed. "I always expect trouble. I found out once, a while back, it's when you don't expect it that it hits you where it really hurts. That ain't never gonna happen to me again."

After putting wood on the fire and sliding down into their blankets, Gundy wondered what prompted him to be certain someone was at the ranch at all times. He'd not had any indication of trouble.

They rode in to headquarters mid-afternoon the next day. He told Joy he'd given the boys a couple of days off. He'd stay with her.

"Trace, you've been working hard, doing the job of two men, why don't you go with them?"

"Reckon I'll stay here, Joy. Ain't much of a drinker so I don't miss it much."

She blushed. "Trace, I know you're broke." The color deepened in her cheeks. "I have a few dollars, go into town with them, get the Levi's you need so desperately, have a beer or two, and — and whatever else men do when they go to town."

He knew what she meant, but how could he tell her he wasn't interested in "having" another woman, maybe she hadn't meant that at all.

"Joy, want you to know somethin'. A trip to town, for me, is a couple o' beers, talk to folks on the street, an' come home. Don't do no carousin' around."

Joy's face turned a fiery red. She looked at the ground, gripped her hands tightly in front of her, and raised her eyes to look him squarely in his eyes. "Trace, I didn't mean to infer that you did other than that, but some men do, you know, and I can't blame them. The hard, lonely days and nights, often filled with danger, are enough to make any man seek whatever comfort he can find. I — I'm just glad you don't see the need for that kind of escape."

Gundy wanted to ask her why it made a difference what kind of solace he chose, but was afraid of her answer. He wasn't ready for what might follow. "No, ma'am. Ain't never seen no need to do nothin' I figure I'd feel dirty for doin'."

He glanced at the bunkhouse. "Reckon I better get me a bath an' shave. Ain't been where I could do them things in the last few days."

A slight smile broke the corners of her mouth. "By the time you're finished, I'll have supper ready. Come on up to the house when you're through."

Gundy nodded. "Gotta heat some water. Take a while so don't be in no hurry."

"Come when you're ready."

While shaving, Gundy thought to ask if he might not sleep in the ranch house, save firewood, lamp oil, and would give him a better feeling for her safety. He turned the

141

thought around in his mind a moment and shook his head. Joy was lonely and vulnerable, and he was just as much as she. He'd better stay in the bunkhouse, no point in doing something they'd both be sorry for the next day.

Two days later Baden and Lawton returned from town, bleary-eyed, smelling like sour, fermented corn, and not fit to ride for a good day at least.

"You men clean up and crawl in your bunks the rest of the day. Be ready to ride come daylight." Gundy watched them head for the bunkhouse, each wearing a satisfied, idiotic grin. He envied them the ability to shed the hardships of ranch life with a couple nights drinking, and the "whatever men do" that Joy had brushed on the other day.

Gundy rode close to headquarters the rest of the day, circled it, and studied the ground for tracks not of his or his riders making. He didn't expect to see anything unusual, but looked anyway.

The next morning he sent Baden and Lawton in the opposite direction, and he returned to the point he'd left off the evening before. He'd ridden only a quarter of a mile when he saw pony tracks. A shod horse had made them, and the horse was not from one of those in their remuda. He rode his gelding to the other side of the sign, ground-reined him, and came back to the scene.

Stubs of three cigarillos lay on the ground close to marks made by boot heels, as though someone hunkered there for a long time. Gundy figured the man smoked and watched the house from here. The cigarillo stubs were between the heel marks and the house, so the man smoked, watched, and threw the stubs out in front of him.

He went back to the pony tracks; they were familiar, but not one of the ranch ponies. Where had he seen them before? He memorized the area, mounted, and followed the tracks to the fence. It had been cut and shoddily mended.

Riding the fence line, he found three more places where it had been cut and mended, and the same tracks were there as at the scene from where the snooper watched. Why would anyone sit in the cold and watch the house? There wasn't anything there worth stealing. Horses and cows could be taken from a distance.

Joy! The thought exploded in his head. Someone watched for a glimpse of Joy. Was there anyone in the West dumb enough to harm a woman? Did they figure to take her away, or attack her there in the house?

He thought of one man who would do such, and at the same time it came to him where he'd seen the familiar horse tracks. He'd followed them mile after mile out of Texas. The gringo.

All the hate and desire to kill flooded back into him. Gradually, during the past months, Gundy knew he had softened on the idea of killing the gringo like an Apache would. He had slowly begun to think he'd just shoot him and end it there. But now? Now he knew how he must do it. Not quick and merciful, but slowly, painfully, horribly.

Gundy wanted to erase the picture from his mind of the gringo as he'd looked riding from his ranch yard.

From each shoddily spliced fence wire, Gundy tracked the gringo to the place he'd spied from at that time. At each, he found several cigarillo butts. The Comanchero had been smart enough to change stations from which he watched the house so as to avoid wearing a path, but he'd not shredded the cigarillo butts. There was no doubt the same man watched each time.

Gundy's first impulse was to find the freshest tracks, none of them over a week old, and trail the horse back to where he came from, but that would get him killed.

He hunkered and studied the tracks, the cigarillo butts, and where the gringo's horse had been ground-reined. After a while he knew all he needed to know, but he still squatted. How should he handle this?

He could tell Joy what he'd found and ask to sleep in the house to protect her. *That* would alarm her.

Even though alone, he felt his face redden at the thought of the two of them being in the house with each other through the night — perhaps many nights.

He might track the gringo, somehow get him away from his friends, and kill him. Gundy shook his head. He'd already discarded that thought.

Finally, he came up with a plan, chancy, but one he thought would work.

The rest of the afternoon, Gundy searched for the next most likely spot from which to spy on the ranch house. He found what he looked for, a knoll less than a quarter of a mile behind the bunkhouse. Now, he had to alert the boys.

That night after supper, he told Baden and Lawton to meet him in the bunkhouse, he had something he wanted them to do.

They growled about never satisfying him, each drank another cup of coffee and left. Gundy lingered only a few moments after they left and followed, with Joy's admonishment not to be too hard on them.

Gundy sat close to the potbellied stove, holding his hands as close to the cherry-red heat as he could stand it, and told them what he'd found. "The way I figure to work is this: I want each of you to take turns standing watch, in case I've missed where I figure he'll show up the next time. Don't let Miz Joy know what we're doin', no need to worry her. I'm gonna slip outta here 'bout dark an' see if I can catch 'im." He glanced at each of them. "Got it?" They nodded.

"Don't want neither o' you stayin' awake long enough to get sleepy. You feel that way, wake the one what's asleep." They again nodded. "Okay, I'll roll my bedroll. Y'all decide which one's gonna take the first watch here."

An hour later Gundy lay on the slope of a ravine that cut between the knoll he wanted to give his attention and another slightly behind it. Bitter cold pushed through flesh and gnawed at his bones. He had wanted a fire many times during his life, but he couldn't think of any when he'd wanted one more than now.

146

chapter eleven

Gundy placed his Winchester on the ground in front of him, wrapped himself in his blankets, then pulled his sheepskin coat over all but his head and arms. His ears had to do the watching until his eyes could do the job.

Stars looked down at him from a cold, distant, black sky. Nothing stirred. Gundy smiled to himself. Even the animals had enough sense to burrow in on a night like this, showed how dumb a man could be. About one o'clock by Gundy's best guess, something scraped the ground not too far away.

Gundy moved the barrel of his rifle in the direction of the noise. Teeth tore at the scrubby grass, a grunt, and the cow settled to the ground again. Gundy relaxed pressure on the trigger.

When dawn lightened the sky in the east not more than a shade of gray, Gundy stood, took care of his gear, and rode back to the stable.

Back in the bunkhouse, he cautioned the

men to take care and not let Joy know how tired they were. And to get used to it, because they were going to do the same thing until they found what they wanted. They cleaned up and went to breakfast.

Joy served them fried grits and syrup. Gundy looked up from his third serving. "Here tell them Yankees call these here fried grits johnnycake, down Texas way we call 'em grits, reckon y'all do the same up here since so many folks up here come from Texas."

Joy nodded. "That's what I call them, Trace."

"Anyway, ma'am, they sure are good."

Joy frowned. "If I didn't know better, as red as your eyes are this morning, I'd say you boys had some moonshine hid out in the bunkhouse."

Bob Lawton saved the day. "No, ma'am, the stove wuz smokin' a little. We took care of it."

They finished breakfast and were drinking coffee when Gundy said, "Joy, the boys have been workin' pretty hard, an' cold as the weather is I figure to give 'em the day off. I'm gonna take it off with 'em."

Joy's head bobbed before he could finish. "Good idea. Trace, you need the time off more than either of them. I'm glad you're going to rest a little."

"Don't reckon we'll be needin' any dinner at noontime, least I won't. Figure on sleepin' the day away." Lawton and Baden echoed his words.

That night and the third night were a repeat of the first. The fourth night things were different. About midnight the slow, measured clopping of a horse's hooves against the frozen ground broke the silence. Gundy's position was downwind of the horse so he didn't worry about being detected before the rider got where he was going. He threw off the sheepskin, unwrapped the blankets from about him, and pointed the Winchester in the direction of the sound. As late as it was, Gundy figured the rider had come to do more than watch. Energy pumped through every part of him. His muscles came alive, tensed for something to happen.

The horse stopped, leather squeaked, a curse, and Gundy picked up a ghostly shape, afoot, moving toward the top of the knoll.

At the top the rider stopped, squatted, and lit a smoke. Gundy choked back angry bile. It was all he could do to keep from firing into the rider. He held his emotions in check, remembering the special treatment he planned for the gringo.

The Comanchero — Gundy had no doubt it was him — finished his smoke, ground the fire out against his boot heel, stood, went to his horse, and gathered the reins in his hand. He led his horse toward the house.

Just a little punishment wouldn't hurt, Gundy thought, and lined his sights on the back of the rider's leg, right at the bend of his knee. He squeezed off a shot.

The gringo stumbled, went to his knees still holding the reins in his left hand, and pulled his horse to his side. Flame spewed from his right hand, searching for the one who'd shot.

The barrel of Gundy's rifle followed every move. His one shot should have blown the gringo's kneecap off. He'd be a cripple until Gundy could end his misery. The rider put his foot in the stirrup and pulled himself into the saddle, digging the spur at the end of his good leg into his horse's flank. The horse leapt forward and lined out for the fence.

Gundy relaxed pressure on the trigger and realized he was trembling. He sucked clean, cold air into his lungs and let it out twice before he settled down and stood calm. He'd never wanted to kill a man so badly. But that would have to wait until he could do it his way. He took the gelding's reins and led him down the hill.

After stabling his horse, he ghosted his way to the bunkhouse, making no more noise than the sigh of wind across the prairie. He stood behind Slim Baden, reached over his shoulder, and covered the hammer of Baden's rifle with his hand before he whispered, "Go to bed. Won't have no trouble tonight. Get some sleep."

The next morning before daylight, about time to roll out of his blankets, Gundy heard Baden talking to Lawton. "I tell you, Lawton, that there man alayin' yonder's a danged Injun. He wuz right behind me, grabbed the action on my rifle, and I ain't heered nothin' yet. Oh, yeah, I did hear a shot in the night, soon after is when Gundy showed up here an' told me to get some sleep. Reckon he took care of whatever trouble he wuz expectin'. Shore am glad I ain't the one he's lookin' for. That man's scary." Gundy smiled into his blankets and stole another fifteen minutes sleep.

He told the men before going to breakfast that they wouldn't be standing guard the next few nights. He knew they wanted an explanation of the shot during the night, but he would have to explain not killing the prowler and he wasn't ready to do that.

Rance Barton, his leg shooting pain throughout his body, clung to the saddle horn wondering why the rifleman hadn't killed him. He'd had the opportunity, yet had shot to cripple.

By the time he reached the outskirts of Milestown, Barton slipped in and out of consciousness. He had to make it to his brother's saloon, Soldier's Haven. He vowed that when he could get two legs back under him, he would get the boys and wipe that persnickety widow woman and her ranch off the map.

He drew rein in front of the saloon, slipped to the side, and was falling from the saddle when two soldiers grabbed him and lowered him to the ground. "Get Lem out here, an' get a doctor. My leg's damned near shot off." He passed out before he could answer questions the two threw at him.

He was aware that time passed. A couple of men carried him into the Haven and placed him on a table, the doctor came, his brother, Lem, shot questions at him, none of which he answered, someone poured a slug of whiskey down his throat, and he began to feel better. He looked up into the eyes of the doctor.

"Mister," the doctor's voice sounded like he talked into a drum, "Mr. Barton, I'm laying it on the line for you. I argued with myself when I saw that leg of yours whether to amputate or try to save it. It was a mess, but I think you'll be able to keep it. Although" — he hesitated a moment — "I better tell you right now. It'll never be the same. It's going to be stiffer'n a board the rest of your life."

Barton lay there feeling the impact of the doctor's words, each word hitting him like another bullet. He felt no gratitude. Anger churned his stomach. "Oughtta kill you, you damned butcher. Get outta here 'fore I do."

The doctor washed his instruments, keeping a wary eye on Barton while he did. He placed each of his tools carefully in his black bag, speared Barton with a poisonous look, spat on the floor, and left.

Barton looked at his brother. "Get me in the back room, and call in the boys, them what ain't out at the ranch. Got somethin' to say."

An hour later twelve men gathered around the bed they'd had brought in. Barton told them on which ranch he'd been shot, and that he'd figured on stealing the widow woman for his own use. He glanced at each man there. "What I want you men to do is go out there, burn the ranch, and take that woman to the Box LB. When my leg gets all right, *I'll* take care of *her.*"

Brad Crockett — a tall, rawboned Texan, tough as a boot, and one of the men Barton had never figured was really one of them — spoke up, "Barton, I done stole cows for you and your brother, but I don't make war on or harm women. Deal me out."

A chorus of "me too" echoed around the room, and at the same time seven of the twelve moved to the side of the bed with Crockett.

"What's the matter, you scared?"

The room quietened. Crockett stared into Barton's eyes. "I'm gonna tell you somethin', Barton, you get well and say that again, I'll blow your other leg out from under you, then I'll kill you. Now" — he looked at Lem — "figure my time." He glanced at the others. "You boys comin' with me?" He walked toward the door. All seven followed.

Lem Barton followed them from the room. "No need for you boys to feel this way. My brother's just mad 'cause of his leg. He'll be all right once he gets over it."

"Figure our time." Crockett's words fell like ice shards around them.

When the eight had their pay in hand, Crockett led them to the Range Rider Saloon in the middle of town. "Sit down, I'll buy the drinks, then I got a proposition for you."

Drinks in front of them, Crockett glanced around the table. "Every one of you men come up from Texas, got here when the weather started turnin', an' looked for a place to winter. Way I got it figured, ain't a single one of you really cottoned to stealin' cows."

"You got that right, Crockett," Stick Turner — young, skinny as broom straw, and a good hand with cows — said. "We all rode up here with the same trail herd. Figured on headin' back 'fore now, but like most, reckon we swung a wide loop from time to time, an' when Barton offered us a job we wuzn't too squeamish 'bout stealin' cows, so we took him up on his offer. But I draw the line at hurtin' womenfolk."

Crockett swept them with a glance. "All right, men, from what I'm hearin', ain't a one of us what wants to ride the owlhoot, so here's my proposition."

155

★ ★ ★

The evening of the second day after the shooting, Gundy, standing in the hayloft, pitched a last fork of hay down to the horses, stood, arched his back to get the kinks out, mopped his brow, and cocked his head. "Riders comin'," he said to Lawton.

"Yeah, I heered 'em."

"Stay here, keep outta sight, an' check your rifle for loads. I'll go down an' talk."

At the bottom of the ladder, he tied holster thongs to his thigh and stepped through the door.

A tight-bunched group of riders approached the house, looked his way, and reined toward him. The one in the lead, older than the rest, drew rein a few feet from Gundy. "The man of the house in?"

Gundy, never taking his eyes from the rider or his hand away from his .44, said, "Ain't no man of the house. Reckon 'til one comes along I'll sit in for 'im."

The older rider nodded. "Good. Want to talk to you. First off, my name's Crockett." A vague wave of his hand included the remainder of those with him. "These here men are my trail partners. They come up from Texas with one herd, me with another."

Gundy flicked each of them with a

glance. A hard-bitten crew, but most Texans who'd come up the trail would fit that description. "Climb down, rest your saddles."

When they'd dismounted, Crockett introduced each of them. The first two stuck out a hand to shake. Gundy locked eyes with them. "We'll shake after we're better acquainted. Name's Trace Gundy. What's your business?"

Crockett's eyes raked Gundy from head to toe. "Gundy, eh? Well, Mr. Gundy, we need a job, all eight of us."

Gundy studied Crockett a moment, and liked what he saw. Crockett was cut from the same mold as the crew he'd had on his own ranch. Every man that stood behind Crockett looked like they came from the same kind of background. "Mr. Crockett, I got a lady boss here. She needs hands all right, but all eight o' you? Hell, I don't know whether she's got enough food to feed you through the winter, an' I *know* she ain't got enough money to pay even one o' you a month's wages. Rustlers been strippin' her calf crop."

Crockett squatted, picked up a pebble, and rolled it around between his fingers. The rest of the men relaxed, a couple rolled smokes, some packed their pipes, others studied the ranch yard. Gundy figured Crockett as the leader when they rode in, and now Crockett was thinking deeply on something. Gundy let him think.

Finally, Crockett looked up. "Got a proposition for you."

"Let's hear it."

"S'pose we, all of us, agree to work for a place to sleep and food, 'til the weather warms. What you say to that?"

Gundy's gut tightened, he felt like he'd felt one time down in Mexico, surrounded by a whole town that wanted his scalp. Why would those men agree to anything like Crockett proposed?

"First off, Crockett, we ain't got enough work to keep but a couple o' you busy; second, I got a job in mind that says I need all o' you. Got you an' your crew figured for fightin' men. That's what I need, and if I can't pay you regular wages ain't no way I can pay you fightin' money."

Crockett stood. "Give me a little time to talk to the men. If they agree with what I got figured, you an' me'll talk some more."

Gundy nodded. He still felt like he'd been surrounded. Crockett had something in mind, but for him to think for a minute he was going to get Crockett and his crew for the price of winter's feeding made him suspicious. There had to be more in it for this bunch than that.

Crockett called his men into a circle, out of hearing distance for Gundy. They talked no more than five minutes before Crockett came back.

"Told 'em you needed fightin' men, but without fightin' wages. Fact is, I told 'em they wouldn't be *no* wages, but the little lady what owns this ranch needed help." He smiled, and every sun wrinkle a man ever thought to have broke his face into a patchwork that somehow, when put together, made up his face. Gundy decided he liked the man. "They bought it. Didn't even ask questions."

Crockett's men had stayed out of earshot. Gundy stared at the man in front of him, packed his pipe, and lit it without ever taking his eyes off him. "Why would you do this? You haven't even met Miz Waldrop yet; you don't owe her anything, an' I got every one o' you figured for a top hand. You don't need no grub-line job."

Crockett continued smiling. He nodded. "Yeah, we owe the lady something, and I'll tell you about it, you and her, if she'll let us put our feet under her table for supper."

"We'll prob'ly eat late. I'll go see if she's fixed enough. You men clean up an' make yourselves to home in the bunkhouse. Be down in a while." Gundy headed for the house.

Joy met him at the door, a worried frown creased her brow. She stood the Winchester she'd been holding against the wall. "Trace, who are those men? What do they want? I was afraid for you standing out there alone with them."

Gundy smiled. "No need to worry. Lawton had them under his rifle all the time I stood there." He glanced at the table already set for supper. "You got enough fixed to feed them men what rode in?"

"Won't take long to fix more, if you can keep them busy down at the bunkhouse."

"You got a jug o' whiskey hid away somewhere? If they take me up on what I'm gonna talk about, I figure to offer 'em a drink to seal the deal."

Joy studied him quietly a moment. "Yes, I think Jim had a bit in the cupboard." She made as though to turn away, then faced him squarely. "Trace Gundy, I don't know why I put so much faith in you, but I do. You — you always seem to be so in control of everything, and I've never seen a flicker of fear in your eyes. You handle this and I'll back you."

"No need to worry. I'll send Lawton an'

Baden up here soon's I get to the bunk-house. Station 'em outside the kitchen, out of sight, with shotguns in case we need 'em. They can eat later." He smiled again. "See, long's I have the edge I'm real brave. Call us when you have supper fixed."

chapter twelve

On the way to the bunkhouse, Gundy signaled Lawton to come out of the hayloft, and told him to go see Joy. When he walked into the crew's quarters, Crockett's men lounged about on unmade bunks. Baden was there, also.

"Gotta wait 'til Miz Waldrop gets a little extra supper fixed. She'll call when it's ready. Baden, Miss Joy wants to see you. You may miss dinner."

Stick Turner spoke up, "Baden, ain't gonna hurt you none to miss a meal or two, hell, you could share your weight with me and we'd both still be too fat."

Baden cast him a sour look and left. The good-natured joshing told Gundy these men would fit in.

Five of them started a penny-ante poker game and asked Gundy to sit in. "If y'all was gonna play for matches, I'd still have to say no, thanks anyway."

They played poker on one of the bunks. Gundy and Crockett sat at the one table. Crockett looked at Gundy's faded and

162

patched jeans, his shirt in no better shape, and said, "You broke, Gundy?"

Gundy felt his face warm. "Nope, I got a couple o' bucks, but I'm takin' right good care of it. Don't like bein' without *any* money."

Crockett's eyes crinkled at the corners. "Somehow, I figured you'd have all the money you needed."

Gundy wondered why Crockett would make such a statement. Broke cowboys were a dime a dozen during any fall and winter.

About two hours later Joy called them to supper. During the meal a lot of good-natured banter passed around the table. Gundy couldn't help thinking that this table should always have a goodly number of hands around it, and suspected it had before the rustling started, and that the conversation had been as lively and fun-filled then as now.

Supper finished and coffee poured, Joy sat at the head of the table. Gundy, sitting at the other end, said, "All right, Crockett, you got somethin' to say, let's hear it."

Crockett took a swallow of coffee, glanced at his men, rolled a cigarette, and nodded. "Miz Joy, we done talked this over, and every man here agrees we'll do it, but there's a catch in it."

Oh, hell, Gundy thought, wonder what that is? "What you agree to do, an' what's the catch?"

That crinkly smile broke Crockett's face again. "Now don't get excited. I'm gonna tell y'all somethin' what's gonna make you mad as hell — 'scuse me, Miz Joy, but I figure to lay all our cards on the table so's you can see why we're makin' this offer.

"First off, we got in this territory too late to start home before winter hit, so we got a job — rustling cows. Didn't sit well" — he shrugged — "but like most cowboys, at some time or other they done swung a wide loop. None o' us are any different. We been stealin' yore cows, ma'am, an' want to make it up to you. 'Sides, we done split from that bunch."

Gundy leaned back in his chair. "*If* we can trust you, that still don't change nothin' about bein' able to pay you, an' the job I got in mind might put you up against the very men you worked with. Could you do that?"

"Gundy, we never was a part of that outfit. We just worked there. We held to ourselves, didn't join in on trips to town with any, didn't play poker with 'em, didn't do nothin'. They just wasn't our kind of people, and when the chance came to split off from 'em we took it."

Gundy stood and again filled their coffee cups. "Crockett, let me get this straight. You're offerin' to work for Miz Joy for nothin', maybe even gun work?"

Crockett nodded. Gundy continued, "Why would you do that? All of you could just ride out and nobody would know the difference. What's the catch?"

"That's what I was workin' up to, Gundy, we want you to give us a job workin' for you when we get back to Texas. You got one of the biggest spreads down yonder, and we want to work for an outfit what ain't gonna lay us off after roundup. We're every one top hands."

Gundy glanced at Joy to see how she reacted to Crockett's announcement. She was staring at him.

"So you know who I am. Anybody in that outfit you rode for know I'm in this part of the country?"

"*We* didn't know 'til you told us your name out yonder at the stable, Gundy — or Blanco, whichever you want to be called."

Gundy again looked at Joy. "Reckon I got a lot o' explainin' to do, an' I'll do it soon's these men go to the bunkhouse."

He shifted his attention back to Crockett. "Call me Gundy around here, but anywhere else, don't call me nothin'. I stopped by Marshal Bruns's office and told him I was here, and why." He stood and walked over to stand by Crockett's chair. "You hear what happened to me down Texas way?"

Crockett again nodded, as did every man at the table. "Then you know I'm gonna raise a brand o' hell ain't nobody seen before. You men, or anybody else, better not get in my way."

"Blanco," Stick Turner spoke up, "you're looking at maybe the saltiest eight men in Montana, but I don't reckon they's a one, maybe even two or three of us, wants to tangle with you. We all cut our teeth on Colt .44s, but none o' us can handle one like you. Why, I seen you down El Paso way take on —"

"Tell the crew about it later," Gundy cut in. "Don't think Miz Joy wants to hear that kind o' stuff."

Joy's eyes were spitting fire. "Oh, yes, Mr. Gundy — or Mr. Blanco, whatever your name is, I want to hear that kind of stuff. Seems like I have a lot to learn about you."

"Yes'm, reckon you do, an' I'm gonna

tell you my story soon's I get this taken care of, if you're still trustin' me to take care of it."

"Go ahead, Mr. Gundy, take care of it."

Gundy included the men in his next words. "Here's the way it stands. You got my word on the job when you get back to Texas. Here, your job's gonna take on fightin', gettin' every cow back what Barton's outfit stole." He stopped, realizing these men didn't know where Barton fit into his past. "Rance Barton's the one I'm after for what he done to me down in Texas. Before we go after the cows, I'm gonna take care o' Barton in the way I learned from the Apache. They ain't gonna be no pay on this end o' the line. Ain't no money here. Miz Joy ain't got none, an' I ain't. But, I promise you, when I get back to Texas I'll pay you fightin' wages for the time you spend workin' for her."

"That ain't necessary, Gundy," Crockett said. "We figure we owe her, an' we'll fight or whatever's needed."

"Thanks, men, but you'll *earn* fightin' pay, an' I'll see you get it. Now get on back to the bunkhouse and stow your gear, you gonna be here awhile."

Gundy watched them troop out, then called Lawton and Baden to the table.

"Eat, and get to bed. Want you to take the buckboard into town in the mornin' for supplies. I'll write a note to Mr. Leighton. He'll let you have them."

They had heard every word while Crockett and the men were at the table. Gundy noticed they looked at him strangely, and with new respect. He drank coffee while they ate, and when they had finished, he closed the door behind them. He went back and sat at the table. "Reckon you want to hear 'bout me 'fore another daybreak."

Joy nodded. "Why haven't you told me before?"

He rubbed the back of his neck, trying to get the stiffness from it. "Wasn't the right time. Was too soon after my wife was killed." He glanced at her and again stared at the table. "You didn't know I'd been married, did you?" He didn't wait for her to answer. "No, don't reckon you did. You don't know nothin' 'bout me, an' I come in here an' started runnin' things like some rambunctious bully, an' you let me get away with it."

"Oh, Trace, I let you do it because I was at the end of my rope with a twelve-hundred-pound steer on the end of it. I didn't know what to do, and you did. I was glad to have you take charge. Now tell me about *you*."

"Ma'am, it's a long story, you sure you want to hear it tonight? Would you let it rest if I tell you I ain't done nothin' wrong — nothin' the law wants me for?" He again rubbed the stiffness from his neck. "Tell you this much for tonight. Yeah, I got one of the biggest ranches in the Big Bend o' Texas, still buildin' it. I come to you broke, 'cause I run outta money trackin' the man what killed my wife. I been months on the trail. I *did* need this job, still do, but I'll go into town in the next day or two and send a wire to the ranch for money. Didn't want to do that, but reckon we gotta pay Mr. Leighton for them supplies, so might's well send for it now. I'll write home an' let them know what's happened so far."

"Trace, if I get my cows back, Leighton will carry me until then. Don't send for money."

He shook his head. "No. These men will need drinkin' money, an' I need some clothes. We'll pay as we go, as much as we can."

"What's this about your name being Blanco?"

"It's part of my story. I'll tell you when I tell the whole thing. Think I'll get some sleep now."

Long after Gundy crawled between his blankets, he lay staring at the flickering light the stove cast on the rough beams overhead. If Crockett's men knew him, there would be others who would. He would have to do something about Barton soon, or he'd be warned, and on the lookout for trouble. But should he try getting the cattle back first, or should Barton come first? He studied on that awhile, and shifted his thoughts to Joy.

He owed her an explanation, and he admitted it had begun to make a real difference what she thought of him. There were things on his back trail that might turn her against him, and his determination to deal with Barton might also disgust her. About daylight he decided the only way to find out Joy's attitude was to tell her and let the chips fall where they would. He pushed the blankets off and tiredly crawled from under them. It would be a long day.

Around the wash bucket, all the riders looked bleary eyed. The late hours of the night before sat heavy on their shoulders. Gundy finished washing first, and when they'd all finished, he said, "Men, they's somethin' you need to know, anytime you gonna go in Miz Joy's house, I want you to be clean."

170

Stick grinned and said, "Hell, Blanco, we heered 'bout you an' Senegal while we wuz down Texas way. Reckon when that leathery faced old bastard sort o' adopted you, trusted you to take his trail herd north, he spoiled you, made you stay clean. Yore men was always clean, too. Also heered the bunkhouse smelled a whole lot better'n most. Stayin' clean ain't gonna be no problem with none o' us."

Gundy nodded. "Good, didn't 'spect no trouble 'bout that. Before we go up to breakfast, I'll lay out the day's work."

"Gundy," Crockett said, "somethin' you oughtta know. Better keep four or five of us close by. Barton was sayin' before the Doc got through with him, he wanted this ranch burned, an' Miz Joy turned over to him *for his use.* He don't know who shot up his leg, but he blames Miz Joy." Crockett slanted Gundy a know-it-all look. "You done that job on him, didn't you? Why didn't you kill 'im?"

"Don't want 'im dead. Got other plans for 'im."

Crockett's face went real serious. "If he could see yore eyes right now, he'd be smart to leave the country."

"He cain't run far enough or fast enough to get away from me." Gundy's voice came out silky quiet. He then laid out the work for the crew. "Crockett, you, Stick, an' a couple other men stay here. Two in the hayloft with rifles, two in the bunkhouse, and I'll stay in the house with Miz Joy. I don't look for nothin' to happen 'til Barton can ride, but we'll play it safe."

Nothing happened. Two weeks went by and all remained quiet. Gundy had to tell Joy why they took the precautions, and about the sign he'd found that led him to set a night watch. He still didn't tell her about himself.

He and Crockett were working on the corral fence when Gundy stopped his hammer in midstroke. "Hold it a minute. Think I hear horses."

Crockett cocked his head. "Don't hear nothin'."

"Horses!" Gundy said, and ran for the house. Crockett cut in the other direction for the stable. "If Barton's with 'em, leave him alone. *I* want 'im."

chapter thirteen

Gundy and Crockett had their rifles with them at the corral, and had both grabbed them when they ran. Gundy jacked a shell into the chamber when he went through the doorway. "Get on the floor and stay there," he yelled at Joy.

The riders rode into the yard, between the house and bunkhouse. They reined in and looked around, surprise showing on their faces that it had been so easy getting this close.

Gundy, standing behind the doorjamb, yelled, "What you men want?" He wanted to open up on them, but he'd not yet fired on a man unless the man had a chance, and these men had no idea they faced more than a couple of old broken-down punchers.

Instead of answering, every man there reached for a gun. Some made a sweep at their holsters, others raised their rifle barrels. Gundy fired at the rider closest to him. That saddle emptied. A quick count showed Gundy six riders, not counting the

173

one on the ground or two others falling.

He drew a bead on another raider and emptied that saddle. The others broke and ran. Gundy searched the retreating gunmen for a sight of Barton, saw him in the lead, and fired at his horse. The horse stumbled, went down, throwing Barton over his neck. The rider behind Barton rode alongside and held out his hand. One of Gundy's men in the bunkhouse dropped that horse.

Gundy fired as fast as he could jack shells into the chamber. His men were filling the air with lead. Horses fell, and the three riders left hit the ground running.

Gundy bounded out the door, yelling for his men to leave Barton for him. Before he could clear the porch, the last of Barton's men fell. Barton ran a zigzag course from the yard toward Milestown, on one good leg, the other stiff and dragging. Gundy dropped his rifle and stretched out, running as he had when an Apache warrior. He caught Barton at the top of a swell.

Barton turned his head to glance at the man chasing him. Gundy saw instant recognition flash into his eyes, and then horror. Gundy launched himself at the killer's knees, hit the backs of them, and

Barton let out an unearthly scream. He sprawled facedown on the ground, both legs bent now. Gundy had torn up everything the doctor had rebuilt in Barton's knee. The wife-killer rolled and came to one knee.

Gundy, still on all fours, crawled toward his prey. The Comanchero fought like a cornered mountain lion. Both of them standing on their knees slugged it out. Gundy took a right to the cheekbone and felt it split. His left went inside Barton's swing. The raider's nose flattened and spurted blood. He tried to stand, but his bad leg buckled under him. Gundy threw a right that caught him on the side of his head. He fell sidewise and Gundy caught him with a left hook to the chin. Barton went flat. Gundy lurched to his feet and sent a foot to Barton's throat. The outlaw choked and tried to stand. Gundy let him get to his one leg, stepped in close, and swung from the ground. His fist caught the killer in the teeth. He went down, and out.

Gundy, rubbing his knuckles, stared down at him a moment, fighting the bile that surged to his throat. He'd never wanted to kill a man so much in his life, but he'd promised himself his wife's killer would not die easy. He swallowed a couple of times, took two deep breaths, picked up his handgun, and shoved it in his holster. Then he twisted his hand in the monster's collar and dragged him back to the yard.

Crockett had the men cleaning up when Gundy dragged his trophy into the yard. The tall Texan glanced at Barton, then swung his gaze to Gundy. "Got 'im, huh. Didn't figure you wanted any help." He glanced at the horses lying about the yard. "Never liked killin' a horse, but seemed the only way to make sure these men didn't get away."

Gundy nodded. "Collect their guns an' take them to the bunkhouse. Have somebody clean 'em. Load what's left o' Barton's men on the buckboard and haul 'em to that deep ravine out west o' here 'bout two miles an' cave dirt over 'em. Go through their pockets. If we can find out who they are, we'll write and tell their folks."

Joy stood on the porch, staring at him. He walked toward her. Crockett called, "They sure 'nuff figured to burn this place. Them horses was carryin' three one-gallon tins o' coal oil."

"Keep it. We need it," Gundy threw the words over his shoulder.

When he stepped to the porch, Joy threw

herself into his arms. "Oh, Trace, I've never been so scared for anyone in my life. What made you chase that man like that?" She stepped back and blushed. "I — I didn't mean to . . ."

Gundy shook his head. "Don't worry 'bout it. Didn't put no meanin' to it 'cept you was worried 'bout one o' your men." For the first time he admitted that he wished she had meant more than that. It had felt good having her in his arms. He held her away from him and looked into her eyes. "That man I run down? Well, he was the one what figured to steal you. He's the one I shot in the leg out yonder the other night."

"Why would anyone want to do such a thing, Trace?"

"Well, first off, Joy, you're a beautiful woman. Any man would want you. But it's right lucky we are that the world is made up of only a few like him, or we'd be fightin' all the time."

When he was certain Joy came through the fight unscathed, he went back into the yard. Crockett and the men were loading the last corpse into the wagon. "Crockett, want you to take charge here the next few days. If Miz Joy asks where I am, tell 'er I had a job the other side o' the ranch

177

needed takin' care of. I'll be back soon. Don't figure we gonna have more trouble, but keep a watch anyway." Gundy saw Crockett wanted to ask what he was going to do, but wouldn't ask. He saddled two horses, went to the quivering hulk that was Barton, threw him across a saddle, tied him to it, and rode out.

That night at the supper table, Joy looked down its length at Gundy's vacant chair. "We better wait for Trace. He must've had a last-minute chore to take care of."

"No, ma'am," Stick Turner said, "he had a job needed takin' care of the other side o' the ranch, said he'd be gone a few days." Turner had his knife and fork poised to make a stab at the steak. "Reckon we can go ahead an' eat."

"So that's who you came in and packed a few days' provisions for."

Turner flushed. "Yes'm."

After supper Joy hummed while cleaning the kitchen and doing the dishes. She'd liked the feel of Gundy's arms about her, although he *had* held her like she might break. And he had told her he thought she was beautiful, and that *any man* would want her. She wondered if Gundy was one of those men.

178

She had never known a man like him. There seemed always to be an aura of confidence about him that whatever came he could take care of it, and the odd thing was that people let him do it. Her breath caught in her throat. She realized how much danger this constantly placed on his shoulders. It wasn't fair.

She continued humming and a slight smile broke the corners of her mouth. He *was* handsome, perhaps the most handsome man she'd ever known, and so efficient. Men, horses, and cows seemed to do his bidding without question. She wondered if women were as willing as men to cave in to his wishes.

Her face turned hot at the thought, then a pang of guilt shot through her. Here she was thinking about a man, not just any man, but Trace. Thinking thoughts a *lady* should not think. Was she being unfaithful to the memory of Jim? No, she decided. She'd always been a faithful and loving wife. But now, still young, she admitted she needed and wanted a man. But the man she wanted seemed not to know she was a woman. He would not take Jim's place. There was a special room for Trace in her heart without taking anyone's place. She wondered what had taken him away from the ranch on such a cold night.

Miles away, at the back side of the ranch, Gundy drew rein on the bank of a deep ravine, dismounted, went down its side, and found a place to camp. Farther down, he found an animal trail to lead the horses down. Then he went back and got the horses.

Barton moaned when Gundy untied him from the saddle and dumped him on the ground. He put the horses on tether, came back and made camp, not until then did he turn his attention to Barton who stared at him with wide, terror-filled eyes. "Wh-what you gonna do with me, Blanco? I didn't shoot your wife, Manuel did it."

"You ain't got 'nuff words in you to worm outta this, gringo. You know they call me the Apache Blanco, and far as you're concerned, I *am* Apache. Gonna give you a full lesson in everything I learned from 'em."

"Come on, Blanco, you're a white man," Barton whined. "You ain't got it in you to be a savage, no white man has." Gundy stared at him a moment, and went about collecting wood for his fire, built it, patted out a couple of biscuits and put them close to the flame, opened a tin of beans, pushed a stick through several slices of side pork, and hung it over the fire.

That done, he sat back and waited for his meal to cook. After a while he stood, went to Barton, and stepped on his mangled knee. An inhuman scream issued from Barton's throat.

Gundy stared down at him. "That ain't even the beginnin', Comanchero." He went back to his saddle, sat, and slumped against it. All the cold fury and gut-wrenching hate he thought had mellowed were upon him.

After a while he ate, cleaned his pan, and sat drinking coffee. He never took his eyes from Barton's face.

"My God, man, you look at me like a snake charmin' a bird. Stop lookin' at me. I — I cain't stand it."

Gundy never spoke, just stared. Then, finished with his coffee and after-supper pipe, he went down the bank and cut two stakes, about two inches thick and a couple of feet long, from a willow. Then he cut another about an inch thick. It, too, was about two feet long. He came back to the fire, dragged Barton far enough from it so the fire's heat wouldn't reach him, then staked him to the ground just as he had done the Comanchero outside of Trinidad.

The inch-thick stake he sharpened to a point on one end and placed it close enough to the fire to harden, but not burn. That done, using his Bowie knife he cut all the clothes from Barton, including his boots. Naked and shivering, Barton watched his every move. "I'm cold, Blanco. Put a blanket over me," Barton pushed the words past chattering teeth.

"You gonna be colder in a day or two, if you last that long — dead cold. You took away from me the only woman I ever loved. Cain't get 'er back, but I can make sure you're sorry you ever rode onto my ranch and shot my wife an' baby."

"I never killed no baby, Blanco. They weren't a baby nowhere abouts."

"Our baby was still in my wife's stomach. When you shot her in the stomach, you shot through our baby. That's what I'm gonna do to you, gringo, only it ain't gonna be no bullet goes through your guts."

Barton's eyes shifted to the sharpened stick laying by the fire. "No, Blanco. You wouldn't do that, would you?"

Gundy saw in his eyes he knew the answer.

Dark settled in. Gundy put more wood on the fire and crawled between his blankets. He was in no hurry to finish Barton. Let him think on what he'd done, think on what was in store for him. *That* would cause him to suffer as much as what Gundy planned.

Gundy lay there, awake long into the night. What kind of man was he? Could he really do to Barton what he planned, what he'd thought out while crossing two states and two territories? He thought of Dee, fun-loving, strong, loyal, his woman. He could — he *would* do it.

Then he thought of the woman he found in his thoughts more as each day passed. What would Joy think of what he was doing? Would she be repulsed by the very thought of his actions? He thought of the way she felt in his arms after the gunfight. He'd not had feelings for any woman in a long time. Maybe it was wrong that he had them now, but somehow, he believed Dee would want him to get on with things. He'd have to make up his mind by the time this was over. And over meant looking out the window of Joy's ranch house and seeing cattle: calves, yearlings, heifers, and bulls dotting the landscape.

He closed his eyes with only one problem solved. He would do to the gringo what the gringo had done to Dee.

chapter fourteen

The next morning, before throwing more wood on the fire, Gundy glanced at Barton. He lay there shivering, his body blue, almost black in some areas. "Get much sleep, gringo? Hope not. Hope you thought all night long o' what you gonna get. Course that wouldn't worry you. You gut-shot my wife. That didn't worry you, so gettin' your worthless hide punctured a bit shouldn't bother you none either."

He ignored Barton and his whiny pleas while he fixed breakfast, ate, and had coffee. He didn't bother to tempt the gringo with food close to him, just out of reach. The gringo had more serious things to think on.

"Why don't you go on an' shoot me, Blanco? Know you gonna kill me, so go on, shoot me."

Gundy squatted by his side. "Gringo, I thought of leavin' you tied out here to freeze to death, or for the coyotes to chew on during the night." He shook his head. "Freezin's too easy. At some point you'd just go to sleep an' not wake up, an' with the coyotes I couldn't be sure they'd find you — so, reckon I gotta make sure, but ain't gonna do it right away. You gotta have time to think 'bout what you done to my wife."

Gundy stood, poured himself a cup of coffee, and came back to squat by Barton. "Thought 'bout turnin' you over to the law, but a man cain't be sure 'bout the law. They might not believe me, might turn you loose. Or if they did believe me, they might put you in prison, or they might hang you." He shook his head. "Finally decided I better take care o' you myself. That's the only way o' knowin' you hurt bad as you made my wife hurt."

He pulled his Bowie and placed the razor-sharp edge on Barton's chest, letting only the weight of the big knife rest on the blade. He pulled it down the gringo's chest and across his stomach. It cut barely through the skin, but blood welled to the surface and ran down the blue body. "Huh. You ain't so cold you cain't bleed. Have to wait 'til tonight to try that again."

"Oh, Lord, Blanco. What kind o' man are you? Kill me, get it over with."

Gundy locked eyes with Barton. "You know what kind o' man I am, gringo. You

185

knew that when you attacked my ranch. You knew the Apache raised me. You shoulda known I ain't gonna ever forget most o' their trainin'. You shoulda thought of that, gringo. An' you shoulda known an Apache never forgets or forgives a hurt."

By sundown Gundy sickened of what he was doing, then he looked at Barton and remembered his face when he rode from his ranch so many months ago; the triumphant, gloating look in his eyes. Then he'd think of Dee lying on the floor, bleeding to death while he held her. Each time his resolve stiffened.

The next morning when he looked at Barton, he knew he'd better get the job done or the gringo wouldn't be lucid enough to know what was happening to him. He picked up the one-inch stake and a blanket, thinking that after driving the stake into Barton he'd cover him, maybe keep him warm enough to live longer, suffer longer.

Back to Barton's side, he squatted and looked him in the eyes. "Gringo, I'm gonna drive this stake into your gut. Gonna make sure it punctures your bowels. Gonna leave you out here alone, tied, to wait for blood poisonin' to set in, then you gonna know what pain really is.

Think about what you done to my wife an' baby while you die."

Two hours later Gundy looked back from the crest of a ridge. He felt no sorrow for what he'd done. But he did feel ten years younger. A weight had lifted from his shoulders. He had done what he had to do. Now Dee could rest easy in her grave.

He had other things to do; get Joy's cows back, take care of the scum Lem Barton gathered around him to steal from and kill the young soldiers stationed at Fort Keogh. And he had a ranch to run in the Big Bend. He had better get on with it.

When he rode into the ranch yard, he went straight to the well and drew a bucket of water. He needed a bath and shave. While waiting for the water to heat, Crockett came over.

"Take care o' Barton?"

Gundy nodded. "He won't be killin' no more women."

"Figured as much when you left here. I'd a done the same myself."

Gundy slanted a look at Crockett. No, he didn't figure Crockett would have done the same. It would end up with the same results, but Crockett hadn't been raised by the Apache. Crockett brought him up-to-date on the happenings at the ranch while he shaved, bathed, and dressed.

"Miz Joy ask any questions 'bout what I was doin'?"

Crockett shook his head. "Nope. Stick 'splained you had some ranch business to take care of at the back side o' the ranch. She didn't push it any further."

After talking with Crockett, Gundy went to the house to check in with Joy. She met him at the door.

"Trace, where in the world have you been out in weather like this? You'll catch your death of cold."

Gundy smiled. "No, ma'am, reckon a little weather ain't gonna hurt me. Come to tell you I'm goin' to Milestown. Need to send for money to carry us 'til we get your cows back." His face warmed. "Need to get some clothes too. Reckon you noticed I just about done wore these I'm wearin' plumb out. Soon be shameful for me to walk around where womenfolk could see me."

"Trace, don't send for money. We'll make do until we can sell our gather."

"No, ma'am. Figure we need money now. Know Leighton'll carry us, but it don't set well with me to owe no one for very long. I'll send for money."

188

She stood back, hands on hips. "Trace Gundy, you're the hardest-headed man I know, but I suppose I've learned by now you're going to do it your way."

"Yes'm, now if you'll feed me I'm gonna head out. I'll put Crockett in charge while I'm gone."

After eating he told Crockett his plans, saddled a fresh horse, and left.

Lanterns cast a soft golden glow on windows when Gundy rode into Milestown. Looked kind of warm and friendly, he thought. Surprising how nightfall could camouflage the harsh reality of weathered, unpainted buildings, muddy or dusty streets littered with horse droppings. He drew rein in front of the marshal's office.

Bruns was pouring a cup of coffee when Gundy opened the door and walked in. "Howdy, Gundy," he said and reached for another cup.

"Howdy, Marshal. Stopped in to let you know I done took care o' the one what killed my wife. Gotta stay overnight, got business to 'tend to in the mornin'."

Bruns finished pouring the coffee, set a cup on the corner of his desk in front of Gundy, and sat down. "Pull up a chair and tell me about it."

Gundy told him Barton had been trying

to do the same thing with Miz Waldrop as he'd done to Gundy's wife. He told him about Crockett, and verified it was Barton's bunch stealing cows.

"Marshal, them riders I just mentioned are all good boys. They gonna help get *all* the stolen cows back when the time is right. For now, I got some things need takin' care of 'fore I call the ranchers together. Just wanted to let you know what's been happenin'. 'Preciate it if you don't hold nothin' against Crockett and the other boys."

Bruns took a swallow of his coffee. "Glad you told me, son, and you got my word I ain't holding nothin' against Crockett, or the others either. You need any help?"

"No, sir. Reckon they'll be plenty of us to do what needs doin'."

"Good. Now, where you sleepin' tonight, boy? You can't stay out in this weather. Why don't you hold down the jail for me?"

Gundy grinned. "Aw, now, Marshal, why didn't I think o' that."

Bruns's eyes crinkled at the corners. "Ahead of me on that, huh?" He stood, went to a cabinet in the corner, and tossed Gundy a couple of blankets. "Gonna make the rounds, see if everything's quiet. Make yourself at home."

190

"Thanks, Marshal, but first I'm goin' over to Leighton's an' do some shoppin'."

They walked out the door together.

"Hey, Gundy. Where you been so long?" Leighton yelled from the back of the store.

Gundy shut the door behind him, closing out the icy gust that tried to follow him in. "I been around, Leighton, just ain't been to town none. Thanks for lettin' the boys have them supplies I sent for. Need somethin' to put on my nekkid bones though. They couldn't buy *them* for me."

"Sure, Gundy, anytime. From what the marshal tells me, you got plans to get a bunch of stolen cows back to them that own them."

"Don't spread that around, Leighton."

"Aw, boy, you don't need to worry about that. Just Bruns and I know about it. Now, what you need?"

"Levi's, shirts, tobacco, boots, you name it. Figure I'll owe you half o' my cow sale when I get through."

"Get what you need. We'll worry about that later."

A half hour later Gundy went back to the jail and deposited his packages in the first empty cell he came to. He dug his fingers deep in his pocket and pulled out his remaining money. He counted it — seventy-eight cents. Allowing two bits to stable his horse, he had fifty-three cents left, enough for a couple of beers and breakfast.

He left and headed across the Tongue to the Soldier's Haven. He thought no one there would know him and he wanted to see what it was like — *had* to see what it was like in order to plan his next step.

At the door he stepped around a young soldier lying on the boardwalk and went in. He pulled his hat brim low on his forehead, walked to the end of the bar, and pushed his way close enough to get the attention of the fat bartender working the bar at his end. Men stood two deep around the polished surface. Looking at the long mahogany surface, Gundy thought Barton must have had it brought up the Yellowstone by steamboat. It sure hadn't been made by anyone in Milestown. The wood wouldn't have been available even if a craftsman was.

He stood there a moment waiting to be served and studying the men standing there. Many were soldiers from Keogh, a few were punchers from surrounding ranches, several were hard cases, guns tied low on their thighs, dirty, unshaven. Gundy smiled grimly to himself. He would fit that last description if he hadn't been clean and had a shave recently.

The fat man looked at him and said, "Whatcha want?"

"Beer."

The man filled a mug and slid it down the bar to him. Before it reached him, a hand shot out and pulled it in. The man who had short-stopped his beer looked at Gundy, daring him to say anything.

Gundy wasn't looking for trouble, didn't want any. The nerves at the base of his skull tightened. His gaze slid from the hard case back to the man behind the bar. "Better fill me another one. That one you sent my way didn't get here."

The bartender filled another and slid it down. "Twenty cents."

Gundy pinned him with a gaze. "Uh-uh. Ten cents. I been watchin' what you charged these here other men."

"Yeah, but you just bought Slagle there the beer I slid to you."

Gundy went quiet inside, his nerves tightened even more. He was being set up. A cold anger built inside his head. "Friend, when I buy anybody a drink, *I'll* be the one what tells you 'bout it. Here's a dime." Gundy tossed the coin in the air. The bartender caught it.

"B'lieve you owe the man for my beer,"

the gunny down the bar said.

Gundy wondered how to avoid having to fight this man in case anyone in here knew him, but he wasn't going to let this pass. "If I want to drink with hogs, I'll go to the hog pen. Pay for your own drinks." He said it quietly, but all between him and the gunslinger heard and backed away.

"You callin' me a hog?"

"Reckon if I knew what hog to apologize to I'd do it. Any hog I ever seen was cleaner an' smelled better'n you. Reckon I'll take my beer to a table where the air's cleaner." He gripped the handle of his mug with his left hand and made to move from the bar. The gunny made a swipe at his side as though going for his gun. Gundy threw the contents of his mug into the trouble hunter's face, stepped in, and dropped him with a short right uppercut.

The hard case again reached for his gun, but was staring into the bore of Gundy's .44. He let his hand settle slowly to the floor. "Holster your gun, an' we'll start even."

Someone standing at the bar said, "Don't do it, Slagle, he'll beat you."

Another said, "Damn! Did you see that draw?"

A man at his side said, "Naw, I didn't

see it an' neither did you. One second his hand's empty, the next it has a gun in it. Ain't never seen the like."

Slagle stood and went to the bar, his back to Gundy. The cold fire of Gundy's anger pushed caution aside. Anybody in here wanted trouble, he'd give them trouble. "Give me a beer, bartender. Slagle's payin'."

Slagle turned slowly to look at Gundy. "Damned if I am."

Gundy walked back to his original place at the bar. He had plenty of room. And no one stood between him and the trouble-maker. Gundy stood where the bar tied into the wall. His back was protected. He slipped his Colt into its holster and stood there. "Buy or die, Slagle, your choice. Don't make a damn to me either way." Anger, white-hot now, burned his gut, his throat, his head.

Slagle twisted as though to say something to the bartender. His hand flashed to his side. His gun half out of the holster, two black spots magically appeared side by side in the middle of his chest. The roar of gunfire sounded simultaneously with the appearance of the holes in his chest. His hand loosened its grip on his pistol. His gun slid back into the holster. He stared at

Gundy. His mouth worked a couple of times, then a thin stream of blood trickled from the corner of his mouth and worked its way down his chin. A red circle spread around the two holes. He fell, straightened his legs convulsively, pulled them tight to his chest, and again straightened.

Gundy turned his eyes on the bartender. "Ought to kill you, too. You backed his play."

"No, no, mister, I was just funnin'. Didn't mean nothin' by it." Gundy felt his face relax a little. "Draw me another beer, on the house."

The bartender filled another mug and sat it in front of him. Then he motioned to two swampers at the other end of the bar and nodded toward the body.

Gundy drank slowly. He'd thought of a cold beer for a month and figured to enjoy every drop of it. While drinking, the swampers dragged the body out the back door. The tension in Gundy melted, only to be replaced with wonder that a man could be killed so quickly, so easily, and not a soul seemed to give a damn — including him.

He studied the people in the room, trying to estimate how many worked for Lem Barton. By the time he'd finished his drink, he'd concluded that no more than eight or nine were Barton's men.

During the attack on the Flying JW, he and his men had killed seven. He figured, at the most, Barton had had maybe twenty-five riders. The seven they'd killed plus these eight or nine left another eight or nine at Barton's ranch, the Box LB. If he and the ranchers were lucky, they wouldn't have to face over eighteen men, and if luckier still, half that number would be here in Milestown drinking. He finished his beer and held up the glass for another.

Gundy had taken only a couple of swallows when Lem Barton walked behind the bar, pushed his way past his bartenders, and stood across it from Gundy. "Hear you killed one of my men."

"Just shot a man. Don't know who he b'longed to. Why?"

Barton stared at Gundy a long moment. "You act right salty, friend. Come off your high horse. I got eight men in here. Any one or at the most two of 'em could take you. All I gotta do is give them a motion."

All the anger returned in Gundy. This time it was a cold, frigid lump in his gut. "Mister, you just spiked out three dead men. You'd be the first o' them to buy it. You want to give that signal, do it, otherwise leave me to finish my beer, that's all I come in here for."

197

Barton's attitude changed abruptly. "Not gonna give no signal. You don't seem to give a damn whether you live or die. You want a job?"

Gundy was tempted to hire on with Barton. He'd like to know what the Box LB was like: what the layout was, how many men stayed there all the time, where most of the cattle grazed in the winter. He thought on that only a moment, then figured, when the time came he needed information such as that, Crockett and the men that rode in with him already knew everything he wanted to know.

"Ain't lookin' for no job. Ain't lookin' for no trouble neither. All I wanna do is drink my beer peacefully an' leave. Make no mistake about it, mister. I'm gonna drink my beer, even if I gotta drink it lookin' through gunsmoke."

chapter fifteen

Barton stared at Gundy a moment. "Mister, I don't know who you are. Don't want to know 'less you want to tell me, but I got a bunch o' men you'd fit right in with. Think about it. You want a job, you got one with me. You don't take it, I'll have you arrested for murder."

Icy anger still burned in Gundy's gut. It threatened to come to a white heat again. "Mister, they's not many men in here what didn't see your man draw on me. No judge is gonna convict me for self-defense."

Barton smiled a cold, confident smirk. "I doubt if there's a man in here what don't owe me his next month's pay. All I gotta do is tell 'em the way it happened, and they'll testify to it that way."

Gundy felt his eyes go cold, his face stiffen. "Barton, you try that and I'll gut-shoot you. I'll stand trial like a good citizen, but after it's over . . ." His words trailed off. The silence hung heavy between them. "I'll be in town 'til tomorrow morning. You want to bring charges, do it before I leave."

Using his left hand, he hoisted his mug and downed the last of his beer, then keeping the wall at his back went to the door and left.

Ten minutes later he entered the jail. Bruns looked up from a stack of wanted posters. "Back, huh?" He opened the top drawer to his desk, shoved the posters in it, and said, "Keys are on the wall peg yonder, if you need 'em. I'm goin' home and get some sleep."

"Marshal, you might want to lock me in one o' them cells. I just shot a man up yonder in the Soldier's Haven. Barton says he's gonna have me arrested for killin' him."

Bruns sighed and sat at his desk. "Tell me about it."

Gundy went through the whole happening, not leaving out a thing. "That's the way it happened, Marshal, but Barton says almost every man in there owes him a month's pay, and will tell the story any way he tells him to."

"The way you tell it, Gundy, it was self-defense. I have no reason to doubt you. I have every reason to think Barton would lie about anything that would benefit him — or for pure spite, but if he brings in a room full of witnesses . . ."

Gundy frowned, staring at the floor, feeling sick to his stomach. He had done nothing outside the law. *He* knew it, but against Barton's trumped-up charges he wouldn't stand a chance. He looked up and locked gazes with Bruns. "What can I do, Marshal? Ain't gonna run. Had enough o' that while the whole New Mexico Territory was lookin' for me."

Bruns sat there a moment, frowning, then obviously came to some decision. "Barton know where you're workin'?"

Gundy shook his head. "No. He don't even know my name. Thinks I'm just some salty gunslinger what's ridin' through. But bet you my next month's pay he'll be in tomorrow to get you to put out a John Doe warrant on me."

Bruns smiled. "From what I figure Miz Waldrop's payin' you, I don't figure you stand to lose much in bettin' a month's pay."

"Well, dang it, Marshal, this ain't no jokin' matter."

Bruns sobered. "I wasn't makin' light of it, son. Tell you what. In the mornin' take care of your business, send for your money, leave town, but watch your back trail. I'll get your money to you at the ranch. Stay there until I send for you. I'm gonna see if

I can dig up some witnesses what don't owe Barton. The circuit judge'll be through here in a couple of weeks. By then I might be able to do something." He stood. "Now, I'm going to spend the night with the loveliest woman I know — my wife."

Gundy locked the door behind the marshal, walked around his desk, blew out the lantern, and sat in the marshal's chair, in the dark. He had some thinking to do.

He couldn't blame this latest gunfight on being the Apache Blanco. It was all because of a ten-cent beer, a terrible price to put on a life. But if a man took water from anyone these days, he might as well run, and keep running. His cowardice would follow him wherever he went. But he had not backed down, he had killed a man who had no friends, but who had a boss who would buy witnesses with a credit ledger.

He would have to tell Joy about the fight. She might not understand. But he had eight men who *would* understand, men who rode for the brand. If he could come up with a plan, they would follow.

He tried to formulate a course of action. His first was to take his men, ride in, and blow Barton and his men into the next territory. He shook his head. He'd only get his men on wanted lists all over the West, and maybe get some of them killed.

He thought to slip into the Soldier's Haven, find the ledger, take it, and burn it. He again discarded the thought. If he got caught stealing, that would be as bad a name as coward.

One thing he knew, he would keep his men out of it if he could. Finally, he thought he had something that would work. He stood, spread his blankets in the first cell he came to and went to sleep.

By ten o'clock the next morning he had sent the wire to Texas, gathered his packages, and departed Milestown in the opposite direction from the ranch.

Not that Bruns would have had to caution him, but he did watch his back trail. About an hour out of town, he knew he was being followed. Two miles or more in back of him, he spotted two men on horseback. To make sure they were after him, he changed directions a couple of times. They took his cue each time.

It wasn't Gundy's nature to hurry when his life was at stake, but he didn't want to spend the day trying to avoid men sent after him. He took cover behind a large tree at the crest of a hill, ground-reined his horse below the rise, out of sight, and waited.

They rode, one looking at the ground for tracks, the other searching ahead for sight of him. Every few minutes they cast back and forth to make sure they still followed his horse's tracks. They rode to within ten feet before he stepped from behind the tree. "Make a move for them guns an' your horse ain't gonna have a rider." His Winchester pointed in their direction, but not *at* either of them. Neither rider made a move that indicated he thought he could beat the .44 slug Gundy would trigger his way.

Gundy stepped closer to them. "Between your thumb an' finger, lift them pistols outta their holsters an' drop 'em, then turn the left side o' your horses toward me an' get off 'em."

The two looked at each other. The one farthest from Gundy shook his head, only slightly, but Gundy knew he directed that they not chance being killed. They dismounted. "Now step off a few steps to the side there, an' go flat on your bellies."

When they had done as told, he searched each for other weapons, gathered the guns they had dropped, and pulled their rifles from saddle scabbards, a Spencer and a Winchester. "Now get up an' start walkin' back toward Milestown."

Gundy gathered their horses' reins in his hands and stood there a full twenty minutes, watching them become smaller with distance. When he judged they were far enough, he slapped each horse on the rump and sent him in the opposite direction. Not until then did he mount and ride in a wide circle toward the Flying JW.

It was the next day about noon that he rode into the ranch yard. He went directly to the bunkhouse after taking care of his horse. Crockett met him at the door. "Better wash up, we already been called to dinner." He glanced at the guns Gundy had tied to the back of his saddle. "Looks like you had some trouble."

Gundy shook his head. "Nope. Two o' Barton's riders had a little though. Didn't even have to fire a shot. They were real nice, give me their weapons without a hiccup."

Crockett gave him that leathery smile. "Just shows how nice people can be when you talk right to 'em." Gundy liked the tall Texan more all the time.

"Got somethin' need to tell all o' you after we eat. Miz Joy needs to hear it, too."

Hungry men do little talking while eating, and these men were no different. Gundy finished before they did and drank coffee waiting for them to finish. Joy served each a healthy slice of apple pie, still steaming from the oven, with coffee. Finally, Gundy lifted his pipe from his pocket and looked questioningly at Joy. She nodded, so he packed and lit it. The rest of the men did, too.

"All right, folks. What I got to tell you is this: I've got the money comin'. We're outta that kind o' trouble for now. But I got a lot more trouble ridin' right square on top o' me." He then told them about the shooting in the Soldier's Haven, and Barton's threat. Joy surprised him.

"We can't let him get away with that, Trace. We'll take the crew in and read to him from the book."

Gundy choked, and set his cup on the table before spilling his coffee. He laughed. So did the boys.

"No, Joy. We ain't gonna take *you* or the boys to town for any kind o' fight. I got an idea 'bout what to do, an' I'm gonna do it alone. Don't want nobody but me to be in trouble from somethin' I done."

Crockett looked over the rim of his cup. "Gundy, would your men down in Texas let you face this alone?"

"Course not. But that's my brand down yonder. This here's Miz Joy's. Don't want none o' you gettin' hurt; besides, you men gotta help get her cows back."

"You done told us we got a job with you when all this is finished," Stick Turner said. "Far's I figure it, this here brand an' the one down yonder's ours. We gonna help."

Gundy smiled. "You got everything figured, Turner, 'cept one thing: you do what I tell you."

Turner's face reddened. "Yes, sir. Reckon I just flat don't want you ridin' in there alone."

Crockett glanced at Turner. "Reckon you done forgot Gundy's also Blanco."

Joy stood and proceeded to clear the table. "We'll talk about this more, Trace. You're *not* going to handle it alone."

A week passed. The boys went about the ranch business as though nothing had happened, but Gundy had the feeling there was always one of them not far away so he could watch Gundy.

That night, he stood by the corral fence, alone, his head pulled down into his sheepskin, and *it* wrapped tight about him. He puffed on his pipe. Only a week now until the circuit judge held court in Milestown. It was time he carried out his plan. First, he had to let the ranchers know when he wanted them here for the ride to Barton's Box LB.

The marshal had brought Gundy's money out the day before, and told him he'd had no luck finding a witness in his favor. *That* firmed Gundy's resolve to carry out his plan.

He had to see Bilkins also. Let him know to join the fight for the stolen cattle or lose them.

The next morning at breakfast Gundy told the men to stick around awhile. He told Crockett to head for the ranches and let them know he wanted their men at the Flying JW two weeks from that day — Saturday. And he would go as far as Bilkins's ranch with Crockett. He'd handle Bilkins himself. And from this day until it was all over, he wanted every man to have his weapons in shape and an extra box of shells in his saddlebags. He pinned Joy with a gaze few *men* could argue with. "And you, young lady, will stay put right here at the ranch until we get back."

Her chin set, then relaxed. "Mr. Gundy, I don't like doing it that way, but I'll do as you say."

Gundy stared a moment longer. He had a queazy feeling in his gut. She had given in too easy.

Several hours later Gundy and Crockett rode into Bilkins's yard. "You go on, Crockett," he hesitated, "no, you better hear this in case the judge don't turn me loose."

At Bilkins's kitchen table, Gundy laid it out for him. "Bilkins, we're gonna get our cows back. You can join us or lose yours. We ain't fightin' your battles for you."

"You can't do that, sir. It would be stealing just as much as the ones who took them."

Gundy's face set. "Bilkins, I'm tellin' you right now. We can and will do it. Are you sayin' you still ain't gonna join us?"

"Mr. Gundy, just because I live here in this uncivilized corner of the world is no reason to become the savages that you people are. No, sir, I will not join you."

"All right, Bilkins, one more offer. We'll sign a contract here and now. I'll promise to pay you two dollars a head for your cows we get back . . ."

"Two dollars? That's robbery."

"Like I started to say, Bilkins, we pay you two dollars for each of your cows we get back, or I'll personally shoot every cow what b'longs to you, 'fore we start the drive back to our home ranches."

They argued another hour before Bilkins

folded. "Well, two dollars is better than nothing. Write up the contract." He fidgeted. "I'll say something, Mr. Gundy, you're not the kind of neighbor I relish living close to."

Gundy gave him a cold smile. "And I'll tell you, Bilkins, you don't need to worry 'bout that. You won't be livin' close to me. Fact is, you won't be livin' close to nobody 'round here. Men like you don't last. You'll go broke and go back east."

Gundy wrote out the contract, they both signed, and Crockett witnessed it.

Before Crockett went his way and Gundy his, Gundy felt Crockett studying him. "Gundy, they ain't no way you could've shot Bilkins's cows. You wouldn't be able to tell what was his from anybody else's."

Gundy grinned. "You know that — an' I know that. He don't."

"You're right down hard, Gundy," Crockett said. "But I agree with you, a man what won't fight for what's his don't deserve to be treated no better." He reined his horse in the direction of Bob Runnels's ranch. "See you back at the ranch."

Gundy rode toward the Flying JW only long enough to get out of Crockett's sight, then he turned his horse's nose toward

Milestown. A cold hard knot rested between his shoulders from the time he rode out of Bilkins's yard.

He studied his back trail. There was no sign of danger or anyone watching. He'd been on the trail to Milestown about an hour when the knot disappeared. Probably nerves, he thought. What he was about to do would make any man jumpy.

When he got to town, he didn't go to see Bruns, didn't want to get him involved in something he could lose his badge over. He went first to Leighton's. "Got a few more things I need, Leighton, then I'll settle Miz Joy's tab."

"No hurry, Gundy."

Gundy went to the stack of coal-oil cans and picked up two. "Better pay up now, Leighton, or I might be broke again. Fill these cans with coal oil, then I'll settle up."

"You going to carry these all the way to the ranch, riding horseback?"

Gundy shook his head. "No, sir, I got use for 'em right here in Milestown. An', sir, I'd shore appreciate it if you just handily forget I ever bought any lantern fuel."

Leighton looked puzzled but nodded. "I never sold you anything that even looked like coal oil."

chapter sixteen

Gundy steered clear of Bruns's office. In town, he was in the marshal's jurisdiction, and didn't want to put Bruns in the awkward position of having to arrest him or look the other way. It could jeopardize his badge, and he was too good a man for that.

Gundy made sure his oilskin packet was full of lucifers. He struck one to make sure they hadn't gotten damp and rolled the oilskin packet around the rest.

In front of Leighton's, he untied his horse and led him to the livery stable. "Feed an' water 'im. I'll pay you now for one night, but I might need 'im 'fore daylight so put 'im in that there front stall."

"All right, young fella. That's where he'll be when you need 'im."

Gundy had gotten a week-old paper from Leighton. "Mind if I sit around in here an' read my paper?"

"Anywhere you want."

Gundy sat in the hayloft, his two coal-oil cans between his knees. He napped awhile, read awhile, and studied the people who rode or walked past on the trail below. Soldiers, cowboys, riverboat men, and a smattering of city folk came under his gaze. He thought Milestown might become a good-sized city one of these days, considering the riverboat traffic and the railroad. It was a right nice town, and would be nicer once rid of the likes of Barton and his bunch. He nodded off again.

When he awoke, cold and stiff, the sun had set. Night had pushed its way into the sky. He looked at his watch, almost seven o'clock. Another hour and he'd get on with the job he'd cut out for himself.

Finally he stood, stretched, twisted his newspaper into a ropy length and stuck it in his pocket, picked up his cans, and walked toward the Yellowstone. Reaching its banks, he wended his way through the bare limbs of willows and past giant cottonwoods to the water's edge, now crusty with a two-foot ledge of ice along the bank. The river would most likely freeze solid before winter was through. He worked his way upstream until the black square of the saloon stood between him and the translucent cobalt sky.

He stood silently a moment, staring at the back of the building, then walked toward it. The hour was still early, and the month was tired with age. It had been a long time since the soldiers had a payday. He hoped lack of money and the weather had kept most of the young soldiers at the fort. He walked down the side of the building and turned the corner to head for the front door. Before reaching it, he pulled his head down into his sheepskin and jammed his hat down on his head such that only his nose and eyes would show. He sucked air deep into his lungs a couple of times to try to stop the queazy feeling in his stomach. Then he pushed the door open and went in.

Men lined the bar, mostly Barton men by Gundy's guess. A few soldiers stood there, and even fewer riverboat sailors. Only three tables had men at them, one with three men playing a desultory game of stud poker. Gundy slid along the wall to a table in back, far from the bar. He pulled a chair to a table next to the wall and leaned back. No one paid attention to him. He studied every man there, looking for Barton, and failed to find him.

He sat at least fifteen minutes before a saloon girl noticed him still covered with his coat and hat. She came to his table. "Whatcha sittin' back here all alone for, mister? Want a drink?"

"You the only girl workin' tonight?"

She nodded. "Yeah. Weather cold like it is, an' so far from payday, Barton figured wouldn't be much business. He was right."

Some of the tension went from Gundy's neck and shoulders. He didn't have to worry about girls or soldiers being trapped upstairs.

"Bring me a beer, an', uh, is Barton here tonight?"

"Naw, he's out at the ranch. You gonna buy me a drink?"

Gundy gave her a quarter. "Yeah, get yourself a drink, too." She brought his beer and he sat there, drinking it slowly, thinking of the best way to do what he intended. After a while she came back to see if he wanted another. "Yeah, bring me one more, no need to walk all the way back here again as this'll be my last one." He paid her and she went to the bar and rested her elbows on it.

About ten o'clock the crowd thinned, most of the soldiers were gone, as were the river men. Gundy figured most of those left were Barton men, and they'd probably be there the rest of the night.

He unscrewed the cap from the spout on each of the cans of lantern oil, then, wishing it didn't smell so strong, poured

215

one can along the base of the back wall. No one seemed to pay attention to him. Maybe the rotgut whiskey these men had swilled all night had deadened their sense of smell. The fumes floated up from the floor and wrapped around his head until they threatened to choke him. He struck a lucifer and touched it to the paper he'd twisted into a rope. He dropped the paper into the puddle of oil. As soon as it flared, he yelled fire and beat at the floor, as though trying to put the fire out. He held the empty can and the full one in his left hand. Everyone around the bar ran toward the flames, including the bartenders.

Gundy sprinted to the door where he judged Barton's office to be and emptied the other can. No one took notice of him. All were busy fighting the fire. He dropped another match in the puddle this can of oil made. It caught fire and spread around his legs. He ran through it, yelling that the fire was on this end, too. He held the two empty cans in his left hand by their handles, leaving his right hand free to use his gun if he needed it.

By now, the fire ate into the back wall. Smoke came from between the wallboards all the way to the ceiling. A few men broke off from beating at that fire and ran toward the bar area. Gundy watched a moment longer, now certain there was no way they'd put the fire out. "Get buckets. Get water from the river," he yelled, grabbed a bucket from behind the bar, and ran out the back door. They had seen him grab the bucket and, he hoped, would assume the oil cans in his left hand were also buckets. He kept running. At the river, he threw the cans as far out into the stream as he could heave them.

At the livery stable he slowed, walked casually to the stall where his gelding chewed a mouthful of hay, and saddled him. The liveryman came out of his room.

"Sounds like some sort o' commotion outside. You notice anything?"

Gundy nodded. "Yeah. Sounded like it come from that saloon across the crick yonder. Pro'bly a fight goin' on. I stay away from them sort o' things."

The grizzled old man nodded. "You're right in doin' so, young man. Don't never know when a stray bullet might find you." He glanced at Gundy's horse. "Leavin', huh?"

"Yeah. Ain't got 'nuff money left to sleep warm tonight, so figured I'd head out." He climbed aboard and rode through the doorway. He rode about a half mile out of

217

town before he drew rein at the top of a hill and looked down on the fire. It had engulfed the entire building.

Flame ate at the roof, running fingers along each line of shingles. Every window showed bright orange-red, some of the fire licked from them and started the outside walls burning.

Gundy watched until the walls fell in on themselves. And finally, nothing was left but a smoldering heap of ashes. And there, he thought, ended Barton's hold on the soldiers. His ledger should have burned in the fire, but whether it did or not, his robbing, killing, and beating the soldiers ended with the fire. He turned his horse and headed toward the ranch.

He'd ridden about a half hour when he thought he heard horses, a large bunch of them. He wasn't sure because of having his head pulled down into his sheepskin. He threw it back from his shoulders and listened.

Horses, and they weren't but a short distance from him. He pulled off the trail, not too worried because of the direction from which they came. He could see pretty well in the murky light and counted eleven riders, the one in the lead smaller than the rest. He grinned and rode into the trail.

"Whoa, now. What brings the Flying JW crew out on the trail at such an ungodly hour, and in this cold, too?"

"Trace? Is that you, Trace?"

"Why sure, Miz Joy, and who else would it be, ridin' peacefullike along a night trail?"

"Trace Gundy, where have you been? We expected you home hours ago. Then we figured you'd gone to Milestown to create some more trouble. Just thought we'd ride in and back you up, if you needed it."

A lump swelled in Gundy's throat. Talk about ridin' for the brand, that young lady, the entire crew, even the two stove-up old punchers rode out in bitter weather to help him. He cleared his throat.

"Ma'am, I ain't started no trouble with no one I couldn't handle. Ain't even fired my gun since I see all o' you."

Crockett spoke up, "We seen a redness in the sky a while back, lasted 'bout an hour, then died away. Anything in Milestown burn down?"

Gundy fidgeted. "Let's head for home, fix some good hot coffee, an' I'll tell you about it. Yeah, somethin' did burn down. Bein' we're this close to town, why don't 'bout half o' you go on in town an' have a few drinks."

Baden and Lawton volunteered right away to wet their whistles. "Ain't had nothin' to cut the dust in more'n two weeks. We better go with whoever's goin'," Baden said, "just in case they ain't no more good whiskey comes up the river 'til spring thaw."

Gundy nodded. "You go, too, Crockett. Take Stick and a couple others with you. You ain't had a break from work in a while."

"Why you slick-tongued son of a gun, you jest talked me right into that," Crockett said. "Come on, Stick, Levy, Brown, let's go 'fore he changes his mind."

They rode off, and with Gundy and Joy in the lead the others headed for the ranch.

The eastern sky had turned pink when they rode into the ranch yard. "You men take care of the horses. I'll get breakfast started," Joy said, dismounted, and handed her horse's reins to Gundy.

After breakfast, Gundy told the men to get some sleep, he'd ride out and break the ice on water holes. What snow they'd had, had long since evaporated, so the cattle could still find grass. He went to the door to leave when Joy stopped him. "Trace Gundy, you're not getting off this easy. Sit down, I'll pour us some coffee and you can tell me what happened in town last night."

"Aw, Joy, you don't want to hear 'bout such doin's."

She pinned him with a look he hoped he'd not face too many times. He'd looked down the barrel of a .44 and not felt more like running. "Trace, don't you tell me what I want to hear. You've got a trial coming up with the deck stacked against you. I know you killed Rance Barton, Lem's brother, and you're going to tell me about *that* when this is all over, but for now I want to hear what happened in Milestown tonight. You didn't just ride in there for the hell of it."

Her use of a mild cuss word surprised Gundy. He'd never heard her do that before and he was beginning to realize how little he knew about this spunky woman. "Ma'am, I'm gonna tell you exactly what happened, and why I did it. First off, I've seen them young soldiers from the fort rooked outta their money, thrown out of Barton's saloon, beat up, and I'm sure some of 'em killed. The Army don't have the authority to close Barton down, an' the marshal can't go out of his bailiwick an' do it.

"I wouldn't a done anything, but when Barton threatened me with trumped-up charges and to use witnesses that he owned because of money they owed him it made me mad as hell." He looked her in the eyes. "Yes'm, it made me mad as *hell*. I decided to do somethin' 'bout it. Tonight I did."

"You did what, Trace?"

He stood and poured them each a cup of coffee. "Joy, you know that orange glow you and the men seen in the sky? Well, that was the Soldier's Haven. It burned slam down to a pile o' ashes. I went in Barton's place with two full cans o' lantern oil, spread it around, and set it on fire."

"And you tell me you did all that without firing your guns? Hogwash."

Gundy took a swallow of coffee and shook his head. "It's a fact, Joy." Then he told her how he did it, and he believed not a person in the place could say he'd been there. "Not even the tired little woman who brought me my two beers could say I was there. I stayed hunkered down in my coat like I was cold, an' kept my hat pulled down. No, ma'am, I don't figure anybody knows it was me in there." He grinned. "You know, I bet the book Barton kept tally on what the soldiers owed him was in his office. If it was, an' it burned, he ain't got a thing to hold over the heads of them boys."

Joy stared at him a long moment. "Did it ever occur to you that you might have been killed going in there like that."

"Well, yes'm, I give it a little thought. That's why I didn't want you or the boys to side me when I went in. Figured to do it by my lonesome." He grinned. "I'd say I done it right slick, wouldn't you?"

Joy stared into her coffee cup, rolled it around on its bottom, and hit him with that hellfire look again. "Trace Gundy, if you ever ride out of here again without taking some of us with you, to help in case you need it, I'll — I'll . . ."

"Ma'am, I'm sort of a stranger to most o' you, an' when things like that need takin' care of, well, I don't want nobody gettin' hurt, an' ain't nobody gonna miss *me,* so I figured to do 'em alone."

"Stranger? Stranger, you say? Trace, I don't know how you did it, but yes, you rode in here a stranger, and in less time than it takes to top off a bronc, everyone on this ranch loved you." Her face turned a fiery red. "Well, we all *liked* you an awful lot. Missed? Oh, yes, you'd be missed. I repeat. We're going to side you from here on no matter the problem."

"Yes'm, but I'm tellin' you right now, *you* ain't gonna be where no gunfire's goin' on."

She smiled and said, "We'll see."

Knowing that to argue the point was a loser, Gundy changed the subject. "Wish I knew how to tell them soldier boys Barton cain't hurt 'em with no debts they might owe him. Far's I'm concerned, when he asked 'em to lie, that canceled the debt."

"Not really, legally that is, Trace. We'll think of something though. We have a few days yet."

He glanced at a window. "Full daylight. You ain't had no rest, an' I need to go fix some water holes so the cows can drink."

"Trace, get some sleep. The cows will break the ice themselves. It hasn't frozen so thick they can't walk into a pond without breaking it. Go to bed."

He ran his hand across his face, felt the stubble, and felt weariness drain his bones of the will to do anything. He stood. "Think I'll take you up on that, Joy. I want to hear what the boys have to say when they get back from town."

chapter seventeen

Late afternoon, Crockett and the crew got back from town. To Gundy's way of thinking, they didn't look like town had been too rough on them. A good night's sleep would do them good, but none, except Baden and Lawton, looked like they'd crawled into a bottle the night before.

Gundy met them at the corral. "Supper's ready. Wash up and come up, wanna hear what all went on in town."

Crockett slanted him a sour look. "You know damn well what went on in there. For a good part o' the night, *you* was the one what went on. Least I figure it was you. One o' them saloon girls told Bruns that a tall, slim man, all bundled up with his hat pulled low, started the fire. Said she didn't know who it was an' wouldn't know 'im if she saw him again."

Gundy felt a ton of worry lift from him. If that girl couldn't identify him, no one could. "Come on up to the house soon's you get ready. We'll talk 'bout it then."

Joy had food on the table when the boys

got there. Gundy sat drinking a cup of coffee. Stick Turner pulled up to the table and picked up his fork. "Miz Joy, them what went in town headed for the first saloon. I went with 'em, but after the first drink, I wanted to head for home. Kept thinkin' 'bout yore cookin'. More I thought o' them golden brown biscuits, meat, vegetables, an' yore apple pie, reckon I just couldn't wait to get here."

"Stick," Gundy said, "I ain't never seen you when you wasn't hungry. Don't know how you do it. You eat enough for two, maybe three men, an' you're still so skinny you have to stand in the same place twice to cast a shadow."

"Aw, Gundy, jest tryin' to keep from gettin' sick. Gotta make you a good hand down yonder in Texas."

"If eatin'll do it, you gonna make a top hand someday."

"All right, men," Joy spoke up, "leave Stick alone. Let's eat, then I want an account of what happened in town last night."

Crockett was the first one finished. "Miz Joy, old Gundy here was right slick the way he sent us in town to get a few drinks. What he really wanted was for us to find out if anyone knew he was in town."

"Well, did anyone know?"

Crockett glanced at Gundy. "She know what you did?"

Gundy nodded. "Yeah, I told 'er."

Crockett continued. "Two people know. One hasn't put it together yet, but he might. I'm talkin' 'bout the liveryman. The other is Leighton, an' he ain't gonna say nothin'. He was glad, as was every other man, woman, an' child in Milestown, to see that den of wolves burn to the ground." He shifted in his chair. "I talked awhile this mornin' with the C.O. at the fort. He was ready to give the man what done it a medal. Never seen a man so happy for a happenin'.

"Bruns, he didn't say nothin' much, jest looked at me an' growled that the Lord worked in mysterious ways. But it was a knowin' sort o' look."

Joy went to the stove and picked up the coffeepot. "When Crockett got back the other day from seeing the ranchers, we got right on the road to find you, Trace. What did our neighbors say?"

"Well, Crockett done most o' that. Tell 'er, Crockett."

Crockett sucked in a deep breath. "Seems like I'm doin' most o' the talkin'. They'll all meet us here when you said, Gundy. 'Cept o' course you know Bilkins ain't gonna show. An' you took care o' that right handy. Figure you gonna sell his cows to Miz Joy." He looked at Joy. "You gonna own a whole bunch more cows when we get 'em back than you ever had in the first place."

She looked at Gundy, long and hard. "You're still set on not giving his cows back?"

He nodded. "Yes'm, sure am, but I ain't gonna take 'em for nothin'. Gonna pay 'im for them."

Crockett choked and set his cup on the table. "What he means, Miz Joy, is he's gonna steal 'em for two dollars a head."

Gundy mumbled under his breath, "Ain't got the guts to fight he don't need no cows."

A week later the Flying JW crew, Joy and Gundy in the lead, rode into Milestown. They had received word the circuit judge was there and waiting. They reined in and tied their horses in front of the marshal's office, then gathered around Gundy.

"Don't know what to say to you folks, sidin' me like this. Always done things alone. Reckon I oughta tell ya, I'm gonna stand trial, but I ain't done nothin' wrong. If they don't let me go at the end, I ain't goin' to no jail. Y'all stand clear. Don't want any o' you mixed up in it, but I'm gonna fight my way outta there. Understood?"

"Oh, Trace, please don't do that. We'll get you free somehow. I — I don't think I could stand to lose you now."

Gundy looked at her. She was lovely, standing there, proud, her eyes glistening with unshed tears, ready to fight *for* him, or *with* him. He choked up, but would do it his way. "Let's go see the marshal. Get this thing over with."

Bruns met them at the door. "C'mon in. Figured you'd be in about now. Joy, the missus wants you to be sure and come by 'fore you leave town."

"I wouldn't miss seeing her for the world, Ted. First, though, we've got to get this friend of mine free."

Bruns looked at Gundy. "Boy, I ain't gonna kid you. It don't look good. I haven't found one man who will admit to seein' Slagle draw on you. And Barton's got all them soldier boys buffaloed. Most o' them who were in there the night o' the shootin' are out on patrol, s'posed to be back late today. If they get back, maybe one or two of them seen the fight and will tell it like it happened."

"You gonna lock me up for the night?"

Bruns smiled. "No, but sort o' figured on you spendin' the night here." He looked at Joy. "Why don't you spend the night with the missus an' me. We can visit while Gundy holds down the jail."

"Sounds good, but what'll the judge say, you turning the jail over to a wanted man?"

"Prob'ly ain't gonna know, but if he does, I done told him Gundy an' me are friends. I also told him Gundy ain't no liar, and that if he said Slagle drew first, then in my mind that's the way it came off."

Bruns offered them coffee. Most of them looked at the blackened, dented old pot sitting there. Crockett asked, "When you make that coffee, Bruns?"

"Yesterday mornin'. Why?"

Crockett grinned. "Just wondered, Marshal. No thanks, I ain't got a hankerin' for coffee right now."

All the rest said they didn't want any except Gundy. He poured himself a cupful, took a swallow, and said, "Ahhh, that would cut a month's trail dust outta a man's throat."

Joy stared at him a moment. "I'll remember that, Trace Gundy. I won't ever try to have fresh coffee for you."

"Ah, Joy. Just wanted to show Bruns I

'preciate the offer. You keep fixin' it like always an' I'll drink it the rest of my life." Gundy thought he heard her mumble, "I wish."

Bruns spoke up again, "Don't want none o' you to get the wrong idea. What I said to Judge Buckner ain't gonna hold any water. He runs things within the law. He might b'lieve a man's innocent, but he's bound by law to go by the decision o' the jury. Who's gonna defend you, Gundy?"

Gundy clenched his fists inside his sheepskin pockets. Defend him? Hell in his entire life *he'd* been the one he depended on to defend him. He gave Bruns a straight-on look. "Marshal, ain't never asked no man to stand in for me. Reckon if they was a man anywhere what I'd ask such of, it would be you or Mr. Leighton."

Bruns held his eyes on Gundy's. "I'd be willin' to take my badge off an' stand for you, Gundy. I ain't never heard of such, but I'd do it. But settin' that aside, Leighton's got more schoolin' than me, he's respected in this town, an' to be honest with you, I think he could do a better job than me. I'll get him over here to talk with you tonight, after we all get outta here."

They went to supper at the cafe, and

after eating, Gundy went back to the jail. Leighton was waiting for him.

They sat long into the night talking. Leighton made notes, and when they were through, Leighton thought awhile and told Gundy his plan. "It's the best we have, son. I'll do as good as I can by you, but I'm not a lawyer — never read the law. We'll give it what we got and hope for the best."

"That's all I could ask of any man, sir. And thanks for doing this for me." Neither of them brought up the two cans of lantern oil Gundy had bought.

They shook hands and parted. Gundy went in the first cell and went to bed. There wasn't much night left. Gundy never figured to worry about things when he'd done all he could do. His last thought before closing his eyes was that for now he'd done his best. He went to sleep.

The next morning Gundy and Bruns walked shoulder to shoulder toward the Range Riders Saloon. It had the largest open room of any business in town. Town meetings were held there, as well as most public functions.

Gundy glanced at the slate-gray sky, clouds bulging toward the earth, with large, quarter-size snowflakes drifting from them. He hoped the weather wasn't an omen as to the outcome of his day. Bruns looked at him across his shoulder. "Gonna have to check your weapons when we go in, Gundy. Everybody will."

"So long's you keep yours, Marshal. Don't want none o' Barton's crowd pullin' one on me, tryin' to get even."

"Don't worry 'bout that, boy. I'm gonna search 'em for guns and knives when they go through the door."

As soon as they entered the room, already about half full of spectators and witnesses, Bruns told them all to go outside and come in one at a time. He had Crockett help search them when they came through the door. Judge Buckner sat on a stool behind the bar. There would be no drinking until after the trial.

When Bruns locked the doors behind the last person to enter, the judge pulled his Colt .44, rapped it sharply on the bar, and said, "Let's get on with choosing the jury. And I'm telling you now. We're not gonna go looking for a unanimous decision. Whatever the majority says is the way it's gonna stand." The jury ended up evenly split, six townspeople or ranchers, five of Barton's men and one young soldier, who Gundy was certain was one who owed Barton.

Judge Buckner rapped on the bar again. "Court's in session." When he rapped on the bar with his pistol the second time, it hurt Gundy two ways. It would dent the polished surface, he liked polished wood, and it wouldn't do the Colt any good either.

Barton had hired a town shyster, Percival Abernathy, to present his case. Buckner called both representatives to the bench. "I'm going to tell you how I hold court. I don't want any arguing, don't break in when a witness is testifying, one person talks at a time, and no swearing. Got that?"

They said, "Yes, Your Honor," simultaneously.

Bruns, acting as bailiff, read the charges. "Trace Gundy" — he nodded in Gundy's direction — "sittin' right yonder, is charged with the cold-blooded murder of one Slagle, first name unknown. Mr. Lem Barton, yonder, says Gundy drew his pistol and shot the deceased without no argument takin' place. Barton says Gundy started his draw, Slagle seen what he was gonna do and went for his gun, but he seen Gundy's intent too late. He caught a big chunk o' .44 lead. That's what killed 'im."

The judge cleared his throat. "That's all right, Bailiff. The charges and defense will be brought out in the trial."

Abernathy presented the case pretty much as Bruns had read. Then he called witnesses. He mixed the soldiers in with Barton's men. Every one of them said Slagle was peacefully standing at the bar talking with friends and drinking a beer when Gundy bumped him and spilled some of his beer on him.

Slagle had cursed, but then admitted it was an accident and apologized. Gundy wouldn't let it rest. He knocked Slagle to the floor, drew his gun, then must have thought better and told Slagle to stand and go for his gun. Slagle stood, but Gundy, seeming to want every advantage, never put his gun away. As soon as Slagle stood, Gundy fired — three times.

Gundy studied each of them as they testified. They had been well coached. He noticed once in a while the soldiers would glance at Barton, he would nod, and they would continue.

Leighton cross-examined each and could not crack their testimony. But he did establish that every soldier who testified owed Barton at least a month's wages and the other witnesses worked for Barton.

When it came time for Leighton to present the defense, he leaned close to Gundy and whispered, "Don't look good,

Gundy. There's not a single honest man in here who saw the fight. We got no witnesses." Gundy nodded. When he sat at the table, he'd set his face so as not to show any feelings; he showed none now.

Leighton walked to stand in front of the jury and faced the judge. "Your Honor, I'm gonna ask you to let me tell about Mr. Gundy's past. In order to defend him I think the kind of man he is, and how he came to be the way he is, has relevancy."

Barton's lawyer jumped to his feet. "I object, Your Honor. His past has no bearing on the case."

Leighton smiled. "If I tell you Gundy was an outlaw for thirteen years, will you withdraw the objection?"

Stunned, the shyster, his mouth working like a fish, nodded. "Objection withdrawn."

Judge Buckner said, "Proceed, Mr. Leighton."

Leighton walked down the row of jurors and looked each in the eyes while doing so. "Gentlemen, Mr. Gundy, when a lad of six years, was taken prisoner by the Apache when they killed his parents. He lived with them as the son of the Mescalero chief who raised him until he was nineteen. He fought, raided." Leighton raised his arms, palms up. "He did everything an Apache warrior would do. As a result, when the Apache were forced onto the reservation, Gundy ran to Texas. The Territory of New Mexico branded him an outlaw. Thirteen years later, after an extensive investigation, the territorial governor, Lew Wallace, gave him a full pardon. He has done nothing since leaving the Apache that was beyond the law. He is a hard man, gentlemen, not a man to cross, but not a man who would take unfair advantage of another. Now, with the judge's permission, I want to show you something."

He walked to the bar, leaned over, and whispered to Buckner. At his nod, Leighton faced the court. "Who out there is the fastest gunhand in the room?"

All of Barton's men looked at each other, and finally pushed one of their bunch to his feet. "Who would you men say was the fastest, this man or Slagle?"

"Ain't no doubt, mister, Mallory could beat anybody in this here territory."

Leighton looked at the man they'd pushed to his feet. "You Mallory?"

The man nodded. "Blacky Mallory."

Gundy had seen Mallory in action along the Mexican border. When he stood, acclaimed to be the fastest gun among them, Gundy figured they had made a good choice. He wondered what Leighton was up to.

"Now, Marshal, I want you to take Gundy's and Mallory's guns and shuck them of all but one shell each. Pull the loads out of those two shells and put those shells one in each gun."

Bruns did as he was instructed. "Now bring me their holsters and guns." He looked at Mallory, then at Gundy. "Come to the front of the room, gentlemen."

Leighton handed each their own gunbelt. "Strap these on and stand about ten feet apart." The courtroom was so quiet you could hear a man two rows away breathe — if they hadn't all held their breaths. "Mallory, I want you to draw first. Gundy, hold your draw until Mallory starts his draw. I want you both to treat this as a real gunfight. Fire when your weapon's lined up on the other."

Abernathy yelled, "I protest. This is a court of law, not a side show in Buffalo Bill's Wild West Show."

Barton sneered and leaned back in his chair. "Let 'em go, Abernathy. You're about to see a real gunslinger. Nobody ever come close to beatin' Mallory. I heard 'bout Blanco a long time. Always figured he was just another big mouth, all talk and no show."

238

Gundy stared at Barton only a moment, but saw fear and belief leap into his eyes.

Buckner said, "Continue, gentlemen."

Gundy didn't like doing this, it was sort of like bragging about his quick gun, and he'd never done that. There was always someone faster. But if Leighton had a motive, Gundy figured to play out his hand. He stood, relaxed, his right hand hanging loosely at his side. He watched Mallory's eyes. Abruptly a tightening at the corners of the gunfighter's eyes gave the clue. Almost lazily, Gundy drew. Mallory's gun was still clearing the holster when Gundy grinned — and fired. Mallory didn't bother to finish his draw. His gun slipped back into his holster. He walked to Gundy and held out his hand. "Blanco, I can only say I'm shore as hell glad this wasn't for real."

Gundy nodded. "So am I, Mallory. I never liked killin' a man. Well, they has been three or four I sorta enjoyed blowin' to hell, but I had a reason."

Mallory, his face serious, said, "Take my word for it, Blanco, I'll never give you a reason."

Leighton cut in, "You men return to your seats. First, give the marshal your hardware." He waited until they were again seated, then faced the jury. "This, as you've probably guessed by now, was not just a side show. I wanted to prove that Gundy doesn't have to shoot a man without giving him a break. I think I proved that, and I want *you* to think about it when you consider your decision. I have no witnesses who'll testify in Mr. Gundy's behalf. It is reported that Barton bought the prosecution's witnesses for a month's salary each."

Abernathy, his face livid, bounded to the center of the floor. "I object," he shouted. "This circus has gone on long enough. Now he's libeling himself."

Buckner's eyes crinkled at the corners. "Forget Mr. Leighton said that, gentlemen of the jury." He looked at Leighton. "Unless you have proof, don't make a statement of that sort in my court again."

Leighton nodded. He'd accomplished what he wanted. "The defense rests, Your Honor."

The judge charged the jury to consider the evidence they'd seen and heard, he stressed the "seen," and to bring back a verdict.

As soon as the jury seated themselves in the room set aside for them, Bob Runnels, owner of the Circle BR, said, "Let's not get in too big a hurry to make a decision. It's comin' on to dinnertime, and I'm hungry. They gotta feed us for free."

He had been elected foreman, so he stuck his head out the door. "Bruns, have somebody go down to the cafe and bring us twelve steaks. We'll work on the decision after we eat."

chapter eighteen

The jury argued late into the afternoon. Every time one of them thought he made a strong point in favor of his opinion, he asked for a vote. Every ballot came out six to six.

Runnels studied each man there. There was no way to break the tie. "Don't look like any o' you men are gonna change your mind. You know what's gonna happen. We gonna have a hung jury, an' then we gonna have to do this all over again, only they's gonna be twelve different men sittin' in here. Now I don't like that. Six of us here are taxpayers, the other six ain't never paid no taxes, an' most likely never will. The taxpayers have to pay for the grub we eat an', and other things, don't rightly know what them things are. But, no matter what it costs, we gonna sit here 'til after supper, then we gonna argue . . ."

"Mr. Runnels," the young soldier interrupted, "reckon you got a minute? Need to talk to you sorta private."

Runnels nodded. "Come over here in the

corner, we can whisper." He wondered what the youngun could want, it was obvious the kid's opinion had been bought, and even more obvious that he was afraid of Barton's men. Runnels didn't blame him. Barton wouldn't let the kid live long enough to get back to Keogh if he crossed him.

Out of earshot of the other ten men, the kid shuffled his feet a couple of times and looked squarely at Runnels. "Sir, I know Mr. Gundy killed that man in a fair out fight. He let Slagle get his gun nearly all the way outta his holster 'fore he even started his draw."

"Well, son, why don't you change your vote?"

The soldier blushed and hung his head. "Mr. Runnels, I'm scared. If I don't do like they told me I ain't gonna live much longer'n to jest git outta this here room. They done told me that."

Runnels had a habit of rubbing his jaw when he had a problem. He did it now. "Son, let me think on this awhile, then you an' me'll get together back here in the corner again. All right?"

The youngster nodded. "Yes, sir. I'd shore appreciate it if you could figure somethin'. I ain't never been a liar in my life, an' here I done told several."

"Don't worry about it, son. I'll think o' somethin'." Runnels needed time, and it was getting late. He looked at his watch, six o'clock. To hell with the taxes.

"Men, 'fore we take another vote, reckon we oughtta have them set us up to 'nother meal. We'll eat supper, then reckon we gonna argue some more."

Supper came and Runnels sat silently, picking at his food. The others were wolfing theirs down. About midway through the meal, Runnels nodded. "That's it," he said to no one in particular. He picked up his fork and ate like any normally hungry man.

When they finished eating, Runnels said, "Take your time with coffee. I'm gonna step outside the door for a minute."

He opened the door, and the two guards just stared at him. One of them was a Barton man, the other was not. "Where you think you're going?" Barton's man asked.

"Nowhere. I need to ask the defense lawyer a question. Get 'im up here."

He stood there a few minutes, rolled a cigarette, lighted it, and had almost finished his smoke when Leighton came down the hall. "Whatcha want, Runnels?"

"Step over here to the side, Leighton, need to talk." Leighton looked at the two guards. "This is court business. We need to talk in private." They stood aside, and Runnels pulled Leighton down the hall a short distance.

"How well do you know the C.O. out at Keogh?"

Leighton said, "Why?"

Runnels speared Leighton with a look. "Because two men's lives, Gundy's and that young soldier's, will depend on what he does."

"Well, reckon I'd stack 'im up with most men. He's fair, hard, and doesn't let anyone mess with his men."

Runnels grinned. "That's about the way I had 'im figured. Now, tell me, court's in recess while the jury argues — right?"

Leighton nodded.

"Okay, I need you to go out yonder, an' get the papers made out all legal like so that young soldier in there don't get in no trouble 'bout bein' AWOL. I b'lieve I can get 'im to change his vote."

Leighton's grin was a joy to see. "Runnels, don't allow a vote until I come back. I'll tell the guard out here to let you know if everything's all right."

Runnels went back in the room and

called the kid to the corner again. "Son, I ain't askin' you to do nothin' but stick in an honest vote. We ain't gonna let nobody hurt you."

He told the youngster what Leighton was doing and how he planned to keep him safe. "Ain't sayin' they ain't no danger for you, son, but I *am* sayin' you gonna be able to look at yourself in the mirror 'thout bein' ashamed. Ain't even askin' you to put yourself in trouble with the Army, so we'll wait 'til Leighton gets back with your C.O.'s okay. Now you think about it a little while an' let me know what you decide. We ain't gonna vote again 'til Leighton gets back no way."

Abruptly the kid seemed to stand taller, straighter. He looked at Runnels with a hard straight-on look. "Mr. Runnels, I don't need time to think about it, done made up my mind. Even if my C.O. don't give me leave I'm gonna do what's honest. Figure my ma and pa would be proud o' me, and that's what counts. Let's wait for Mr. Leighton."

Runnels stalled until he thought he'd have a rebellion on his hands, from his own men as well as Barton's. They were ready to hang the jury and go have a drink. "No, men, we'll wait until I'm sure the next vote is the final one, whether it's a hung jury or not. We vote one more time, then we let the judge know we've made a decision."

They smoked, drank coffee, grumbled, and, Runnels noticed, Barton's men measured the soldier with long, threatening gazes. When he was about to give up controlling them, footsteps sounded in the hall, and someone tapped on the wooden panel. He opened the door a crack. Leighton stood there, a sheaf of papers in his right hand. He held the papers out, shook them, smiled, nodded, did an about-face, and left.

Runnels walked back to the table. "All right, men. I told you: win, lose, or draw, this is your last vote."

When the vote was counted, without exception Barton's men looked at the kid. He sat pale and straight. Runnels couldn't have been more proud if the kid had been his own son. He opened the door and told the guards to notify the judge they'd made a decision.

He wrote the jury's decision on a slip of paper and they returned to the courtroom. Judge Buckner called the court to order and asked for the decision.

Runnels stood and read: "The jury, by a

count of seven to five, rule the defendant 'Not Guilty.' "

As soon as the verdict was read, Barton's men in the audience bounded to their feet, cursing, and headed for the door. Joy ran to Gundy and threw herself into his arms. He hardly had time to stand, and his chair fell over.

Bruns stood in the doorway, a Colt .44 in each hand. "Every damned man in here sit down. We're gonna leave this here courtroom when and the way I say." He pointed toward the seats with each pistol. "First off, the Flying JW crew, come get your hardware and stand by to back me. Next, I deputize each one o' you. Consider yourselves swore in." He looked at the judge. "You got somethin' to say, Judge?"

Buckner cleared his throat, pounded on the bar with his gunbutt, and stood. "Bailiff, hold each man who swore under oath that Gundy had his gun out before Slagle began his draw. The charge is perjury. We'll build the case by the time I return in about three months." He looked at Barton. "Unfortunately, Mr. Barton, I can prove nothing on you in that you didn't testify. Change your ways, Mr. Barton, or you'll be sitting where Mr. Gundy has sat all day, only with different results."

Gundy wasn't sure he had heard the verdict rightly, but one thing he read right was the beautiful woman he held in his arms. That alone told him he'd been freed. He looked at Buckner. "Sir, am I free to leave?"

The judge only smiled and nodded. Gundy took Joy by the elbow and steered her toward the door. Bruns handed him his gunbelt when he passed by, and at the same time told Crockett to gather the witnesses and lock them in jail.

Thirty minutes later, Joy's crew, the kid — his name they found was Will Harvey — Leighton, Bruns, and the judge sat in the front of the jail, Bruns's office, drinking coffee. Joy made the coffee; nobody in the room trusted the task to Bruns.

Gundy shook his head slowly. "Leighton, don't know how you did it. Figured I was gonna be an outlaw again. I owe you."

"Young man, you owe Mr. Runnels the thanks. He was the one who came up with the whole idea. And young Harvey, there, said he never counted himself a liar."

Gundy swept the group with a hard gaze. "Folks, we ain't outta the woods yet. If I get it right, Runnels promised to keep this young fella safe. We got a long ride back to the ranch, an' Barton ain't gonna let this rest. Figure he'll try to ambush us on the way." He looked at Joy. "Ma'am, reckon you better stay here in town, stay with the marshal's wife 'til this is over."

"Why sure, my missus an' me'll be glad to have you, Joy."

Joy sat quietly a moment. She looked at each man. "I'm going to say something here and now. It's been a long time since anything as good as all you men has happened to me. I love every one of you. You've given me hope again." Her voice had been soft, now it hardened. "You tell me you ride for the brand, well, I'm here to tell you it's my brand, you're my men. I'll not let you do *anything* I'm afraid to do. *You fight, I fight. You're not leaving me behind.*"

They sat staring at each other. Gundy thought he might be the only one in the room not surprised. The only side of Joy the men had seen, or bothered to look for, was the "woman of the house." She made certain they were fed, made certain they had a clean house to come into when they had reason to talk with her, and for meals. She did all the things you'd expect of a young, pretty woman.

When she'd tried to track the rustlers, with no help, Gundy knew then she would do whatever she knew how to do. She wasn't limited by lack of nerve — only knowledge. He sat back in his chair. "Ain't gonna do no good to argue, men. Miz Joy's gonna go with us. You men find a place to stay tonight. I want full daylight when we head out in the mornin'. I'll scout. When we get on the trail, I want Harvey an' Miz Joy to ride in the middle o' the pack. Saddle an' be ready to ride . . ." A knock shook the thick panels of the door.

Bruns looked at the men. They took stations about the room. Gundy pulled Joy into a corner. Bruns opened the door a crack. "What you want, Mallory? You alone?"

"Yeah, Marshal. I'm alone. Jest want to talk to you folks."

Bruns pulled the door open. "Come on in."

Blacky Mallory walked to the center of the floor, taking the room in at a glance. "Glad to see you folks are leaving nothing to chance. Ready for a fight, huh?"

Gundy grinned at him. "This ain't no new breed, Mallory. We're always ready to fight. What you got on your mind?"

Mallory centered his eyes on Gundy. "You seen me down Texas way. You heard 'bout me. You ever hear I was a back shooter?"

Gundy shook his head. "No, to be honest, I heard a lot o' things 'bout you, Mallory, not a helluva lot o' them good, but I always heard you give your man a chance."

Mallory, never taking his eyes off Gundy, said, "I done quit Barton. I ain't askin' no favors of any o' you. Just want to let you know Barton's figurin' on an ambush tomorrow. Fact is they done rode out."

"You know where?"

Mallory shook his head. "Nope. Just know they gonna do it."

Gundy's face broke into a hard smile. "We figured on such, already made plans. You want to ride with us?"

"No. Cain't rightly fight against men I been ridin' with. Just thought y'all should know." He tipped his hat and left.

Gundy stared at the door a moment and said quietly, "There but for the grace of God goes any man in this room. He took the wrong fork in the trail. We didn't."

The meeting broke up soon after. Bruns kept two of Joy's riders to guard the jail; the rest went searching for a place to stay the night. Most would sleep with their horses at the livery. They agreed to meet at the cafe for breakfast before heading for the ranch.

The next morning dawned gray and cold. Gundy glanced at the sky, thinking they would ride in snow before reaching the ranch. He finished saddling his horse and rode him to the cafe. Looks like I'm the first one here, he thought.

Welcome warmth hit him in the face when he walked in. He sat on a bench at a corner table.

He drank coffee, waiting for the others. He figured Barton's bunch would find a place to hide between town and the ranch. That being the case, he thought to have Crockett and the men take Joy and the kid out by Keogh, and circle northwest toward Runnels's ranch. They'd ride with rifles across their saddles.

Joy was the first to arrive. She sat next to Gundy. They talked quietly until all had shown up. The waitress brought them breakfast. "Chickens stopped laying, so you'll have to take what I can put together." None of them cared what they had; they said all they wanted was to get on the trail.

When all were finished eating, Gundy stood and told them his plan. "I'll go first, be sure they ain't outguessed us. If I find them, I'll try to let you know where they are." Joy looked at him and placed her hand on his arm. "Be careful, Trace."

He smiled. "Ma'am, you heard 'em say in that courtroom I was the Apache Blanco. They ain't gonna know where I am, let alone hurt me." He wished he felt as confident as his words sounded. "Y'all wait 'til I'm gone 'bout a half hour, then hit the trail." He left.

Figuring Barton's men would head for the fork of the Tongue and Pumpkin to take advantage of the trees and riverbanks as cover, he headed out of town in that direction, then pulled off the trail and sat his horse below the crest of a hill. From here, the town lay below him. Soon, Crockett and his bunch left town in the direction he'd laid out for them. Within minutes a lone rider followed. Gundy, squinting against the cold wind, cut a trail parallel to them, keeping to the slope side of the hills, not wanting to skyline himself.

The lone rider followed until Crockett led his bunch off the trail and headed northwest, then he broke off and headed almost straight west. Gundy nodded to himself. He'd been right. The rider headed toward the fork of the rivers. Right now everything was shaping up the way Gundy thought. He reined his horse to intercept the rider.

His angle on the rider would let him cross his path, even if he had to do it on foot. He followed, staying below the crest of hills, losing the rider when he had to circle one, then he would spot him again. The rider rode in a straight line for the forks of the Tongue and Pumpkin.

Finally, Gundy reined in, climbed from his saddle, and ground-reined his horse. There was a shallow ravine ahead. Barton's man would have to cross it to reach the forks. He made sure his horse couldn't be seen from the rider's path, and headed for the gully. Snow, widely spaced, began to fall in large, feathery flakes. Gundy ignored it.

A cow path crossed the ravine, and figuring a man on horseback with any sense would follow the path, Gundy slipped down its side far enough to keep his head below the cut-bank. He went flat on his stomach about ten feet from where the animal path cut down the side. He lay there and waited.

The soft thud of the horse's hooves reached his ears. The man, his head pulled down into his sheepskin, wasn't looking in either direction. Gundy waited until the horse was almost past when he stood, .44 pointed at the man's chest. "Rein in. Don't want to kill you."

chapter nineteen

The rider's hand made a sweep for his gun. It was buttoned under his coat. "Dumb move, cowboy. I could've killed you right then. Now unbutton your coat and drop your hardware." Gundy hoped the man didn't try for his gun. They were close enough to the forks for a shot to be heard. His hope was futile.

The cowboy slowly unbuttoned his coat, giving the appearance of being careful. He reached to his belt buckle with both hands, then swung his right hand toward his holster. Gundy hadn't time to reach for his throwing knife. He thumbed off a shot. The heavy slug knocked the rider back into his saddle. He straightened and tried to get his gun in action. Gundy fired again. The man jerked when the slug tore into him, and almost in slow motion sagged to the side and fell.

Gundy ran to his side, pulled his gunbelt and gun from him, went to his horse, took his rifle, and ran for his buckskin. Barton's men would be coming.

Gundy put heels to his horse and headed toward the Flying JW. A straight course to Joy's men and he'd lead the ambushers directly to them. But he had to get to them. They had to be warned that Barton knew they weren't coming the way he'd planned. If they had taken a straight course to the JW, they would have already reached Barton and his men at the forks. Maybe Barton would follow him instead of looking for the JW crew.

Six men, riding hell for leather, topped a hill to his left. In seconds a slug whined by his head. He leaned flat to his horse and let the buckskin run. He had to find some sort of cover, but could think of none closer than the ranch. If he could keep these men chasing him, then Joy and the kid would be safe.

At a dead run, he pulled his Winchester from its scabbard. Without hope of hitting anyone, he fired the rifle, pistol fashion, to the rear. His chest tightened. Fear gripped him, not for himself, but fear that if he failed Joy might get hurt.

His shot must have come close — they slowed. He didn't want them too far behind, they might have second thoughts as to where the main bunch of JW riders were.

Gundy rode into the ranch yard about three hundred yards ahead of his attackers. He didn't hesitate, but rode his horse to the porch overhang and swung to the roof. He needed a field of fire.

Bent over, Gundy ran to the roof's crown and put it between him and the attackers. He jacked a shell into the chamber, lined his sights on the lead rider, and fired. "One down, five to go," he muttered, jacked another shell into the chamber, and brought the second one out of his saddle. "Four."

Barton's men split, two going to each side. Now it would get harder. Rapid fire, he knocked the two men to his right from the saddle. One of them, Gundy knew he had a solid hit on; he thought he had no more than winged the other. The barn was now between him and the two men who split to the left. Gundy gave a moment's thought to swinging from the roof and seeing if he could catch them trying to enter the barn, and decided time wouldn't allow him to get there first.

He rolled to his back and searched the area where he'd knocked the third rider off his horse. The mustang stood, head hanging, at about a hundred yards from the house on a flat stretch of ground.

Gundy looked from the horse back toward town. The wounded man crawled, using one arm to drag himself along, clutching his rifle in his good hand.

Gundy first thought to let him go, thinking he was not a threat, and not wanting to kill if he didn't have to. He looked at the barn, then back to the man on the ground. He couldn't afford to split his attention. His rifle came to his shoulder, he drew a careful bead on the man and pressed the trigger. Now he could pay full attention to the other men, either behind or in the barn. He rolled back to his stomach, shook his head, and slipped down the roof to the back of the house.

On the ground, he looked across the yard to the bunkhouse, wishing he were in it. He'd have a much better chance to see the attackers from there without exposing himself. He thought to try to reach the barn or the bunkhouse with a surprise sprint, and shook his head. He hadn't lived this long by being a damned fool.

If he was the attacker, what would he do? He decided at least one of them would climb to the hayloft for a better chance to see him. The other would probably stay inside the stable at ground level. Gundy watched the loft door.

He was beginning to think they had as much patience as he did when a rifle barrel poked around the side of the haymow door. Pointed at the roof's crown, three shots in quick succession spouted from the rifle's bore. The barrel withdrew to the side.

The rifleman had nothing to fire at; he was hoping to flush his quarry with those shots. Gundy knew he might have done the same thing. He studied the door a moment. There would be a thick wooden beam supporting the door frame, and to the side of that he thought the gunman would stand until he thought it safe to fire again.

Careful not to make a sudden move that would draw attention, Gundy lifted his rifle and sighted at the second flat, gray board from the door's frame. He triggered off three shots as fast as he could jack shells into the chamber, then withdrew behind the shelter of the house's corner.

From ground level, bullets knocked splinters from the wall where he had stood but a moment before. Gundy's stomach muscles tightened. If those splinters hit a man, they would tear him apart. No shots came from the loft. Maybe, Gundy thought, just maybe, he'd scored a hit on the man in the haymow.

The man at ground level would probably be looking for a rifle barrel to poke around the corner of the house, and he was most likely right. A pistol from this distance wouldn't hit anything unless pure luck made it happen.

Gundy thought to lie down and try for a shot. He discarded the idea. The man in the barn would be raking the whole corner with his gaze. Abruptly he drew his .44, stuck his hand around the corner, thumbed off two quick shots, turned, and ran for the back of the house. He circled the back and ran up the other side. Coming to that corner he went flat on his stomach and peered around it looking straight into the barn door.

The last of the attackers stood behind the upright supporting the door frame, his rifle held with the barrel pointed toward the roof, his head twisted for a quick look at the corner of the house Gundy had just left.

Gundy eased his rifle forward, drew a bead on the rifleman, and squeezed the trigger at the same time the man shifted his gaze to look at the corner behind which Gundy lay. In the split second it took for Gundy's rifle to spit its bullet, Gundy saw the man's eyes widen. Even if it wasn't possible to see the bullet coming at him the rustler saw death, and knew he couldn't avoid it.

The slug took him in the chest, picked him up, and flung him backward. That should be the last of the six, but Gundy held his position. That man in the loft still worried him. Gundy raked the opening with a searching gaze. He saw no sign of the man he'd tried to shoot through the board alongside the loft door. Maybe he'd hit him, but the man could be playing possum. Gundy decided to wait and see.

He waited, motionless for over an hour by his watch, and decided to try to get to the barn.

Again he sprinted around the house and without stopping cut across the open space to the bunkhouse. He made it without drawing fire.

In back of the bunkhouse, he crawled through a window, went to the front, threw a shot at the last place he'd figured the man to be, again ran to the back, and climbed out the window. He ran to the corner of the bunkhouse, gauged the distance to the stable, and ran. He made it to the side of the barn. No shots came his way. He was almost positive now that the last man was down, if not dead, then badly hurt.

Gundy circled the stable to the back. Two horses stood ground-hitched there. Whatever shape his attackers were in, they had not left. He catfooted to the back opening, slipped through it and stood in the semidarkness, taking slow, deep breaths, not wanting his breathing to give him away. A horse in one of the stalls stomped a hoof, one of the barn doors squeaked on a rusty hinge, small feet skittered across the loft floor. None of the sounds bothered him. His ears and senses were attuned to heavier movement, movement made by man — or smells, sour sweat, maybe mixed with tobacco, and as much as anything, Gundy wanted his sense of not being alone to warn him.

He first looked toward the front door. One of his attackers sprawled there, on his back. Gundy watched a few moments, saw no movement, but wanted to make sure. As silent as a shadow on a sunny day he moved to stand over the man. Sightless eyes stared at the ceiling. His chest didn't move, and the hole in it had stopped oozing blood. Dead.

Two ladders went to the loft, one close to the front doors and one at the back. If the man who had been by the loft door was only wounded, he might be waiting for a shot. Gundy decided to chance using the back ladder.

One rung at a time, he tested with his weight, then put his foot down solid, then another until his head was even with the floor. His scalp tingling, his back muscles tense and knotted, he inched his head above the floor level until he could scan the floor.

The first place he looked was at the framing at the side where he'd shot through the wood by the door. A man lay there on his stomach, his rifle by his side and a pistol in his hand. A pool of blood spread from the man's side, but he faced the door, still alive. Gundy thought if he spoke softly, letting the man know he was covered, he'd not have to kill him.

"Don't move. I got a six-gun pointed at your head."

The gunman moved only his head. His hand holding the pistol didn't move. He stared at Gundy. "Partner, them slivers from that board done tore me up somethin' fierce. You might's well go on an' shoot, stop me from hurtin'."

"Let that pistol slide off your finger, an' don't make any sudden moves."

"Mister, I don't feel like I could move fast or slow." He straightened his finger and opened his hand. The handgun slipped from his grip. Gundy walked softly to his side and moved his weapons from his reach with his foot. He squatted at the man's side.

"Gonna turn you over, gotta see how bad you're hit."

The gunman, his face pasty, grimaced and nodded. Gundy slid his hands under the man's side and as gently as possible turned him onto his back. Then he opened the blood-soaked shirt. "Looks like my slug only creased you, but them wood slivers shore made a mess." He ran his fingers over each place that bled. "Mister, you gonna hurt awhile, but if I can get them slivers outta you I figure you gonna make it."

Hard blue eyes bored into Gundy's. "You ain't funnin' me, are you, partner?"

Gundy shook his bead. "I wouldn't fun a man 'bout somethin' like that. Yeah. I b'lieve you gonna make it." He holstered his Colt. "Gotta see if I can pull them sticks outta you. Gonna hurt 'bout as bad as anything you ever felt."

The largest sliver stuck through the man's right side, between two ribs. Gundy pulled the gunman's shirttail up and wiped the lips twisted in pain, then looked at the part of the shirt he'd used to wipe and saw no blood. "You're lucky. That big sliver didn't hit your lung. Now, hold tight, partner. I'm gonna pull it out."

He grasped the piece of wood close to the man's chest and pulled. He did it fast, and glanced at the putty colored face that had only moments before been twisted in pain. The gunman had passed out. While the man was unconscious, Gundy worked as quickly as he could, removing the splintered wood.

When he finished, Gundy glanced at his attacker's face. Pain-filled eyes stared back at him from a face pouring sweat. "Why you doin' this for me, Blanco? If you was lying' here, I'd a probably let you die."

"Ain't made that way. What's your name?"

"Mike Brady." His voice came out thin, strained.

"Well, Brady, I done about all I can for you. You figure you're up to ridin', your horse is still out back. Gotta find Miz Waldrop, get 'er back here now your bunch ain't no problem."

Brady studied Gundy a moment, then said, "Blanco, you been good to me so I'll tell you. They wuz twelve of us. You only took care o' six. The others went after Miz Waldrop."

chapter twenty

Gundy ran from the barn, grabbed the saddle horn, and the buckskin was running all out by the time he got his foot in the stirrup.

About a mile from the house, he reined in to listen. Between the gelding panting for air, Gundy thought he heard a faint crackling that might be rifle fire. He kneed his horse into a run again, heading north by northeast toward the sound. Another mile and he reined in again. This time he was certain. His chest muscles tightened. Joy was in danger!

He again rode toward the shots until he could hear them above the pounding of his horse's hooves. Now he was sure the fight was taking place over the brow of the hill in front of him.

Gundy pulled his Winchester from its scabbard, dismounted, and trailed the buckskin's reins. Bent low, he ran toward the top of the hill and went flat on his stomach. Using his elbows, he dragged himself up far enough over the coarse stubbly grass to see over the crest. A quick swipe of his hand and he knocked his hat to the ground. No point in making a bigger target than he had to.

Gundy hoped Barton's bunch was on this side of the swale, with their backs toward him. He inched up until he could see to the far side against the rise of the next hill. The Flying JW crew, along with Joy and the young soldier, Will Harvey, were forted up behind four large boulders. Didn't any of them seem to be hurt. He inched higher.

Barton's bunch had found a similar place for protection. A jumble of large rocks lay about fifty yards below him, and none of Barton's men looked his way. Both groups were neatly pinned down. Gundy breathed a silent prayer for that. If they hadn't been, a man could have climbed to where he lay and poured shots directly into the JW bunch.

He pulled his head down below the crest and glanced in both directions, hoping to see cover of any kind he could hide behind. No luck.

A brassy taste formed under his tongue and in the back of his throat. He had learned long ago it was the taste of fear. To fire into Barton's men he would have to expose himself from the waist up. Nothing came easy. He sucked in a deep breath and raised to his knees. As soon as he could draw a bead, he fired into the rustlers, jacked another shell into the chamber, and fired again. Two men jerked and bent against the ground. They would never trouble anyone again. His third shot did no more than wing one of the scummy bunch below. That was the man who rolled to his back and yelled, "Behind us — on the ridge!" He fired at Gundy.

Gundy dropped to his belly again and rolled below the crest. He ran about twenty feet to his right, and again poked his head above the rise. The four remaining Barton riders ran for their horses. The JW crew brought another two of them to the ground. By the time Gundy could get his rifle lined up on one of the two left they were out of sure shooting distance. He threw a couple of shots their way to hurry them along.

Gathering the reins of the buckskin, he walked down the hill to meet his men. They ran toward him, Joy in the lead. Gundy had never seen her look prettier. She had a smudge down one cheek, her skirt was stained with dirt, and dried grass clung to it in several places. She flung herself into his arms.

"Oh, Trace, where have you been? We've been so worried about you."

"Not now, Joy. I'll tell you about it on the way home."

He looked at Crockett. "Have a couple of men check those you knocked down. They's a couple more over yonder behind them rocks. Bury the dead ones, throw the others across their horses, and slap 'em toward Milestown." Gundy waited while Crockett carried out his orders.

Crockett came back, shook his head, and said, "All dead."

"All right, find a cut-bank and cave some dirt in over 'em." He swept them all with a glance. "Let's go home."

While they rode, Gundy told them about leading the six riders toward the ranch, thinking they were the only ones Barton sent after them, and of the wounded man who had told him differently.

When they rode into the ranch yard, Joy sighed. "You men get washed up for supper."

"No," Gundy said, "you go on in the house and clean up, you've had a hard day. We'll fix supper out here and bring it to the house." Joy opened her mouth to say something. "Don't want to hear no arguin' outta you. We're fixin' supper. That's it."

Joy stood there a moment, staring at Gundy, then her mouth crinkled at the corners in the beginning of a smile. "Yes, sir, Mr. Gundy." She turned away, but Gundy heard her mutter, "No doubt about who's in charge here."

When the crew had cooked supper and brought it to the house, they pulled up to the table, talking too loud, laughing at unfunny things, and jumping up from the table to do things not needing doing. Gundy understood why they acted as they did. Most men and women did these same things as a way of relieving tension after any harrowing experience. Gundy was not one of those who acted this way. The Apache had not allowed it.

After they'd eaten, Gundy told them each man would clean his own dishes and put them away. He looked at Joy. "I'll help clean up the kitchen."

He wiped the table with the dishcloth, swept the kitchen with a glance, and nodded. "Everything looks pretty clean, Joy. Don't figure it'll take long for you to fix it the way you want it. I'm gonna turn in so you can get some rest." She stood next to him when he stepped toward the door. She placed her hand on his forearm.

"Trace, please stay awhile, sit with me. I'm tired, but I don't want to be alone right now. I know it's selfish of me, but I need your company."

They sat in the front room. Gundy watched the firelight play across the drapes, the curtains, and paint Joy's face a golden hue. Strange the only two women he'd ever been close to were also the most beautiful he'd ever known. He'd never put much stock in beauty until he realized that most of it came from the inside. And Dee and Joy were both strong and beautiful from the core out. He glanced at her only to see she was looking at him. "You feel like hearing some of the story about the Apache Blanco?"

She smiled. "That's what I hoped for when I asked you to stay, Trace. I'm not too tired, if you aren't."

"Ain't much of it pretty, Joy. You might hate me when I finish."

Her eyes locked with his. "Trace, you may not have noticed, but I'm not one of these milksop women who faint at the sight of blood. Yes. I want to hear it all. I doubt there's anything in the world that could make me think less of you. Tell me."

He told her about his folks being killed by the Apache, about the Mescalero war chief who raised him to be an Apache warrior, about the raids he went on, about the Apache being relegated to reservations, about him running and being branded an outlaw for doing so, about meeting Dee, her mother and father, Alejandro and Maria Kelly, and her brother, Paul.

He told her about Lew Wallace, Territorial Governor of New Mexico, pardoning him at his and Dee's wedding, about the Comancheros and Matt and Hillary Ross who planned the Comanchero raids and controlled the Comanchero bandit leaders. He told her about killing Matt, and Hillary getting killed when the law raided the Ross ranch, and about his taking over the Ross ranch as his own. As a result of all this, he became the most hated gringo along the border.

He told her about the Comanchero, Barton, raiding his ranch and killing Dee. "Joy, he shot my wife in her stomach, shot right through our baby she had been carryin' there for seven months. That's why I tracked him slam across two states and two territories. When he showed up here, you know I rode off with 'im slung across his saddle." Gundy stood, went to the kitchen, poured them each a cup of coffee, and brought it back.

"Joy, when I took him to the back side of the ranch, I killed 'im. Killed 'im like he killed my Dee. I drove a stake through his guts, and sat there and watched 'im die." He again stood. "You know the rest of it, Joy. Reckon if you're ever gonna hate me, be disgusted with me, you are now. You're tired, I'm tired. Gonna go to bed." He put his hat on and walked toward the door. "Good night, Joy."

She never acknowledged his words, never looked at him. She sat staring into the fire, her arms folded tightly across her breasts.

Gundy slipped between his blankets and lay there staring at the ceiling, listening to the wind play around the eaves, hearing the rafters creak and settle, feeling warmth creep close to him under his blankets. But sleep didn't come. He'd told Joy as much about him as he himself knew. He'd told her everything except how he felt about her, and now that he admitted his feelings to himself, it made no difference. He was a savage. She had shown she thought of him that way. She had not looked at him when he left, had not even acknowledged his words.

Maybe he shouldn't have told her, but he knew they couldn't have gone through life with that between them. She'd had to hear his story.

It had been late when he left Joy, now a gray dawn pushed its wan light into the room. He made up his mind. He'd not make it any harder on either of them. He'd saddle and leave.

Gundy pushed his blankets down, tugged his hat onto his head, dressed, rolled his bedroll, and headed for the stable. The men were still in their bunks.

Gundy pulled the second cinch strap tight and sensed someone behind him. He looked over his shoulder. Joy stood there, her hands twisting, pulling and wadding her skirt on each side. Tears slipped down her cheeks. "Where are you going, Trace? You've not eaten your breakfast."

He straightened and faced her. "Didn't figure you'd ever want to see me again, Miz Waldrop. Not after what I told you. Don't reckon no decent person would want me in their house."

"Please, Trace, please don't go back to calling me Miz Waldrop. Please don't go, Trace. I want you to stay. I don't know what I did to make you feel the way you're feeling. Whatever it was, I'm sorry. I — I don't think I could stand to lose you." She stepped toward him — and in the next instant she was in his arms, sobbing as though her heart would break.

"Trace, when you left I sat there crying, thinking of the little boy who had never known a mother's love, probably scared to death. And then being raised to never show emotion, and finally discarded by his own people until he met a woman strong enough to stand with him against the world." She drew in a ragged breath. "Oh, Trace, I *couldn't* answer when you told me good night. I was hurting for you inside so — so badly I would have done then what I'm doing now, b-b-blubbering like a baby."

He stood there, smoothing her coat against her back. Crooning to her like a mother with a hurt child. "Now, now, Joy. Stop cryin'. Dry your eyes, cain't let the men see you like this. I don't b'lieve the men are at the house yet. I figured to get an early start. They was most of 'em still in their bunks when I left. You go on to the house an' fix your face. Some cold water on them eyes might help."

She pulled away from him, the shadow of a smile showing behind her eyes. "Trace, I'll go now if it means you're staying." She stepped toward the door and turned back. "Trace, I want you to know. I

276

don't blame you for what you did to Rance Barton. I'd like to think a man would feel that strongly for me someday."

As soon as she cleared the door, Gundy pushed his hat back and muttered, "Well, what do you know. She don't know it yet, but they's a man right close by what feels that way."

During breakfast Gundy told Crockett he had something needed doing at the back side of the ranch and for him to take over until he got back. Crockett stared at him a moment. "Figured you'd want to go back there one o' these days. I wuz over there a couple weeks ago, seen the job you done an' wuz gonna take care o' things, but figured it was a job you wanted to take care of yourself. Now all you gotta do is tidy it up a little."

Gundy read the full knowledge of what he'd done to Barton in Crockett's eyes and saw no condemnation. His throat tightened with feeling for the range-hardened man he faced. Maybe most people, those worth knowing, were a little harder than he thought, and maybe *he'd* lost some of his savagery.

When the crew left to go about their daily chores, Gundy tarried a moment. "Joy, I'll be back tomorrow evenin'." He studied the floor a moment, then locked gazes with her. "Ma'am, want you to know I 'preciate you understanding me so good. You're a good woman, a strong woman, a woman any man would be proud to ride the trail with. Thank you, ma'am." She stared at him through tear-filled eyes, and afraid she was going to cry again, he left.

Joy wasn't going to cry. Her chest and throat were so tight she had to swallow, and then swallow again to keep from showing her happiness and pride in this man who'd appeared out of nowhere and taken over her life. She didn't know how he felt about her; didn't know if Dee was far enough behind him that he could even think of another woman; didn't know if he even saw her as a woman to share life with. Right now she didn't care. She needed his strength, and the strength of those men he'd gathered around him.

She walked to the window and watched him ride into the gloomy, cloudy day. The day, despite being sunless, was as bright as any she'd known — and it had started out so badly. Her eyes shifted from Gundy to the men puttering around the corral, the stable. Gundy had done that. He seemed to keep more men than necessary around

278

the ranch house, and she knew he did it for defense. If Barton or any of his men came back, the Flying JW was ready for them.

When Gundy disappeared across a ridge, Joy went to the gunrack, took every rifle and shotgun from it, and proceeded to clean and load them.

It was coming on to dark night when Gundy rode up on the ashes of the camp-fire he'd had when he took care of Barton. He tethered his horse and went about making camp. The night was bitter cold, and it took him more than an hour to collect enough firewood from along the creek bank to last the night. He fixed supper, spread his groundsheet as close to the fire as he figured was safe, and crawled between his blankets fully dressed. He'd need all the covering he had if he wanted to stay warm.

One of the times during the night, when he woke long enough to put more wood on the fire, snow was falling. He'd have to stay away from this section of the ranch. It seemed to him that every time he came this way it snowed.

Over breakfast Gundy cast looks about the area. Less than an inch of snow lay on the ground so he had little trouble seeing what he wanted. The three stakes he'd used on Barton still stood. The two end stakes had the pigging strings tied to them that he'd used to tie Barton's hands and feet, but Barton's bones were scattered about the area. Coyotes had gotten to him after all. He hoped Barton had been dead by then.

Finished eating, he took the shovel he'd brought with him and went to the creek bank. He looked for a cut-bank that would be easy to crumble dirt over. The ground was frozen too hard to try digging a decent burial for what was left of Barton.

He found what he wanted, went back to his campsite, collected every bone he could find, took them to the cutaway under the bank, and shoveled dirt over them.

When satisfied everything was as he'd found it when he brought Barton here, he straightened and stared at the spot he'd packed dirt over, then he looked heavenward and spread his hands out from his sides, palms upward. "Great Spirit, keep this man out of the perfect afterworld you've created for us. He is not worthy of walking among great warriors." Gundy lowered his hands to his sides and brought his eyes back to the world he lived in.

It was over — all over. He put the hate

from him. If he'd had a tipi he'd have built a sweat lodge. He decided he'd do that as soon as he had the skins. He'd have to use cow skins, but they would work, then he would wash in the cleansing smoke and again be clean. He returned to his camp, made his bedroll, saddled his horse, and headed for home.

chapter twenty-one

The day the ranchers were to arrive with their crews, Gundy set his men to tasks that would get them ready for a fight and a trail drive. He figured they'd have both in the next few days.

They cleaned, oiled, and loaded weapons. The metallic click of rifle bolts opening and closing, the scent of gun oil, the soft scraping of cartridges pulled from boxes and stuffed in saddlebags, all filled the bunkhouse with a sense of quiet efficiency and determination.

Finished with weapons, the men broke out extra blankets, clothing, and went from that to getting the chuck wagon ready for a trail drive. Gundy looked from one man to another. "Any o' you men ever cooked for a whole crew before?" No one had. Gundy pushed his hat back and scratched his head. " 'Fraid o' that. Well, reckon I'll pick somebody."

Joy had been helping provision the wagon. "I'll do the cooking."

Gundy gave her a hard look. "You ain't.

You never cooked for as many men as we gonna have. It's gonna be cold enough to freeze the horns off a mountain goat. They's gonna be shootin' — an' you just flat out ain't goin' with us."

Joy's mouth set in a hard straight line. "Don't tell me what I'm going to do, Trace Gundy. I'm saying right now, straight out, I'm going."

"You ain't." Gundy took her elbow and led her off to the side. "Joy, you gotta stay here, watch the ranch buildings. I'm gonna leave Baden an' Lawton here to protect you, an' — an' besides, I cain't have you gettin' hurt. I got somethin' we gotta talk about when I get back."

"Let's talk about it now."

Gundy felt his face flush. "Aw, now, Joy, this ain't the time to say what I gotta say. Need to be alone with you. Not right out here in front of the men."

"Tell me what it's about, and I *might* stay here, *might,* mind you." Her lips were still set in that hard straight line, her eyes half closed. Gundy had seen logging mules less stubborn.

He leaned closer to her. "Dammit, Joy, I need to talk 'bout you an' me." He planted his feet solidly against the frozen ground, leaned close to her, and stuck his chin out.

283

"Now, by damn, that's all you gonna get outta me right now."

Her face softened. "You want to talk about you and me?" Her voice came out almost a purr. "Why didn't you say so in the beginning? If that's a promise, I'll be waiting here when you get back."

Gundy straightened and stepped back a step. "You will?"

Her eyes sparkled. "Why certainly I will. You just didn't explain it to me right in the first place."

"Aw, hell. I still gotta find a cook. Maybe one o' the other outfits'll have one." He walked back to the men gathered around the chuck wagon, wondering what he'd "explained right."

About midafternoon, the Flying JW crew still topping off extra horses for the remuda, Bob Runnels showed up with two men. Before sundown Denton and Purdy rode in with their crews and remudas. Purdy had a fully provisioned chuck wagon with him. Gundy counted twenty-five men, including himself.

Gundy looked sourly at the two wagons. "Looks like we got plenty o' grub, now if we only had somebody who knew what to do with it."

"No problem, Gundy," Purdy said, "I

have at least three men who can handle that job."

Satisfied that problem was solved, Gundy swept them with a glance. "You men all been told what we're here for?" They nodded. "All right. I've already scouted the area we gonna head for. Ain't real rough country like most o' you know from Texas, judging by them Texas rigs you're ridin', but they's a lot o' scrub cedar, so gettin' them cows rounded up ain't gonna be no Sunday sleigh ride. An' first we got a fight on our hands. Shouldn't be as hard as it was when I first talked with your bosses. We done thinned 'em down some."

He told them of the happenings in recent weeks, then looked at Denton and Purdy. "I ain't tryin' to horn in on runnin' your crews, just thought I'd tell all o' you what I know about the situation."

Denton stepped to Gundy's side. "For my part, Gundy, I'd kinda like for you to be in charge."

Runnels and Purdy nodded. "Goes for us too, Gundy."

Gundy looked at the men. "How y'all feel 'bout that?"

One crusty-looking old-timer chewed the wad of tobacco in his cheek a couple of times, spit, and hit a cow pie dead center. "Reckon if the boss tells us to do somethin', ain't a one of us what's gonna not do it." Every man there nodded. The old-timer continued, " 'Sides that, we all been hearin' 'bout the Apache Blanco for years. I'm here to tell you right now, I'm gonna follow you into a fight if for no other reason than to see can you live up to it."

Gundy's eyes crinkled at the corners in the beginning of a smile. He swept the men with a slow, lingering look. "Don't want you men to b'lieve all you heard 'bout me. Fact is, if them stories was even near 'bout true, don't reckon I'd need much help to do the job we're goin' out yonder to do. But the way it stands, they's gonna be enough fight there for all o' us to get a bit of it."

He looked toward the corral to find Crockett. "Hey, Crockett," he yelled, "show this bunch o' stove-up old punchers where to sleep tonight. This'll be the last night they gonna sleep warm for maybe a couple o' weeks."

He turned his attention to Purdy. "Have two o' your men what know how to put a meal together check in with Miz Joy. She'll tell 'em where to find what to cook, and she'll help 'em fix it.

"We'll head out after breakfast in the mornin' an' make it to Ismay sometime the third day. Ain't far from there we tie into the Barton bunch. He's the one what owned that saloon, the Soldier's Haven. An' he's the one that's been stealin' our cows.

"We'll make camp this side o' Fallon Creek, just outside of Ismay, the night before we tie into the Box LB, Barton's outfit."

He stepped off to the side and watched the men get acquainted. It turned out several of them had ridden for the same brands in Texas, and some of them already knew each other. In short order they became one crew riding for a single brand. From behind his right shoulder, Denton said, "Looks like we made the right move putting them in your charge, Gundy."

"Naw, these men would've come together as one crew anyway. A lot of them know each other, an' we got a job to get done where we all gotta work at it. I'm glad though that ain't none o' them had a long-forgotten fight with none o' the others. They might have taken it up right here and now."

The last thing Gundy did before dark

was make sure a spare wheel and axle was tied to the side of each wagon. He didn't have to tell these men how to get themselves and their weapons ready for a fight or a trail drive.

The sun was not yet peeking above the horizon when they rode out. Joy stood on the veranda. She'd never seen a crew as efficient or hard-bitten as this one. There rides the future of most every ranch in this part of the territory, she thought, and it's led by the man who wants to talk about him and me.

She hugged her arms around her breasts and smiled. Now I wonder what that cowboy is going to talk about. She sobered, realizing she had no solid thing to go on that he was going to say anything romantic. Maybe he would tell her it was time for him to head for Texas, that he'd gotten the ranch back on its feet and she would have no trouble running it.

He had never indicated, in any way, he had thoughts about them as man and woman. He always seemed to guard against letting himself think about anything other than doing the best job for her that he knew how.

But would he have done as much for any woman trying to run a ranch alone? She worried that thought until, frustrated, she cast the problem from her mind. Even as much as she wanted Trace to love her, it wasn't something she could say anything about, it wouldn't be ladylike. Abruptly she squared her shoulders, still staring at the cleft in the hills where a cold, distant sun had cast a ray on the trail crew just before they disappeared. She said in almost a whisper, "Ladylike or not, Trace Gundy, you're not riding out of here without knowing how I feel."

The first night Gundy stopped his outfit on the south side of Milestown, and the second night they camped beside the Powder.

"We'll camp alongside o' Fallon Creek tomorrow night. If the boys want a drink we'll all go in town together." Gundy talked to Denton and Purdy. "Don't know how the word could've gotten out on what we plan, but it coulda happened, so we'll stick together. Hope that town's got a marshal. We might need one."

"What you got in mind, Gundy? Why would we need the law?" Denton asked.

Gundy slanted him a look, eyes squinted against the cold wind. "Denton, we might run into some o' them Box LB punchers, an' if we do, I figure we can cut the odds when the fight starts."

Denton nodded.

Late afternoon of the next day they forded Fallon Creek and set up camp on the edge of town. "You men go on in town, they got a right nice saloon. Drink enough to cut the dust, but not too much. We got a lot o' hard days ahead of us. I'm goin' in alone now, see if I can find any law there."

Gundy rode to the center of town, glancing at each building, searching for one with bars on the windows. He saw what he wanted and reined to the hitch rail.

The inside of the jail was dark and musty. A lamp burned on the back side of a beat-up old wooden desk. A tough, capable-looking man about Gundy's age sat on the other side. He looked up. "Don't tell me you already got trouble. You an' that bunch you rode in with ain't been in town long enough."

Gundy laughed. "Marshal, it don't take long to find trouble, but no, we ain't got trouble yet."

"That being the case, what can I do for you?"

Gundy locked eyes with the marshal. "Gonna ask you a question. Don't mean no offense by it, but I gotta know. Who put you in office, the townspeople or the Box LB?"

The marshal's face hardened. "You trying to say I might be owned by somebody?"

"Reckon that's about it, Marshal. Are you?" Gundy held his hands wide of his guns, not wanting to give any idea he wanted a fight.

The marshal stood. "Mister, I'm gonna tell you here and now, don't nobody *own* me. The town pays me to keep the peace. That's what I do, and I don't take orders from nobody as to how I do it."

Gundy smiled knowing he had crossed the line but wanting to salve the lawman's feelings. "Marshal, like I said, I shore didn't mean no offense, but I got a story to tell you an' it will make a lot o' difference what side you're on — if any."

He then told who they were and why they were here. "Marshal, know you ain't got no authority outside o' town. We ain't gonna cause trouble here unless they bring it to us, but knowin' what I done told you, if they's any o' that bunch here in town I want to cut the odds, arrest whoever's here, and keep them in jail 'til we get through with the fightin' out at the Box LB."

The lawman looked at Gundy through squinted eyes. "How do I know what you told me is true?"

"You don't. I'm askin' you to talk to the three owners what's with me. You've prob'ly heard of them: Purdy, Runnels, Denton. They're all solid citizens. I'm ramroddin' the show for them."

"I know of all three. Bring 'em in here."

It took only about thirty minutes for the three ranch owners to convince the marshal of the truth. Gundy looked at them. "Now let's go have a beer."

The saloon was full when Gundy pushed through the heavy wooden doors. Townspeople, cowboys, most of Gundy's riders — and Biggun and Bowlegs from the Box LB. Three other riders were talking with Biggun, so Gundy guessed they were from the same ranch.

Gundy told Runnels to find a table, he had something to do at the bar. He edged his way to the wall at the end of the curved mahogany surface and looked across the curve in it right into Biggun's eyes. He grinned, not showing humor or amusement. He would have to fight this man, with guns, fists, or knives, and he didn't give a damn which. A cold blistering fire built in his head. He hated outlaws, and right now the one he faced was at the top of his list.

"You wuz walkin' last time I seen ya, Biggun. Ever find yore horse?"

Biggun swept those between him and Gundy aside with one sweep of his beefy arm. "Thought you mighta had more sense than to come back this way. Now, I'm gonna kill you, with my bare hands."

"Take it outside," Red Dawson said from across the bar. His words, to Gundy's thinking, were mighty convincing in that he held a double-barreled Greener up where they could see it.

Gundy wasn't sure he could beat the big man he faced, but spending as much time hanging over a bar as the lout seemed to do, Gundy thought he could stay away from punches until the beefy rustler tired.

On the way outside Gundy said quietly to Purdy, "Them other four with the big man, have our men see that none o' them leave. Hit 'em over the head if you have to."

He walked to the middle of the street and faced the doors. Biggun lumbered through.

"If you don't shed your hardware, you ain't gonna have a chance to beat me, big man, 'cause I'll kill you right here."

Biggun shucked his gunbelt and knife

while Gundy did the same. Then he ran at Gundy. Gundy stepped aside, stuck out a foot, swung to the back of Biggun's neck, and stepped toward the hunk of beef when he fell. He kicked Biggun in the side of his head.

The rustler lay there a moment, crawled to his hands and knees, shook his head, and lunged to his feet. Again, Gundy sidestepped and swung a right to the big man's temple. Biggun went to his knees. He was slower getting on his feet this time. Wary now, he plodded slowly toward Gundy, quickened his pace, and swung. Gundy faded back, but not quite out of reach. The outlaw's fist caught him on the side of his jaw. He went down, a red haze marring his vision.

From the corner of his eye he saw his adversary jump. Gundy rolled. Only Biggun's boot toes caught Gundy's ribs. He rolled again and came to his feet, only to catch a hard right against his shoulder. He fell back against the hitch rail. If he caught a blow like that to his heart or head, the fight would be over.

Biggun rushed at him. Gundy dropped to the ground letting the huge man run past him into the rail. Gundy came to his feet and swung at the back of the thick-muscled neck, knocking the animal-like face down against the end of the post supporting the rail. He heard something snap, almost like a pistol shot. The outlaw fell in one loose-jointed heap. He didn't move.

Gundy brought his foot back to kick him. Runnels gripped his forearm. "That's enough, Gundy. I think you killed 'im."

Gundy backed off and held his hand toward Crockett, who held his gunbelt.

While he buckled his belt he never looked away from the mass that lay there. Finally, he raised his gaze to lock with Runnels's. "Think you're right, 'less he's different from most I've seen. Most people cain't turn their head all the way 'round."

"What you want to do with him?"

"Leave him lay. Have somebody take those other four to the marshal an' lock 'em up. I'm gonna have a beer." It was not until then that his anger slowly cooled to a small icy feel in his head. His gut muscles relaxed, and with them tiredness took over. He felt like his bones turned to water. He pushed his way through the crowd slapping him on the back and saying they were glad to see Biggun whipped. Gundy didn't think they realized the big rustler was dead.

Red had a beer waiting for him when he

walked to the bar. "You mess your hands up any?"

Gundy looked at his knuckles. They weren't skinned, but his left hand puffed out above his thumb. "Look all right. Long's I can use a gun."

"What you need a gun for?"

Gundy pinned him with a look that didn't invite more questions. "Tell you about it when it's over." He reached in his pocket for change.

"This one's on the house." Gundy nodded and put his dime back in his pocket. When he finished his drink, he told Purdy he was heading for camp, and not to let the men drink too much.

Back in camp, he checked his weapons again to make certain not a speck of dust marred their action, then he unrolled his blankets, gathered more firewood, and built up the fire after asking the cook if it was all right. They had left Cookie in camp to fix supper. He could go into town after everyone had eaten.

Gundy crawled between his blankets. "Wake me when supper's ready, Cookie." With those words, he pulled the blankets to his neck and went to sleep.

He felt like his eyes had been closed only an instant when the cook touched his shoulder. "Men are on their way back, Boss. How you feelin'?"

Gundy rolled from his blankets, stretched, felt a few sore spots stab at his movement. He grimaced. "I've felt better, but then, reckon I felt worse at one time or another." He went to the creek and washed his face.

After supper Gundy called the men around him. "We gonna have an early get-up-an'-go in the mornin'. I want the ten best rifle shots we got in the bunch to go with me. We gonna surround the ranch buildin's, an' pin down any who are there while the rest o' you round up every cow critter you see.

"Don't worry none 'bout who they b'long to. We'll figure that out when we get every critter back on our home range. They's gonna be more cows than what any o' us lost all put together, but we gonna keep them, too. Don't want none o' you takin' any chances you don't have to. Shoot anybody what tries to leave them ranch buildin's, an' anybody who tries to get into 'em. We got a lot o' cold work ahead of us."

Gundy answered questions, and then told the ones the ranch owners had selected as the best rifle shots in the bunch to take their bedrolls to the spot they'd be lying, that they wouldn't be moving around much and he didn't want them freezing.

When it seemed every question they could think of had been answered, and they had again checked their gear, Gundy said, "All right, men. I b'lieve we're as ready as we'll ever be. Let's get some sleep."

chapter twenty-two

Gundy had set his mind to awaken at two o'clock. He lay still, getting the feel of the coming day, then he opened his eyes and looked at his watch in the flickering few flames from the fire. Ten minutes of two. He rolled from his blankets, stiff and more sore from the fight than he'd been the night before.

He woke the men and told Cookie they would not eat until they were on station. Then they would eat in shifts. After the usual grumbling and growling, they were saddled and ready to go.

"Crockett, want you to segundo this gather and trail drive. I done explained the bounds of Barton's ranch to you, so soon's your men eat, stretch 'em out an' start roundin' 'em up. Purdy, Denton, Runnels, want you to stay with me and them with the rifles."

After putting the fire out and cleaning up the campsite, they headed out, all hunkered into their sheepskins, the air so cold it froze smells before they could reach your nose. The scents of wood smoke, pine, or grass, frozen stiff and brittle, were all wasted. These were a group of hard men, befitting the times that spawned them.

Gundy had Cookie set up the chuck wagon below the brow of the hill. The other side of the crest, at the bottom of the slope, the Box LB stood in ghostly shadows in this before-dawn light. Gundy rode up beside Crockett. "Keep your men here 'til after they eat, then start your gather at the far east side of Barton's spread. Make sure you got plenty o' provisions with you. This's the last time the chuck wagon's gonna do you much good 'til we flush them in those buildings yonder. Once that's done, I'll bring these men to help you."

He took the riflemen to places where they had a good vantage point looking down on the ranch within easy rifle range. He cautioned each of them to fire at anyone moving outside the buildings.

"I'll have Cookie bring you breakfast. After that we'll relieve you to go back to the chuck wagon, by then them what's down there's gonna know they cain't go nowhere. Hope we don't have to kill 'em. Hope after they see we got 'em boxed in they'll give up."

Cookie had breakfast ready an hour before sunrise. Crockett's men ate and he led them out. Gundy and the three ranchers sat by the fire drinking coffee while Cookie took breakfast to the riflemen.

"I figure 'bout sunup, we gonna hear our first rifle shot," Gundy said. "Then we gonna hear some more from around the ring we got around 'em. Then I figure it'll get quiet while Barton's men figure out what's happened to 'em."

Denton nodded. "Think you got it pegged." He slanted a puzzled look at Gundy. "After this's all over, what're you going to do? You need a job, you have one with me."

Purdy chuckled. "Denton, Gundy's got a ranch down in the Big Bend of Texas that could swallow all of ours and then have room for some more." At Gundy's surprised look, he continued, "Yeah, Gundy, I checked you out with Marshal Bruns. You mighta figured I would before committing my men to such as this. Hell, man, I ain't got many cows missin', I just needed the company and a chance to break the boredom. When we get home, you gotta promise to come over an' help me drink another bottle o' my whiskey."

Gundy grinned and shook his head.

"Sorta wondered . . ." The sharp report of a rifle cut him off. He picked up his saddle gun and snaked his way to the crest of the hill. Rifles in the bunkhouse were now answering the fire, all aimed toward where Gundy's man had fired.

When they weren't fired on from any other direction, two men crawled through a window on the ranch house side, and another of Gundy's riflemen got in the act. The two who'd left the window dived back through it. Gundy chuckled. They were getting the idea now they weren't going anywhere.

Another puncher tried to leave by the back door. He didn't make it out or in. He hung over the doorjamb, half in and half hanging out the doorway.

Abruptly those in the bunkhouse opened fire from every window. Gundy knew they could see nothing to fire at, and when they realized they weren't going to hit anything they'd pull back into their hole and wait. They did.

Sporadic firing continued throughout the morning. There was not a chance that any of Gundy's men would take a hit. They were too well sheltered.

Occasionally Gundy heard a shot from one of his men. They fired through the windows of the bunkhouse just to make things interesting. Gundy was glad he wasn't holed up in there with Barton's men. A rifle slug ricocheting around in those four walls could make a man right uneasy.

Gundy kept most of his attention on the house. He was sure Barton was in there. He wanted Barton for himself.

About ten o'clock smoke came from the cook-shack chimney. Gundy drew a bead on the steel cylinder and squeezed off a shot. It shook, but didn't fall.

Someone snaked up to his side. He glanced that way. Purdy lay there grinning. "Ain't had so much fun since I got caught in a stampede." Purdy nodded toward the stovepipe Gundy had fired at. "You know what, Gundy, you're just downright mean. Do it again."

Gundy grinned and drew another bead on the pipe, barely above the chimney. He squeezed off another shot, jacked a shell into the chamber, and fired again. The cylinder canted to the side and fell inward. "Now we wait." His chuckle verified Purdy's words.

At first, thin wisps of smoke curled around the upper part of the window casings. It got heavier, then filled each rectangle. A man Gundy supposed to be the cook scrambled from the cook-shack doorway and ran toward the bunkhouse. Gundy peppered shots around his feet.

"Whoeee," Purdy said, "that man is one fine dancer. You see them fancy steps he was takin', Gundy?"

Gundy allowed a slight smile to crinkle the corners of his lips. "Purdy, you're meaner'n me. You got more of a kick outta seein' that man run than I did."

"Well, one thing for sure, Gundy. Those people down yonder ain't gonna be eatin' anytime soon."

"What I figured. Now, if I could figure some way to wreck their well." He squinted toward the cistern in the middle of the yard, between the house and bunkhouse. "Don't think I'm a good enough shot to hit the bucket rope, but I can sure put 'nuff holes in that bucket they ain't gonna get any water even if they're dumb enough to come outside to try."

"C'mon, Gundy. Let me have some fun. You rest awhile now since you been workin' so hard, an' I'll take care of the bucket."

The old man hardly stopped to draw a bead. His rifle came to his shoulder in one fluid motion and he was firing. His third shot cut the well rope, and the bucket dropped from sight. He lay there grinning like a kid with a lollipop.

"Damn, old man, that there is some of the best shootin' I ever seen."

"Son, I fought the Comanche, Kiowa, 'Rapaho, an' Sioux. I'm still here, so I must of been fair to middlin'."

Gundy shook his head. "Yeah, reckon you could say that."

The day worked its way toward sundown, and Gundy felt a tightening of his nerves. Come nightfall some of those men in the bunkhouse would try to get out. He studied the layout awhile and came up with only one idea. *It* could get him killed.

While daylight waned, he continued to study the buildings and any approach to them. He returned to his original idea. He shrugged. If it had to be that way, so be it.

As soon as it got full dark, he gathered the ranchers around him. "Want you men to go tell our riflemen not to shoot at any shadows they see down yonder. I'm goin' down yonder an' see if I can set a big enough fire for us to see any who might try to escape."

Runnels looked at him. "Man, you've got to be crazy. Can't nobody get that close without getting shot to hell and gone."

Denton agreed, but Purdy stood looking at Gundy. "Men, if there's a man alive who can do it, Gundy can." He turned his look on Gundy. "You gonna let me go along, boy?"

Before Purdy finished his question, Gundy shook his head. "That'd be too many of us, Purdy. I'd shore like to have you with me. One man *might* be able to get the job done without gettin' killed. No way two of us could."

When the three of them set out to warn the riflemen, Gundy rummaged in his possibles bag and pulled his moccasins from it. His hands patted the back of his belt, went up to feel behind his neck, and then to his thighs to make sure his Bowie knife, his throwing knife, and handguns were all in place. Then his moccasined feet made not a sound when he slipped like a shadow from camp.

There were a few scrub cedar between him and the buildings, so he took advantage of their cover. But a hundred yards from the nearest building, the ranch house, there was only bare ground, except for a buckboard parked by the stable.

With the last cedar at his back, Gundy dropped to the ground, and using his elbows to drag himself forward snaked his way toward the house. Every building stood dark and silent in the night. He wanted to see who and how many were inside the house, but without even a lantern to light the interior he'd not be able to.

Gundy reached the house that stood between him and the cook shack. He made his way toward the back. As an afterthought he pulled his Bowie. There might be someone standing outside trying for a better look at the surroundings.

Still on his stomach, he poked his head around the corner and caught only a whiff, but recognized the pungent smell of tobacco smoke. His eyes searched along the wall for the smell's source, and would have missed it had not the man taken a drag on his cigarette. Its tip glowed white against the unpainted wall, throwing the smoker's face into sharp relief. Gundy let his elbows from under him and lay flat. He waited.

The man must be a sentry, because when he ground his cigarette out under his boot, he walked to the far corner, turned, and came toward Gundy.

Gundy eased his head back and got to his feet. Soft footsteps approached, stopped, and then a grinding sound as though the man turned on one foot.

Gundy waited only another moment before slipping around the corner. A wisp of fog made more noise than Gundy.

The sentry stood before him, his back turned. Gundy reached around his head, clamped his hand over the smoker's mouth, dragged his Bowie blade across the man's throat, moved his hand from the outlaw's mouth, and with both hands grabbed him under the armpits lowering him to the ground quietly. A spurt from the man's neck, black in the night, continued for only the few moments it took for his heart to stop beating.

Gundy snaked his way to the other corner. He wanted to reach the cook shack, thinking there would be less likelihood of anyone being there; and some ranches used part of the cook shack for storage. If he got lucky there would be lamp oil there.

He hoped most of the attention of the rustlers would be focused away from the buildings. He could sneak *to* the building, but coming *from* it he'd be running all out, and his bet was that every Box LB gun would be pointed his way.

About halfway between the house and his destination, the back door of the house slammed. Damn! Now they'd find the man he killed. He pushed to his feet and ran the rest of the way. No shots came his way.

He circled the shack, pushed on the heavy door hoping it wouldn't squeak. It gave a slight scraping noise against the framing and opened quietly. Gundy squeezed through the opening as soon as the door swung wide enough.

He'd thought it was dark outside, but in here was almost total darkness. He'd have to search by touch and smell. Groping his way, he located the stove and a stack of wood piled against the wall. Any storage space must be on the far wall.

Feeling his way down the rough boards, he came to the back wall, but could hardly reach it for the boxes and sacks of grain, coffee, or whatever were stacked against it. He thought lamp oil wouldn't be stored close to the food for fear of causing the food to taste of oil.

He moved to the other wall. If it wasn't here, starting the size fire he wanted would be next to impossible. Trusting his hands to find something that felt like a can, Gundy crawled along the floor feeling every object, then moving to the next. He even found a couple of saddles. Knowing he had circled the room almost back to the door, he was about to give up when his fingers touched metal. His heart pumped harder, faster.

Putting both hands on the metal surface, he moved them around the can, then toward the top and found a spout with a potato crammed down on it for a cork. He'd used that device many times to keep oil from spilling. The potato came off easily. He held the can to his nose. No doubt about it — lantern oil.

Now that he'd found what he wanted, Gundy studied the things he knew. He couldn't go back the way he'd come. It was a safe bet there was a man behind the house; he'd heard the door slam when he came out. If he went toward the stable he'd be in a cross fire between the house and the bunkhouse, and the stable might have men in it too.

The end of the bunkhouse didn't have windows. When he thought he'd considered every option, he poured oil around the walls, and starting at the back soaked the floor to within a foot of the door. He swallowed hard, his chest tightened, his mouth was so dry he couldn't spit. He pulled the oilskin packet of lucifers from his pocket and pulled one out. When he struck the match and dropped it in the oil, he'd have only a moment to get out. He counted on a few extra seconds for the fire to get the attention of those in the house and bunkhouse. He'd not have much time to get out of their sight.

He had put the match to his boot sole when he changed his mind and walked to the back of the shack. Start it burning here, and it'll take them longer to see the flame, he thought. He lifted his leg, pulled the lucifer along the seat of his Levi's, shielded the flame in his cupped hands until it caught, then dropped it to the floor. He waited only a second to see the fire catch and begin to spread.

When he left the shack, he pulled the door closed behind him and ran. The door might shield the fire from their view for another few moments. He palmed his Colt while he ran.

He rounded the corner and headed toward the back. Two men were sneaking from the bunkhouse. One of the rustlers saw Gundy as soon as he saw them. He yelled. Gundy fired from a full run, and fired again.

Both men stopped as though they'd run into a wall and went limp. Their momentum carried them another couple of steps before they fell like a wet cloth dropped in a heap.

Gundy ran a zigzag course. Shots peppered the ground around him. Slugs whined like angry hornets past his ears. His sheepskin tugged like someone had yanked it to the fore. Brassy saliva flooded his mouth, and fear washed into his throat. A slug seared his ribs. Then another tore through his thigh. Only a few more feet now. He could see the top of the hill in the murky light.

Now his own riflemen poured lead into the ranch yard. He topped the ridge and dropped to get its protection between him and those who wished him harm. He sat there, not moving, letting the taste of fear wash from him, and along with it the shaking. He had taken at least two hits, but however many, Gundy knew they weren't bad or he'd never have made it this far.

When he finally stopped trembling, he peered over the crest of the hill and saw the cook shack engulfed in flame, lighting the ranch yard like sunshine. He crawled down the hill far enough to make sure he was out of sight, then stood and limped toward the chuck wagon.

When he came into the ring of light from the campfire, Purdy was the first one to his side. "Damn, boy, you scared me to death down yonder. You gotta be crazy."

Gundy smiled tiredly. "Scared *you* to death? You shoulda been with me." He nodded. "And, yeah, reckon I must be a little crazy. Ain't nothin' gonna make me do somethin' like that again." He pulled his pipe out, tamped, and lit it. "By the way, they's three less o' that bunch we gotta face."

They nodded, and Denton said, "Yeah, we saw two of them drop when you ran from the cook shack."

It was then they took stock of him. He had four holes in his sheepskin, not counting the one that creased his ribs, and he had a crease along one thigh plus the hole that cut through the outer part of his leg. When they were through looking him over, he took his pipe from between his teeth and said, "Figure one o' you broken-down old men could get me a cup o' coffee?"

Purdy slanted him an acid look. "Well, broke down as I am, an' as much sympathy as you give me for bein' so old, reckon I still figure to strengthen that coffee with a little somethin' extra. Then I'm gonna dress them scratches you got down yonder playin' with them tenderfeet." He went to his bedroll an' pulled a bottle of rye whiskey from it, emptied a hefty jolt into a cup, finished filling it with coffee, and handed the cup to Gundy. It was then Crockett rode in.

"What in tarnation's goin' on down here? Heered a whole bunch o' shootin' an'

313

figured y'all needed some help."

"Naw," Purdy said, "that danged Injun there went an' hogged all the fun. No wonder they call 'im the Apache Blanco. He's selfish, mean, an' tee-total without feelin's for us older folks. Wouldn't share the fun with me a-tall."

Crockett looked at Purdy. "Sounds like he's done convinced you how he got the name Apache Blanco."

They nodded, but Denton said it best. "Crockett, if the Mescalero had one or two more like him, the Apache would still have all of Arizona, New Mexico, West Texas, and southern Colorado. I never seen the like."

With their every word, Gundy slunk farther down against the saddle he leaned against. "If y'all are through insultin' me, how 'bout one o' you fixin' up my side an' leg."

"I been puttin' it off, Gundy, 'cause I figured I'd have to waste some more o' my good drinkin' whiskey on them little old scratches, an' maybe you'd beat me outta another drink. Don't figure I could stand much o' that do-gooder stuff or I'd give outta whiskey."

"Purdy, I don't want you wastin' yore good whiskey on my scratches. Save it for *us*. I bet the cook's got a bottle o' rotgut stashed away somewhere. Ask 'im."

Gundy shifted his look to Crockett. "See enough today to get an idea what kind a job we got roundin' them cows up?"

"Yep" — Crockett nodded — "figure it's gonna be easy, maybe a week to get 'em all, an' we gonna have cow critters comin' outta our ears when we get through. If Barton figured on keepin' all the stock he's got on this range, it would be overgrazed down to a nubbin'. Course he probably figured to sell most of it come spring, bein' young stuff like it is. It's gonna take every one o' us to finish the gather an' get 'em strung out on the trail." He poured himself a cup of coffee and looked at the three ranchers. "We gonna have a lot more cows than anybody lost — addin' 'em all together."

"We can't keep them all . . ." Denton said.

"The hell we cain't," Gundy cut him off. "Barton stole from us, so we keep any he mighta got honest. 'Sides that, I don't figure on lettin' him stay around to claim 'em anyway."

Crockett looked at the three. "Told you he wuz a hard man." He grinned. "Besides, I agree with him." He scratched his head. "What's that old sayin', you make your bed, you sleep in it? Somethin' like that anyway."

Gundy drank his coffee and had another that Purdy again laced pretty heavy with rye, then Purdy dressed his wounds. After Purdy finished with him, Gundy picked up one of his blankets, poured himself another cup of coffee, and sat by the fire. He shook his head when Purdy offered to doctor his coffee again. He shivered and looked at the sky. "Gettin' colder. Might snow 'fore daylight."

Crockett stood. "Better get back to the roundup camp. Get an early start in the mornin'." Gundy nodded and lifted a hand.

He watched Crockett leave, and again glanced at the sky. "Shore hate to see it snow, but right now it might be the best thing that could happen."

"How's that?" Runnels asked.

Gundy glanced at him and looked into the fire. "That cook shack's gonna burn down to embers 'fore long. We ain't gonna be able to see much down there. Figure if it snows, covers the ground, we'll see a whole lot better. Snow gives off a good bit o' light on its own."

Runnels nodded. "See what you mean, Gundy."

Gundy dropped the blanket from his shoulders, stood, winced, and leaning into his hurt side went back up the hill for a look.

chapter twenty-three

From where Gundy lay, the ranch yard was still highly visible. The fire had consumed most of the building, but the flickering flames still threw the yard into sharp relief. While lying there it began to snow. Gundy couldn't remember ever wishing for snow before tonight, but he did now.

From a few isolated feathery flakes, it began to snow harder. Now the problem might be a white-out. He *didn't* want that. He lay there about an hour, long enough to see the ground become a white sheet. It was then he got the idea. He was going back down there. There was no way he could keep his men sitting in a snipers nest for several days, they'd freeze to death too. They were needed for the roundup. He slithered below the crest of the hill and went back to camp.

The chuck wagon belonged to Purdy, so he aimed his question at him. "You know if Cookie stashed any white canvas in the wagon when y'all packed the supplies?"

"Don't know, but figure he would in case

the top got ripped. Why?"

Gundy scraped his boot sole in the thin layer of snow, studied the small mound he'd made, then locked gazes with Purdy. "I figure to go back down there. We gotta get rid o' Barton one way or another."

"Hell, man. We can sit here an' let 'em starve. They ain't got any groceries, an' no way to cook 'em even if they did have. Less they want to cook on top o' room heaters. Don't go back down there, boy."

Gundy shook his head. "We cain't sit here long enough for them to get that hungry. One o' you men go tell our riflemen to pay special attention an' don't let nobody outta that bunkhouse. If they's a way for them to get closer, 'thout bein' in the open, have 'em do it. I'm goin' after Barton. Gonna kill 'im if I have to, but I'd rather take him to Milestown and let 'im stand trial, then we can hang 'im."

Purdy speared Gundy with a look that brooked no argument. "Gonna hang 'im anyhow. Him an' them cow thieves he's done took around 'im."

Gundy grinned. "Figured you was gonna give me a argument on that. Okay, you done talked me into it."

Purdy squinted at Gundy. "Son, don't know when I'm gonna smarten up. You knowed I was gonna say that all along, didn't you?"

Gundy laughed, slapped Purdy on the back, and said, "Let's find that canvas. When I get back, I want another drink o' your *good* whiskey."

"You get back, boy, you can have it all."

They found the roll of canvas after rummaging through the supplies. Gundy cut a swatch about seven feet long. While looking for the canvas, he spotted a double-barreled Greener twelve-gauge shotgun. He picked it up along with a box of shells. He loaded the shotgun on the way back to the fire, and stuffed the remainder of the shells in his pocket.

"You ain't told me yet what you gonna use that canvas for."

Gundy looked at Purdy, wanting to keep the conversation going, anything to let his stomach settle down. The brassy taste of fear again flooded his throat. He swallowed. "Come to the top o' the hill and watch."

A few minutes later Gundy stood below the brow of the hill, strapped the Greener to his back, spread the canvas, lay down, and pulled it over him, leaving only the crack in front so he could see. Then he inched down the hill toward Barton's house. If the canvas failed to blend with the snow, he'd be a stiff, cold corpse quicker than scat.

He made only a few inches at a time, and to make it harder every muscle in his body was braced against the impact of a rifle slug. He gauged the temperature at about zero, but sweat poured from him.

He called himself a fool at least a hundred times for every foot he made toward the house. About halfway he stopped. His leg throbbed, his elbows raw and bleeding hurt almost as much as his leg, and his ribs felt like a big man had hit him bareknuckled. That rib crease had bruised more than punctured.

Rested a bit, Gundy dragged himself farther. It seemed the gray logs of the house never got any closer. What he had guessed as an hour to get the two hundred or so yards turned into over two hours before he edged close to the base of the wall. He lay there a moment.

Deep breaths washed some of the fear from him. He massaged his arms, then his stomach muscles. Some of the pain went from them. He stood, bent at the waist, and looked for a window. A few feet to his right and no more than chest high, he saw one.

He reached to take his hat off and remembered he'd left it at the wagon. A slow step at a time brought him under the glassy rectangle. He inched his head high enough to peer into the dark interior and could see nothing. The back door would be his safest bet, someone might be asleep or on guard in the room. Too, he'd have full use of his hands to use his weapons if he went in the door. He drifted to the back, peered around the same corner he'd looked around on his last trip, and saw no one in his way, but the body of the sentry he'd killed was gone. They knew he'd been here.

He thought to try to slip in the back door, then discarded the idea. A bold approach might be best. They might think he was one of their own men. Fear again took its muscle-weakening hold on his body.

He shook his head. This wouldn't do, besides, a man could only die once, fearing death every second was what made a coward. He was no coward. Gundy squared his shoulders and walked brazenly toward the door.

Reaching it he pulled the screen toward him and pushed on the heavy wooden inside door. It opened without a squeak. He stepped inside, and someone from a side room grunted. "That you, Ace?"

Gundy held his hand over his mouth and

in a muffled voice said, "Yeah . . . coffee." To muffle his voice wasn't the only reason Gundy held his hand over his mouth. The house stank of dirty socks and dirty bodies. He drew breath in shallow drafts, feeling dirty from breathing it.

"On the stove in the front room. Goin' back to sleep," the voice from the bedroom said.

Gundy went down the hall, and before stepping into the front room, he stopped and searched every inch of it in the slight light from the stove. No one was there. He walked in, warmed his hands, poured himself a cup of coffee, and had taken one swallow when footsteps sounded in the hall, footsteps of more than one man.

They walked into the room shoulder to shoulder, stopped, looked toward him, obviously trying to recognize him.

Gundy rotated the Greener to point their way. "Come on in, men," he said, his voice barely above a whisper, "an' shuck yore hardware. You won't be needin' it."

They must not have seen the shotgun. They both reached for their holsters. Gundy squeezed one trigger, moved the barrel a couple of inches, and pulled the other one. Both men, knocked back a few steps, folded and fell. The one who'd taken the second load of buckshot fell on top of the other. They each had a hole in their chests big enough to put both fists in, side by side.

Gundy ran to the wall next to the hallway, reloaded the shotgun, and waited. He didn't know how many men were in the house.

Someone yelled from a room on one side of the hallway, "Who the hell fired that weapon, it wasn't a pistol or rifle."

"Don't know Peetry. Wasn't me," a voice across the hall said. Now they would look for him. He shifted the Greener to his left hand. He would fire it pistol fashion from that side. The scattershot would take care of what he lacked in accuracy. He pulled his Colt with his right hand. Again footsteps sounded in the hallway.

"Dammit, Crowley. Don't go traipsin' into that room. You don't know who might be there. Wasn't one of our men who fired that shotgun." The footsteps receded. Gundy wanted to twist around the corner and fire down the hall, but caution got the better of him.

Counting the man he had killed outside earlier, there were three down. If they'd had a poker game going before the attack started, he could figure on there being four more. He didn't like those odds. From down the hall, Crowley said in almost a whisper, "Peetry, don't like it in here. Gonna try to make it to the bunkhouse. Wanna come?"

A long silence, then Peetry answered, "Yeah, rather chance them rifles out yonder than a shotgun close range. Let's go."

Another voice cut in. "Don't be a couple of damned fools. Them rifles on the hill will get you."

Then from the one Gundy had learned was Peetry, "Gonna go anyhow. Rifle bullet don't mess you up bad as buckshot."

Gundy didn't try to stop them. He didn't want to kill them. He wanted Barton. The back door slammed. He waited, figuring at the longest odds he still had two guns to face. But they were in one or both of the bedrooms down the hall.

He checked the walls at each side of the doorway leading into the hall to see if they could get out of the bedrooms directly into the front room. There was not a door in either wall.

Abruptly firing sounded from the hills surrounding the ranch. Gundy went quiet inside. Those two who had left the house, unless mighty lucky, were lying out there in the snow.

Gundy's mind returned to Barton. How could he get him out of wherever he was? He hit on an idea, walked down the passageway, turned when he passed the doors to keep them in sight, and walked backward to the outside door. Still eyeing the two bedroom doors, he opened the back door and slammed it, but stayed inside.

"Hey, Barton, sounded like he left." The voice came from the room to his right.

"You wanna be an idiot, Masters, go out there and see." Barton's voice came from the room on the other side.

"Makes it harder," Gundy muttered, "still two sides to watch." He flattened himself against the wall, then decided to catfoot it back to the front room. If they came out, they'd probably come out looking toward the back door. Making less noise than a wisp of smoke, he went back to the front room. He made no effort to shield himself by standing to the side, but stood squarely in front of the passageway looking down it toward the rear door.

The door on Barton's side squeaked slightly. A hand, holding a pistol stuck out into the hall, fired three more quick shots toward the outside door and withdrew.

After those shots, a deafening silence hung in the rooms. Gundy breathed in shallow breaths, fearing even those would bring shots his way. He stood there, waiting, thinking his Apache upbringing had given him more patience than the two in the rooms.

After about thirty minutes, Barton said, "He's gone. Let's get a drink."

"Ain't for sure. Go ahead if you want. I'll come out later."

Barton laughed, and Gundy could tell from the sound of it he sneered contemptuously. "No guts." Then he stepped through the doorway. Gundy rotated the shotgun. "Don't even think about that .44, Barton."

With Gundy's first word, Barton's hand swept for his handgun. He was fast. He got off a shot that tore into Gundy's side, knocked him around so that when he squeezed off one barrel of the Greener, he missed. He swung the double-barreled weapon around and squeezed off the second round. He and Barton fired at the same time. Their shots crossed. Barton's bullet caught the top of Gundy's ear. Gundy's shot caught Barton full in the face. There wasn't much left to recognize above his neck: Gundy opened the breech, removed the spent shells, and thumbed two more into the twin barrels.

"Throw your guns out, Masters, an'

come out empty-handed through that door. Your boss is dead. Throw 'em out, you live, or leave by a window an' them rifles on the hills will cut you down. You stay here an' try your luck against this scattergun they gonna haul you out in two pieces." Gundy tried to keep his voice steady, but the pain in his side made his voice thin. He pressed his elbow against the wound to try to stanch the bleeding.

The door opened a crack and a pistol and knife skidded across the floor. "Those are the only weapons I got, man. I'm comin' out. Don't shoot."

Masters came through the doorway, hands held high above his head.

"Keep your hands where they are an' come into the front room."

Gundy slipped to the side of the doorway until Masters walked to the center of the room. "Anybody else here in the house?"

Masters shook his head. "No. They was only seven of us to start with. B'lieve you got 'em all."

"Some. Rifles got some. Lie down in the middle of the floor." He didn't want Masters to know how bad he was hit until he got him tied.

As soon as Masters stretched out on the floor, Gundy tied his hands and feet, went to the table, poured himself a half glass of whiskey, and took a sip of it. The whiskey must have been some of Barton's private stock. It was good.

He tossed the drink down, went in the bedroom, rummaged through some drawers, and found a clean sheet. Using his Bowie, he slit the sheet into wide strips, made a pad of one of the strips, pressed it to the wound, and wrapped his side with another. He went back to the front room and poured himself another drink. Now all he had to worry about was how to get the rest of Barton's bunch out of the bunkhouse.

He thought to send Masters to tell them Barton was dead, but the rifles would get him before he cleared the back door ten feet.

Gundy thought maybe he could yell to them what Barton's luck had bought him. He shook his head. He couldn't suck in a deep enough breath to muster a yell. Finally, he nodded. Maybe it would work. He looked at Masters.

"Gonna cut your legs loose. You gonna walk to that window yonder and yell out to your friends what's happened to Barton. *I'm* gonna sit in that chair over yonder with this shotgun pointed at you. You make one funny move, you'll be holdin' hands with Barton on the way to hell."

Before cutting Masters's leg bonds, Gundy poured himself another drink hoping it would ease the pain enough to get him through the last hours of night. Then he cut the lashings from Masters's legs, backed away, picked up his drink, and sat in the chair facing Masters and the window.

"Masters, tell 'em to wait 'till daylight, wave a sheet out one o' them windows, wait 'til my men let them know they seen it, then in one bunch walk outside with their hands grabbing for sky. They do that, maybe they got a chance to live. I ain't promisin', but it's the only chance they got."

Masters stared at him a moment. "Who *are* you? I never seen one man who could raise so much hell at one time."

Gundy thought to tell him he was the Apache Blanco, but decided if ever there was a time to let Blanco become only a memory, it was now.

"Masters, let's just say you met an honest cowboy who hated thieves."

Masters continued looking at him a few moments. "That answer ain't very good" — he shrugged — "but reckon it's all I'm gonna get. Yeah, I'll do what you tell me, but it shore would be nice knowin', before they hang me, it took a known man to beat that salty bunch I ride with."

Gundy smiled, knowing it was a cold one. "I'll tell you this much, Masters. The man who beat you was the best you'll ever meet. I say that because he proved he was better. That don't say they won't be somebody tomorrow who's even better. The man who beat you done a lot of bad things, but never a crooked one."

Masters went to the window and did as he was instructed to do. Gundy nodded. "Now tell 'em if they let even one man stay in there to shoot at my crew, I'll kill 'em all." Again Masters relayed the information. Then Gundy retied his feet.

Every few minutes, Gundy stood at the window and searched the yard. Nothing stirred. About halfway to the bunkhouse lay the two punchers who'd tried to make it. Gundy stared at them a long time, hoping to see movement, hoping they were alive, but knowing all the while they were stiff, frozen, and dead. A helluva price to pay for a woman on Saturday night, a few drinks, and maybe a small stakes poker game. His face hardened. He had seen too much of this sort of thing. A few years back and he wouldn't have given it a second thought. But now? He only shook his head.

Daylight came, and as soon as they

could be seen clearly, a bed sheet swung back and forth from a bunkhouse window. Gundy glanced at a side window and saw the same thing. Good. They had at least made certain those on the hill could see from those two directions.

One man took a tentative few steps into the open, and when no shots came his way the rest followed him to the center of the yard. There were only five of them.

A few minutes passed and the riflemen walked down from the surrounding hills, then came the chuck wagon. Purdy followed the wagon on foot, waving a bottle of his good whiskey as he came.

Despite the pain in his side, Gundy dragged Masters out to where the other rustlers huddled. Purdy handed him the bottle.

"Barton's dead, along with a couple o' others inside the house. Reckon if it's all right with the rest o' you, I'd like these men taken to Milestown and put on trial. Time we let the law take care o' things like hangin'. 'Sides, I ain't got the stomach for it. Done had enough killin' to last a lifetime."

They all, including Purdy, looked at each other and nodded solemnly. "I think you're right, son. Time we let this territory grow up," Denton said. "Let's round up some cows."

chapter twenty-four

Runnels, Denton, and Purdy had taken their cut of the Barton herd. Purdy and Gundy loaned Runnels men to help with his drive. Gundy left men to tend Joy's cut and headed home.

Midafternoon, when they rode into the ranch yard, Joy ran toward them, and when Gundy swung out of the saddle, she stood back and studied them, all of them. Then, hesitant, she walked to stand in front of him.

"Oh, Trace, I'm so glad to see all of you. Did we get any men hurt? Did everything go all right? Did — did — did — Oh, damn. I'll ask you every question in the book after supper." Her eyes opened wide. "Supper! I haven't fixed enough to feed the crew. I had no idea when you'd get home."

Gundy grinned. "Take your time, Joy. Purdy gave me a couple bottles of his good whiskey so the boys and I could have a drink. We'll take care of that while you fix supper."

"Trace Gundy, there better be enough of that 'good whiskey' for me to have a hot toddy."

Gundy's face warmed. "Aw, Joy, don't reckon I even thought about you havin' one with us. Uh, what I mean is, well you're welcome. Reckon it'd be all right if we clean up an' come up to the house to have our drinks? You know, sort of a celebration."

"Of course, it'll be fine. I'll get the supper started. You all stash your gear."

"All right, men, you heard the boss, but you ain't heard me yet. This ain't no excuse for not shavin' an' bathin'."

A couple hours later the crew, except those left to keep the herd from straying, sat at Joy's table. They had their drinks, and Joy sipped a hot toddy while finishing cooking.

After eating, Gundy had Crockett send out reliefs for those men at the herd. After the kitchen was cleaned, Gundy asked Joy if she would like him to stay and give her an accounting of the happenings while they were gone.

She looked at him with that straight-on look she had. "No. You'd better get a good night's sleep, and get the men lined out for tomorrow's jobs. We'll talk then."

He felt relieved, but disappointed. He

wanted to just sit quietly, have a drink, and talk. But he knew it was for the best. He was tired and his ribs still hurt. That bullet probably busted a rib, he thought. Besides, he wanted every cow they brought back branded before they turned them loose.

The next morning Gundy put Crockett in charge of the branding. He figured there were about two thousand head, eight hundred of those rustled from Joy, seven hundred from Bilkins, and about five hundred head that had been Barton's.

After breakfast, he told Joy he'd have to put off bringing her up-to-date on the happenings, he had to see Bilkins. "Trace, you're not really going to keep the Bilkins cattle, are you?"

He pinned her with a look that said it all. "Ma'am, I been shot at, hit, froze, an' a lot more you ain't never gonna know. Yes'm, I'm gonna keep them cows. Fact is, Crockett's out yonder right now puttin' Flyin' JW brands on them." He shoved his hat off his forehead. "When I get back we'll sit an' talk, all day an' all night if you want to, but right now, I'm ridin' over to see Bilkins. Gonna spend the night with Runnels, then I'll come home." He stepped toward the door, then turned back to her. "Ma'am, why don't you pack your grip an' come with me? You ain't met Mrs. Runnels yet. Time you did."

Joy's face beamed, then she frowned. "I can't do that, Trace. The men'll expect me to feed them."

He looked at her a moment, shook his head, and said, "Pack your things. We'll swing by the herd and tell Crockett to send somebody in for the chuck wagon. They can eat out there."

Her face looked like a kid he had seen one time, his nose pressed flat against a store window looking at the penny candy in the show window. She wanted to go so bad, but he saw the indecision creep in. Her responsibility to the men won. "Trace, I can't do the men that way. All of you have been on the trail over three weeks now, they deserve better than a bedroll for a bed and slumgullion for food."

"Pack your gear, woman. If you don't, I'll pack it for you."

"You — you wouldn't dare."

"Try me."

She stared at him a moment, her lips set in a straight line, then they softened. "All right, I'll pack. You've taken charge of my ranch, and now it seems you've taken charge of me."

It was coming on to dark when they rode

into the Bilkins's ranch yard. Bilkins and his wife met them on the porch.

"I suppose you got the cattle back," Bilkins said before offering greetings of any kind.

Gundy stared at him a moment. "Bilkins, where I come from it's customary to greet ladies respectfully. Don't give a damn how you greet me, but this here's Mrs. Joy Waldrop. Say howdy."

Bilkins glanced at Joy and turned his attention back to Gundy. "I've decided not to sell my cows at the price you offered."

Blood crept up Gundy's neck and an icy anger settled into his brain. "Decide again, Bilkins. You signed an agreement, and I had a witness to that signature. You're sellin' at the price agreed on, or I give you nothin'. Make up your mind right now. Got no time to tarry."

The starch went out of Bilkins. His shoulders slumped, and his face sagged. "I — I'll make out a bill of sale. It's — it's pure robbery, nothing more, nothing less."

"Call it what you want. Out here we fight for what's ours. You let us do your fightin' for you, so we're takin' what we fought for." Standing there on the porch, Gundy counted out fourteen hundred dollars. "Make out the bill of sale, and I give you this. Quick now, or you get nothin'."

Riding away from the Bilkins place, Joy was unusually quiet. Except for an occasional tight-lipped glance at Gundy, she looked straight ahead.

When they stopped, he made camp in the lee of a cut-bank. He said, "Be at the Runnels ranch by noon tomorrow." He hesitated a moment. "You'll have somebody to talk to then, bein' I ain't fit." He made her a comfortable place to sleep, made a fire, and fixed supper. In normal circumstances he knew she would have insisted on fixing the meal, but now, she was all tight-jawed about the way he'd treated Bilkins. Well, she could get used to him treating anyone that way when they didn't carry their part of the load. They ate in silence, and after he'd cleaned the pans and dishes, he poured coffee for them both and held her cup out for her to take.

Almost sarcastically courteous, he said, "Would you like a cup of coffee, Miz Waldrop?"

She took the cup and, looking across it at him, said, "There isn't a soft bone in your body, is there, Trace?"

"Ma'am, that depends on who I'm dealing with, depends on whether they deserve softness."

"And you've set yourself up as judge and jury as to whether they deserve it?"

His chin set in a hard stubborn knot. He looked at her over the rim of his cup. "Yes'm, I've done that. When I earn the right to be judge an' jury, reckon I take on the job right handily."

Not much more was said until they slipped down in their blankets, one on each side of the fire. Gundy raised his head from his saddle. "Miz Waldrop, you get cold, I got more blankets here than I need." She only nodded.

True to Gundy's estimate, they rode to the Runnels's front porch about noon. "Climb down, rest your saddles. The missus is just now putting dinner on the table. Miz Joy, see you brought a grip with you. Ma will get you set up in the guest room. Gotta warn you, though, she'll talk you right out from under your hair."

"Now what's that lazy good for nothin' tellin' a pretty lady like you? Gosh dang it, Pa, introduce us and quit standing there with your face hangin' out."

"Woulda already done it if you'd a hushed up for a minute. Joy, this is my missus. Martha's her name, but much as she talks, you probably ain't gonna get much chance to use it."

"Oh, come on in outta the cold, child. Lord a mercy, dinner's ready and you ain't had a chance to thaw out yet." Martha glanced at Gundy. "Hello, Trace, come in and set. Pa will get you a cup of coffee while I get this youngun settled."

While Joy was shown to her room, Runnels told Gundy he had sent one of the JW men to Milestown to see if there were any cowhands there needing a couple weeks' work, and he'd return the man to Gundy as soon as he got back.

Over dinner, Gundy thought he'd never seen Joy so animated, so happy. This was the first woman she'd seen since staying with Bruns's wife during the trial. He made a mental note that if she ever spoke to him again, he'd try to see to it that she visited with women more often.

They talked long into the afternoon, and every time Runnels approached the part Gundy played in getting the cattle back, Gundy changed the subject. Then after supper they cleaned up and went to bed. Gundy slept in the bunkhouse.

The next morning after breakfast, Gundy and Joy left with promises on both sides to visit more often. While riding, Joy seemed to want to talk, but Gundy still felt like she had unfairly judged him. He only answered in short sentences, or with a word if it would suffice. That night they camped under the same cut-bank they'd camped at two nights before.

Joy started supper as soon as Gundy had the fire built. He made a move to help and she turned to him, hands on hips. "Trace Gundy, you sit down. I'll fix supper just like I should have night before last. I'm sorry about the way I treated you. There, now I've said it. You satisfied?"

"No, ma'am. I wasn't askin' for no apology. Need to tell you right now, though, when it comes to dealin' with men, that's my job. I'll treat 'em hard, but fair, an' I ain't askin' for no help or complaints silent or otherwise outta you. They was a lot more behind the way I treated Bilkins than you know. An' you ain't never gonna know if I have to tell you."

At his words, Joy seemed to soften; she pushed some dirt around with her shoe sole, stared at it, then looked into his eyes. "Trace, I already know. After you went to the bunkhouse last night, we sat up a long time talking. Bob told me the whole story about how you almost single-handedly took on the Barton outfit and beat them. If I'd known what you were doing I'd have gone out of my mind. You earned every

Bilkins cow you got."

He filled his pipe and lighted it, looking into her eyes all the while. "Didn't take those cows for you, took 'em for us."

"Good, you deserve them, all of them, so have the boys put your brand on them when they get around to it."

"No, ma'am, figure to put *our* brand on 'em. Which says you an' me, we got a problem."

"What problem, Trace?"

He puffed on his pipe a couple of times, worrying how to say what he had to say. "Well, ma'am, we gotta decide where we gonna live. Do we split the year 'tween here an' Texas, or just live in one place all the time?"

Joy's eyes filled with tears. Her puzzled frown didn't hide the fact she understood what Gundy was doing. "What do you mean, Trace? I don't see that anything has happened to make that a problem."

He walked to her and stood close. "Yes'm, somethin's done happened. I been fightin' it a considerable while, what with worryin' 'bout whether I wuz bein' unfaithful to Dee's memory. I done fell in love with you, want to get married."

He gasped, stepped back, and stopped. "Well, dang it. Ain't never said nothin' to you 'bout how I felt. Reckon they's no chance you gonna say you'll marry me, what with me bein' such a hard man. Ain't no way you could love me."

When he stepped back, it wasn't far enough to keep Joy from rushing into his arms, tears streaming from her face. "Oh yes. I'll say it over and over again. Yes, yes, yes. You be hard at the right times, and with the right people. I think I've loved you ever since you stood outside my door, half drowned, wanting a job. Yes, I'll marry you. And I don't care where, or how we live as long as I have you."

Gundy didn't say anything. He just pulled her tighter against his chest.

About the Author

JACK BALLAS served in the U.S. Navy for 22 years, and received 12 battle stars for his service. In his younger days, he ran a honky-tonk saloon in the South (with the help of a 12-gauge shotgun), rode the rails, and found himself lost deep in the Everglades. He was taken in by a band of Seminole Indians, whom he credits with saving his life. Ballas now makes his home in Fort Worth, Texas.

The employees of Thorndike Press hope you have enjoyed this Large Print book. All our Thorndike and Wheeler Large Print titles are designed for easy reading, and all our books are made to last. Other Thorndike Press Large Print books are available at your library, through selected bookstores, or directly from us.

For information about titles, please call:

(800) 223-1244

or visit our Web site at:

www.gale.com/thorndike
www.gale.com/wheeler

To share your comments, please write:

Publisher
Thorndike Press
295 Kennedy Memorial Drive
Waterville, ME   04901